CLASSIC EROTIC TALES

CLASSIC
EROTIC TALES

CASTLE BOOKS

This edition is published by CASTLE BOOKS
a division of Book Sales, Inc.
PO Box 7100
Edison, NJ 08818-7100

First published in 1994 by
Michael O'Mara Books Limited, 9 Lion Yard
Tremadoc Road, London SW4 7NQ

A CIP catalogue number for this book is available from the British Library

ISBN 0-7858-0198-7

Designed and typeset by Servis Filmsetting Limited, Manchester, England
Printed and bound in the United States of America

CONTENTS

BOCCACCIO

from

The Decameron

Giovanni Boccaccio wrote The Decameron *in 1353. The Italian city of Florence is in the grip of the Black Death and among those fleeing to safety are ten young people who tell each other stories to take their minds off their predicament.*

SEVENTH TALE

The Sultan of Babylon sends his daughter to marry the King of Garbo. In the space of four years she passes through many adventures in different lands and lies with nine men. She is finally restored to her father who is made to believe she is still a virgin, and marries the King of Garbo

THE pity felt by the ladies for Madonna Beritola's misfortunes would have made them shed tears perhaps if Emilia's tale had lasted much longer. But when it was ended the queen ordered Pamfilo to follow, which he obediently did.

Fair ladies, it is difficult for us to know what is truly useful to us. Thus, as we often see, there are many men who think they would live secure and carefree if only they were rich. To this end, they not only send up urgent prayers to God but eagerly brave every danger and fatigue to acquire wealth. And then when they are rich, it sometimes happens that they are slain by those who in poverty were their friends, but who are tempted by the hope of acquiring their riches. Again, men of humble birth have risen to the dignity of

Kings through a thousand battles and the blood of their brothers and friends, thinking that all happiness lies in ruling. But they have found their thrones surrounded with cares and fears, and have learned at the cost of their lives that at royal tables poison may be drunk in gold cups. Others have ardently desired such gifts as bodily strength and beauty; and yet these very things have caused them misfortune or even death.

But I do not wish to name every human desire one by one; so I shall only add that we can choose no desire which will certainly bring us happiness. Wherefore, if we desire to labour rightly, we should resign ourselves to accept what is given us by Him Who alone knows what is necessary to us, and is able to give it. Men indeed sin by desiring many things; but you, most gracious ladies, are especially given to one sin, which is the desire to be beautiful. So much so that the beauties Nature gives do not suffice you, and you seek to increase them by wonderful arts. I shall therefore tell you a tale of the misfortunes of a beautiful Saracen girl, whose beauty caused her to lie with no less than nine men in the space of four years.

Long ago there was a Sultan of Babylon named Beminedab, fortunate in all his enterprises. Among his many male and female children he had a daughter called Alatiel, the most beautiful woman to be seen in the world in that age, if we may believe those who saw her. Now, the King of Garbo had given valuable aid to the Sultan in a fierce war he had waged with a vast horde of invading Arabs; and at his request, the Sultan as a special favour granted him Alatiel as his wife. So the Sultan sent her on board a well-equipped and well-armed ship with an honourable escort of men and women and many rich and noble presents; and, having commended her to God's care, despatched her to the King.

The weather was fine, the sailors set every sail as they came out of the port of Alexandria, and for many days their voyage was prosperous. They had passed Sardinia and saw the end of their journey in sight when suddenly one day furious and contrary winds arose and beat so heavily on the ship that more than once they gave themselves up for lost. But, like brave men, they made use of all their strength and every device, and for two days endured the infinite onslaught of the waves. The third night of the storm only increased its violence. The sailors did not know their position; all observation was impossible, for the sky was blotted out with clouds and mist; but they had drifted somewhere near Majorca when they found the ship had sprung a leak.

Seeing no other way of escape and everyone thinking of himself, the officers launched the long-boat and got into it, thinking they had better trust to it than a leaky ship. But although those first in the long-boat tried to fight the others off with knives, every man on the ship tried to jump into it; and, in trying to avoid death, fell into it. In such weather the long-boat could not hold so many; it capsized and everyone in it perished. Nobody was left on the ship but the lady and her women, who lay half dead with fear and the violence of the storm. Although the ship was leaking badly and was nearly full of water, it was driven rapidly by the force of the wind and struck on the coast of Majorca. So great was the shock that it struck firmly in the sand about a stone's throw from the shore, and there remained all night beaten but not moved by the force of wind and sea.

At daybreak the storm calmed down somewhat. The lady, although almost half dead, weakly lifted her head and called one after another of her attendants by name; but she called in vain, for they were far away. Getting no reply and seeing no one, she was greatly amazed and began to feel terrified. She stood up as well as she was able, and saw the ladies in attendance on her and the other women lying about. She called first one and then another, but found that seasickness and fear had so exhausted them that most of them seemed dead, which greatly increased her terror. However, seeing that she was quite alone and did not know where she was, she took council of necessity and so shook those who were alive that she made them get up. Finding they did not know where the men were and seeing that the ship had struck and was full of water, she began to weep most piteously with them.

It was past the hour of Nones before they saw anyone on the shore or elsewhere from whom they could hope for assistance. About that hour a gentleman named Pericone da Visalgo was returning home that way on horseback with his attendants. He saw the ship, realised what had happened, and ordered one of his servants to get on board without delay and to report what he found there. With great difficulty the servant climbed on to the ship and found the lady with her few attendants hiding timorously under the bowsprit. When they saw the man they besought his pity with many tears; but finding he did not understand their language nor they his, they tried to communicate their plight by signs.

The servant went back and told Pericone what he had seen, and Pericone immediately had the ladies and the most valuable things in the ship brought on shore and carried to his castle. He saw that the women were given food and rest, and judged from Alatiel's rich clothes and the respect showed her by the other women that she was a lady of high birth. Although she was pale and dishevelled from the sea, yet her features seemed most beautiful to Pericone. So he immediately determined to make her his wife if she was not married, or, if he could not marry her, to have her as his mistress.

Pericone was a strong, haughty-looking man. For several days the lady was most carefully tended, and thus perfectly recovered. He saw that she was indeed extremely beautiful, and grieved that he could not understand her language, nor she his. But as her beauty moved him immensely he attempted by amorous and pleasant signs to induce her to yield to his pleasures without resistance. But to no avail. She flatly refused to lie with him, which merely inflamed Pericone's ardour. This the lady perceived. She had now been there for some days and guessed from the clothes of those about her that she was among Christians, and also approximately where she was. She saw that it was of no avail therefore to make known who she was, and she also saw that in the long run she would have to submit willingly or unwillingly to Pericone's desires; she therefore proudly resolved to spurn the misery of her fate. She ordered her women (only three of whom remained alive) never to reveal who she was, unless they found themselves in a position where they might reasonably expect some help towards getting free. In addition she urged them to preserve their chastity, asserting that she herself had made up her mind that no man should enjoy her save only her husband. Her women praised her, and said they would obey her faithfully.

Pericone, having the woman he desired ever before his eyes but yet denied him, became daily more ardent. He saw his allurements were useless, so had recourse to cunning and art, leaving force as a final resource. He had several times noted that the lady liked wine, as happens with those who are unaccustomed to it because their laws forbid it; and he thought he would use wine as an aid to Venus. Pretending not to care that she rejected him, he gave a fine supper one evening, to which the lady came. Everyone was very gay, and Pericone ordered the servant who waited upon her to give her various mixed wines to drink; which he did very skilfully. Attracted by the pleasure of drinking and not knowing what she was about, she took more than befitted her chastity. She forgot all about her misfortunes and became very merry; and when she saw some of the women dancing in the fashion of Majorca, she danced for them in the Alexandrian style.

When Pericone observed this, he felt he was drawing near the desired end. He therefore prolonged the supper far into the night, with abundance of food and drink. Finally, when the guests had all gone, he went alone with her to her bedroom. She, being hotter with wine than cool with chastity, unreservedly undressed herself before Pericone as if he had been one of her women, and got into bed. Pericone was not long in following her. He put out every light, nimbly got into bed with her, took her in his arms, and, without any resistance on her part, began to enjoy her amorously. She had never known before the horn with which men butt, but

when she felt it she regretted that she had formerly refused
Pericone's advances; and, thereafter she did not wait to be invited
to such sweet nights, but herself often invited him, not with words
(which he could not understand) but by actions. While she and
Pericone thus enjoyed life, Fortune, not content with making a
King's wife into a gentleman's mistress, was preparing a yet worse
bed-mate for her.

Pericone had a brother named Marato, aged twenty-five, as
handsome and fresh as a rose. He saw Alatiel and she pleased him
mightily, while, from what he could gather by her signs, he was
well in her good graces. In his opinion nothing kept them apart but
Pericone's very strict watch over her, and so he devised a cruel plan
to which he wickedly gave effect.

At that moment there happened to be in the harbour, a ship laden
with merchandise, owned by two young Genoese, just about to sail
for Chiarenza in the Greek Empire. Marato arranged with them to
take him and the lady with them. That night he went to the castle
of the unsuspecting Pericone together with several companions, to
whom he had revealed his project, and hid them in the house as he
had planned. In the middle of the night he called his companions
and went with them to the room where Pericone was sleeping with
the lady. They murdered Pericone in his sleep, and threatened the
weeping lady with instant death if she made any noise. Unobserved
they stole Pericone's most valuable goods, and fled to the shore,
where Marato and the lady went on board, and the rest went to their
homes. The sailors at once started out before a fresh breeze.

The lady grieved bitterly over this her second misfortune, as well
as the first. But Marato, producing that holy crescent which God
had given him, soon consoled her in such a manner that she forgot
all about Pericone and settled down comfortably with him. But just
as she began to feel happy again, Fortune, not content with her
former woes, prepared her a new experience. As I have already said
more than once, Alatiel was most beautiful and her manners graceful; consequently the two young Genoese fell in love with her, and

thought of nothing but trying to please and serve her, though they took care that Marato should not notice anything.

Each perceived the other's love, and, after a secret discussion, they agreed to share her between them, as if love could be shared like money or merchandise. But they found that Marato watched her so carefully that they could not carry out their intentions. So one day when the ship was sailing very fast and Marato was standing at the poop looking out to sea and not noticing them, they crept up behind him and together threw him into the water. The ship had already gone over a mile before anyone noticed that Marato had fallen overboard. When the lady heard of this and saw there was no way to save him, she began to lament once more on the ship. The two lovers at once went to her and tried to comfort her with soft words and big promises; she understood little of what they said, and as a matter of fact, was grieving far more over her own misfortunes than the loss of her lover. After they had talked to her for a long time and felt they had consoled her, they began to argue as to which of them should lie with her first.

Each wished to be first, and neither could agree with the other. So from high words they fell into a rage, drew their knives and attacked each other. Before the other men on board could separate them, they both fell, one dead and the other seriously wounded. This greatly grieved the lady, for she saw herself left without any help and advice, while she dreaded lest the anger of the two Genoeses' relatives and friends should fall on her. But the wounded man's entreaties and their speedy arrival at Chiarenza saved her from the danger of death. She landed with the wounded man and went to an inn with him. The fame of her beauty immediately ran through the town and reached the ears of the Prince of the Morea, who was in Chiarenza at that time. He therefore desired to see her; and, when he saw her, she seemed to him far more beautiful than common report had said, and he fell so deeply in love with her that he could think of nothing else.

The Prince discovered how she had come to Chiarenza, and began to wonder how he could get hold of her. While he was examining ways and means, the wounded man's relatives heard of it, and immediately sent her to him without any delay. This delighted the Prince and the lady too, for she felt she had escaped a great danger. The Prince saw that she possessed royal manners as well as great beauty; he felt she must be a noblewoman (although he could not find out who she was), and this increased his love for her. He felt such love for her that he treated her as if she were his wife, and not his mistress.

Thinking over her past misfortunes, the lady felt she was now happily situated. She felt quite consoled and cheerful again, so that all her beauties blossomed out, and nothing but her beauty was talked about in all Greece. The young and handsome Duke of Athens, a relative and friend of the Prince, greatly desired to see her; and sending notice of his visit, as he was accustomed to do, he arrived with a numerous company at Chiarenza, where he was honourably received with great joy.

Some days later, when the beauties of the lady were being discussed, the Duke asked if she were as wonderful as people said. To which the Prince replied: 'Far more so. But you shall judge with your own eyes, not from my words!'

The Duke eagerly accepted, and the Prince conducted him to her. Being warned of their visit, she received them politely and with a cheerful visage, and sat down with them; but as she understood little or nothing of their language, they could not enjoy the pleasures of conversation. Therefore everyone gazed at her in wonderment, especially the Duke, who could scarcely believe that she was a mortal woman. Gazing at her, he failed to realise how the poison of love was working upon him, and, thinking he was merely satisfying his curiosity, he found he was deep in love with her. When he had left her and the Prince, and had time to think matters over, he concluded that the Prince was the happiest man in the world to have such a beautiful woman at his pleasure. Then, after a great many agitated reflections, his love got the better of his honesty, and he decided to deprive the Prince of this felicity and to get it for himself.

Having a mind to accomplish this, he put aside all reason and justice, and devoted his whole attention to deceit. One day, in collaboration with one of the Prince's most confidential servants (whose name was Ciuriaci) he secretly prepared his horses and everything else for departure. That night, with an accomplice, he was let into the Prince's apartment by the treacherous servant, and, since it was very hot, he found the lady asleep and the Prince naked at a window overlooking the sea, enjoying the faint sea breezes. His accomplice, knowing what was to be done, crept quietly to the window, stabbed the Prince in the back with a dagger and threw him out the window.

The palace overlooked the sea from a great height, and the window where the Prince had been standing was directly above some small houses which had been destroyed by the sea and were therefore rarely or never visited. Thus things turned out as the Duke had expected, and the fall of the Prince's body was not heard by anyone.

When the Duke's bravo saw that this murder was successful, he pretended to embrace Ciuriaci, but in fact threw a rope (which he had concealed for the purpose) round his neck so that he could not utter a sound. Then as the Duke came in, he strangled Ciuriaci and threw his body after the Prince's. When this had been done without arousing the attention of the lady or of anyone else, the Duke took a light in his hand and secretly examined all of the charms of the sleeping beauty. He looked at everything and was highly delighted; she had charmed him when clothed, but when naked she delighted him beyond all expression. Therefore, heated with desire and caring nothing for the crime he had just committed, although his hands were still bloody he got into bed and lay with her, while she was heavy with sleep and thought he was the Prince.

After he had lain with her in the greatest delight, he got up and let in some of his attendants. He warned the lady not to make any noise, led her out by the secret door through which he had entered, put her on horseback as quietly as possible, and set off full speed for Athens with all his train. But he had a wife, and therefore did not take Alatiel to Athens, but to a very handsome residence he had on the seashore not far from the town. There he secretly hid the grieving lady, and arranged for her to be served with every honour.

Next morning the Prince's courtiers waited until Nones for him to get up. Hearing nothing, they softly opened the doors of his apartments (which were not locked), but found no one there. But they felt no alarm, thinking that the Prince had gone off secretly somewhere to enjoy the lady all to himself for a few days.

The next day it happened that a madman wandered among the ruins where lay the bodies of the Prince and Ciuriaci, and came out dragging Ciuriaci behind him by the rope. The attendants were amazed at this sight and persuaded the madman to take them to the place where he had found the body; and there, to the great grief of the whole city, they found the body of the Prince, which they buried with all honours. They then enquired into the authors of this crime, and, seeing that the Duke of Athens was not there but had secretly departed, they realised that he had murdered the Prince and carried off the lady. They immediately elected the dead man's brother as their new Prince, and urged him to avenge the murder. Having collected further proofs of the crime, this new Prince called upon his friends, relatives and servants, and gathered together a large and powerful army to make war on the Duke of Athens.

Hearing of this, the Duke at once began to gather forces for his defence, and many gentlemen came to his aid, including Constantine and Manuel, son and nephew of the Emperor of Constantinople, with a large contingent. They were received with the greatest honour by the Duke and by the Duchess, who was their sister.

Day by day the war became more imminent. The Duchess invited both her relatives to her apartment and there, with many tears, told them the whole story and the reason for the war, and showed how she had been insulted by the Duke who was keeping this woman secretly hidden somewhere. And in great grief she begged them to advise her for the best, in regard to the Duke's honour and her own satisfaction. The two young men already knew all about the matter and therefore, without asking many questions, comforted her as best they could and bade her be of good cheer; they found out from her where the lady was concealed, and then departed. They had often heard praise of the lady's marvellous beauty, which they desired to see, and they asked the Duke to let them see her. Forgetting what had been the Prince's fate through letting him see her, he promised to do so. He ordered a magnificent dinner in a most beautiful garden, belonging to the house where the lady was lodged, and next day took them and a few companions to dine with her.

As Constantine sat beside her, he looked at her with amazement, telling himself that he had never seen so beautiful a woman and feeling that there was every excuse for the Duke or anyone else who committed any treacherous crime to get possession of her. And as he kept gazing at her time after time, the same thing occurred to him as had happened to the Duke. He fell hopelessly in love with her, abandoned all thought of the war, and began to ponder over means of getting her away from the Duke, while he carefully concealed his love from everyone.

While he was burning with desire, the time came to meet the Prince's forces which were drawing near the Duke's territories. So the Duke and Constantine and all the rest left Athens and marched to the frontier to prevent the Prince from advancing any further. While they were there, Constantine's mind and thoughts were filled with the lady. He thought that, since the Duke was away, he could easily achieve his desire, and therefore pretended to be ill in order to have an opportunity for returning to Athens. With the

Duke's permission he handed over his command to Manuel, and returned to his sister in Athens. A few days later he turned the conversation on the insult done her by the Duke in keeping a mistress, and told her that if she wished, he was ready to help her by taking Alatiel away.

The Duchess thought Constantine was doing this for love of her and not love of the lady, and told him that she liked the idea greatly, if only it could be carried out in such a way that the Duke would never know she had consented to it. Constantine immediately gave her a promise, and she consented that he should act as seemed best to him.

Constantine secretly equipped a fast ship and sent it one evening to lie off the garden where the lady was living. He arranged with his friends on board what they were to do, and then went with other friends to call on the lady. There he was greeted by the attendants and by the lady herself, and they all went into the garden. Pretending that he had a private message from the Duke to Alatiel, he went alone with her through a gate which opened to the sea. One of his companions had already unlocked it and gave the signal to the boat; and Constantine immediately had the lady seized and carried on board. Then he turned to her attendants, and said:

'Let no man move or say a word, unless he wants to die. I am not robbing the Duke of a woman, but wiping out the shame he has put upon my sister.'

Nobody was eager to reply to this, and Constantine and his attendants then went on board the ship. He sat beside the weeping lady, and ordered the rowers to start at once, which they did with such speed that the boat reached Aegina the next day. They landed there to rest, and Constantine enjoyed the lady, who wept over her unlucky beauty. They boarded the ship again, and in a few days reached Chios. Fearing his father's reproofs and also that the abducted lady might be taken from him, Constantine decided to remain there, and for many days Alatiel wept over her misfortunes. But Constantine comforted her, just as the others had, and she began to feel content with what Fortune had prepared for her.

While things were going on in this way, Osbech, King of Turkey, who was continually at war with the Emperor, happened to arrive at Smyrna. There he heard how Constantine was living a lascivious life with a lady he had abducted, and was quite unguarded. Osbech armed a number of small ships and sailed to Chios by night, where he silently landed his troops and surprised many of the Greeks in their beds, before they knew the enemy was upon them. The rest, who had rushed to arms, were slain. He burned the whole island, put the spoils and prisoners on the ships, and returned to Smyrna.

Osbech was a young man, and, as he was looking over the spoils, he came upon the woman who had been found sleeping in bed with Constantine, and was highly delighted with her. Without any delay he made her his wife, celebrated the marriage, and lay happily with her for several months.

Before this event occurred the Emperor had been treating with Basano, King of Cappadocia, for them both to attack Osbech simultaneously from different quarters. But they had not come to an agreement because the Emperor would not grant some of Basano's demands, which he thought excessive. However, when he heard what had happened to his son he was filled with grief, and immediately did what the King of Cappadocia had required of him. Urging him to attack Osbech with all his forces, the Emperor prepared to invade him from the other side.

Hearing of this, Osbech collected an army and, to avoid being caught between the forces of two great monarchs, he marched against the King of Cappadocia, leaving the beautiful lady in Smyrna under the guardianship of a trusted friend. Before long, Osbech gave battle to the King of Cappadocia, but his army was defeated and scattered, and he himself slain. The victorious Basano immediately marched on Smyrna, and as he advanced everyone submitted to him as conqueror.

The name of Osbech's friend, who was looking after the lady, was Antioco. Although he was elderly, he also fell in love with her great beauty, forgetting the faith pledged to his lord and friend. He could speak her language, which was delightful to her, since for several years she had been compelled to live as if she were a deaf-mute, for nobody had understood her language nor she theirs. Urged by his desire, Antioco became so familiar with her that in a few days they both forgot their lord away at the war, and became intimate in an amorous as well as a friendly manner, both taking great delight in each other between the sheets. But when they heard Osbech was conquered and slain, and that Basano was coming to pillage everything, they agreed not to await his coming. Taking the greater part of Osbech's treasure, they secretly fled to Rhodes; but they had not been there very long, when Antioco fell mortally sick. A merchant of Cyprus, his friend, whom he greatly loved, was living there; and Antioco, feeling he was drawing near his end, determined to leave this man his wealth and his dear lady. Being come near to death, he called them both before him, and said:

'I see I am certainly failing, which grieves me, for I never enjoyed life so much as I have done recently. One thing will make me die happy. Since I must die, at least I shall die in the arms of the two persons I love most in the world – in yours, my dear friend, and in those of this lady whom I have loved more than myself ever since I have known her. It grieves me to die and leave her here, a stranger, without help and without advice. And it would grieve me still more, if I did not know you are here and did not believe you would take the same care of her as of me. Therefore I beseech you, if I die, take my goods and her, and do with them both what you think will be a consolation to my soul. And you, dearest lady, after I am dead do not forget me, so that I may boast there that I am loved here by the most beautiful woman Nature ever created. If you will give me hope of these two things, I shall depart in peace.'

The merchant friend and the lady both wept when they heard these words. They tried to comfort him, and solemnly promised

they would do what he asked, if he should die. Very soon he did
die, and they buried him honourably.

Soon after this the Cyprus merchant finished all his business in
Rhodes, and determined to return to Cyprus on a Catalan ship
making the voyage. He therefore asked the lady what she wanted
to do, and whether she would return to Cyprus with him. The lady
replied that she would gladly go with him and hoped that for
Antioco's sake he would treat her as a sister. The merchant replied
that this would give him the greatest pleasure; and so that he might
protect her from any insult on the voyage, he gave out that she was
his wife. They went on board ship and were given a small cabin on
the stern, where they slept together in the same bed in order to
keep up the pretence. In this way occurred something which
neither of them had intended when they left Rhodes. They forgot
their love and friendship to dead Antioco, and, stimulated by the
darkness, convenience and warmth of bed, they began to feel
excited with mutual desires, and before they had reached Baffa
(where they were going) they were lying together. After they
reached Baffa she remained for some time with the merchant.

There happened to come to Baffa on business one Antigono, a
very elderly gentleman of great wisdom and little wealth. He had
involved himself in the service of the King of Cyprus, and
Fortune had been against him. One day, when the merchant had
gone on a voyage to Armenia, this Antigono happened to pass by
the lady's house just at the moment when she came to the
window. As she was very beautiful, he gazed at her, and remembered that he had seen her somewhere before, though he could
not recollect where.

The beautiful lady, who had long been Fortune's plaything, now
saw the end of her misfortunes drawing near. As soon as she saw
Antigono she remembered that she had seen him in an important
position among her father's servants. A sudden hope came to her
that through his advice she might return to her royal estate; and so,
since the merchant was away, she sent for Antigono as soon as she

could. When he arrived, she blushingly asked him if he were Antigono of Famagusta, as she believed. Antigono said 'yes,' and added:

'Madonna, I seem to recognise you but I can't remember where I saw you. If it is not displeasing to you, I beg you will recall yourself to my memory.'

Hearing this, the lady wept, threw her arms round his neck (to his great amazement) and then asked him if he had never seen her in Alexandria. On hearing this question, Antigono immediately recognised that she was Alatiel, the Sultan's daughter, who was thought to be drowned. He wished to pay her the customary respect, but she refused, and asked him to sit down with her. Antigono did so, and then respectfully asked how, when and by what means she came there, since the whole of Egypt was convinced that she had been drowned at sea several years before. To this the lady replied:

'I wish I had been drowned, rather than go through the sort of life I have endured, and I think my father will wish the same, if he ever knows about it.'

Whereupon she began to weep bitterly again. And Antigono said:

'Madonna, do not despair before it is time. Tell me, if you please, your misfortunes and the life you have led. Perhaps with God's help we may find some remedy.'

'Antigono,' said the beautiful lady, 'when I see you, I seem to see my own father, and feel for you the love and tenderness I am bound to feel for him. I therefore spoke to you, when I could have concealed myself. There are very few persons whom it would give me as much pleasure to see as yourself. And so I shall tell you, as if you were my father, all the misfortunes which I have kept secretly to myself. If, when you have heard them, you can think of any means by which I can return to my former state, I beg you to make use of them; if not, I beg you will never tell anyone that you have seen me here or heard anything about me.'

Having said this she then told him with many tears all that had happened to her from the time when she was wrecked in Majorca to that moment. Antigono wept with pity, and then, after some thought, said:

'Madonna, since you have always concealed your identity in your troubles, I can certainly restore you to your father, dearer than ever, and see you married to the King of Garbo.'

She asked him how, and he carefully explained his plan to her in detail. And to prevent any delay, Antigono immediately returned to Famagusta, and went to the King, to whom he said:

'Sire, may it please your Majesty, you can do yourself great honour and be of great service to me, who am a poor man on your account, without much cost to yourself.'

The King asked how, and Antigono then said:

'There has arrived at Baffa the beautiful young daughter of the Sultan, who for so long was thought to be drowned. To preserve her chastity she has suffered great hardships. She is now in poverty, and desires to return to her father. If you will send her to him under my protection, this will do you great honour and be of vast service to me. I think the Sultan will never forget such a service.'

Moved by his royal virtue, the King at once consented. He sent for Alatiel and had her brought honourably to Famagusta, when she was received by himself and the Queen with the greatest festivity and magnificence. When the King and Queen questioned her about her adventures, she replied exactly as Antigono had advised her. A few days later, at her request, the King sent her with an honourable attendance of ladies and gentlemen, under the care of Antigono, to her father the Sultan. It is needless to ask whether he received her and Antigono and the rest with delight. After she had rested, the Sultan desired to know how she chanced to be still alive, and where she had been for so long without ever sending any news of herself. The lady had most carefully got into her mind what Antigono had advised her to say, and answered her father as follows:

'About the twentieth day after my departure from you, father, our ship was wrecked in a storm and driven on to the shores of a place in the West not far from Aiguesmortes. What happened to the men on board I have never known; all I know is that next day I seemed to return from death to life. The inhabitants had already seen the wrecked ship, and were hastening from every direction to rob it. I got down on to the shore with two of my women, who were immediately seized by young men and taken off in different directions. What happened to them I never learned. I was caught by two young men and dragged along by the hair, weeping loudly. They were dragging me along a track towards a large wood when four men on horseback passed that way, and when the men dragging me along saw them, they at once released me and fled.

'Seeing this, the four men, who appeared to me persons of authority, rode up to me and asked me many questions. I talked a great deal, but they did not understand my speech, nor I theirs. After a long discussion they set me on one of their horses and took me to a convent of women, living in accordance with their religious laws. There I was kindly received and always honourably treated, and together with them I served with great devotion the Holy Crescent in the Hollow Vale, which is much honoured by the women of that country. After I had been with them for some time and had learned something of their language, they asked me who I was and where I came from. Knowing where I was and fearing that if I told them the truth they might do me some injury as an enemy of their faith, I replied that I was the daughter of a great nobleman in Cyprus, who was sending me to Crete to be married when the ship was thus driven out of its course and wrecked.

'For fear of trouble I often followed their customs in many respects. The chief of these ladies, who was called Abbess, asked me if I wished to return to Cyprus, and I replied that I desired it above everything. But she was so tender of my honour that she would never entrust me to any person travelling to Cyprus until two months ago. At that time certain good men of France with their wives, among whom were relatives of the Abbess, passed through on their way to Jerusalem to visit the Sepulchre, where He whom they believe to be God was buried after the Jews had slain Him. She entrusted me to them and begged them to deliver me to my father in Cyprus.

'It would take long to relate how much these gentlemen honoured me and the joy with which their wives received me. We went on board ship and after many days arrived at Baffa. When we arrived there, of course I did not know anyone and did not know what to say to the gentlemen who were to hand me over to my father, as the venerable Abbess had instructed them. But God perhaps was sorry for me, since He brought Antigono to the shore at the very hour when we were disembarking. I called to him immediately and told him in our language (so that the gentlemen and their wives would not understand) that he must receive me as his daughter. He immediately understood, and greeted me with the greatest joy, showing every honour his poverty permitted to the gentlemen and ladies. He then took me to the King of Cyprus, who received me with honour such as I can never fully relate, and has now sent me to you. If there is anything more to know, Antigono will tell you, for he has often heard me tell the story of my adventures.'

Antigono then turned to the Sultan and said:

'Sire, what she has now related she has several times told me, and the ladies and gentlemen with whom she returned said the same. She has only omitted one thing, because she did not think it fitting for her to speak of it. And this is what the gentlemen and ladies who accompanied her said of the virtuous life she led with the nuns, and her praiseworthy behaviour, and the tears and the regrets of the ladies and gentlemen when they handed her over to me and left her. If I tried to tell you all that they said about her, I should need all the rest of today and the night as well, and then not finish. It must be enough if I say that, according to what they told me and I have observed for myself, you may boast that you possess the most beautiful, the most chaste and most virtuous daughter of any living monarch.'

The Sultan was marvellously delighted with all these things, and piously prayed God to grant him grace to reward fittingly every-one who had done her honour, particularly the King of Cyprus who had sent her to him so honourably. After a few days he pre-sented Antigono with very great gifts, and gave him permission to return to Cyprus, returning the warmest thanks to the King both by letter and by special ambassadors for the kindness shown to his daughter. After this, he determined to carry out the original plan and marry Alatiel to the King of Garbo. He therefore wrote to that King all that had happened and said that if he still wished to marry Alatiel he must send for her. The King of Garbo was delighted, sent an honourable company for her, and received her with joy. And thus she, who had lain perhaps ten thousand times with eight different men, went to bed with him as if a virgin and made him think she was one. And thereafter she lived with him happily as Queen. Hence the saying: A kissed mouth loses no savour, but is renewed like the moon.

CASANOVA

from

The Memoirs of Casanova

Giovanni Jacopo Casanova (1725–1798) was an Italian adventurer. He had dealings with many of the great political and literary figures of his day including Catherine the Great and Louis XV. His scandalous memoirs were first translated into English in full and unbowdlerized as recently as 1966, by W.R. Trask.

> *An untoward night. I fall in love with the two*
> *sisters, I forget Angela. A ball at my house.*
> *Giulietta humiliated. My return to Pasiano.*
> *Lucia's misfortune. A propitious storm.*

AFTER expressing her thanks to me at great length, Signora Orio told me that in future I was to enjoy all the privileges of a friend of the family. We spent four hours laughing and joking. I made such good excuses for not staying to supper that she had to accept them. Marta was going to light the way for me; but a direct command from Signora Orio to Nanetta, whom she believed to be my favorite, obliged her to precede me, candlestick in hand. The sly vixen hurried down the stairs, opened the door, banged it shut, put out the candle and, leaving me there, ran back up to rejoin her aunt, who sharply reprimanded her for treating me so shabbily. I groped my way upstairs to the appointed place, and flung myself on a couch like a man who, having given his enemies the slip, awaits the moment of his happiness.

After spending an hour in the most pleasing reveries, I hear the street door being opened, then closed and double-locked, and ten minutes later I see the two sisters, followed by Angela. I disregard the others completely and spend two whole hours talking only with her. Midnight strikes; I am pitied for having gone supperless; but the tone of commiseration offends me; I answer that, in such happiness, it would be impossible for me to feel any lack. I am told that I am in prison, since the key to the house door is under Signora Orio's bolster, who will not open it until dawn, to go to the first mass. I am astonished that anyone should think I could consider this bad news; on the contrary, I am happy to have five hours before me and to be sure that I shall spend them with the object of my adoration. An hour later Nanetta laughs under her breath. Angela insists on knowing what she is laughing at; she whispers in her ear; Marta laughs too; I ask them to tell me why they are laughing; and finally Nanetta, looking chagrined, tells me that she has no other candle and that when this one burns out we shall be left in darkness. This news fills me with joy, but I hide it. I tell them that I am sorry on their account. I suggest that they go to bed and sleep in peace, assuring them of my respect; but this proposal sets them laughing again.

'What shall we do in the dark?'

'We'll talk.'

There were four of us, we had been conversing for three hours, and I was the hero of the play. Love is a great poet: its matter is inexhaustible; but if the end at which it aims never arrives, it sinks like dough at the baker's. My dear Angela listened, but not being fond of talking, answered very little; she was not particularly clever; instead, she prided herself on showing sound common sense. To weaken my arguments she usually only launched a proverb, as the Romans fired a catapult. She drew away, or repulsed my poor hands with the most offensive gentleness, whenever love called them to its aid. Yet I continued to talk and use my hands without losing courage. But I became desperate when I saw that my too subtle arguments confused her instead of convincing her and, instead of softening her heart, troubled it. I was completely astonished to read on Nanetta's and Marta's faces the impression which the shafts I was shooting straight at Angela made on them. This metaphysical curve seemed to me out of the course of nature; it should have been an angle. Unfortunately I was studying geometry at that period. Despite the season, I was sweating great drops. Nanetta got up to carry out the candle, which would have made an unbearable stench if it had guttered out in our presence.

No sooner is it dark than my arms naturally rise to take possession of the object necessary to the state of my soul; yet I cannot but laugh when I find that Angela has seized the previous moment to make sure that she will not be caught. I spent a whole hour saying the most amusing things which love could invent to persuade her to come back and sit on the same seat. I thought it impossible that she could really be in earnest. 'This joke,' I said at last, 'has gone on too long; it is against nature; I can't run after you, and it amazes me to hear you laughing; such strange behavior makes it seem that you are mocking me. So come and sit down. Since I have to talk to you without seeing you, at least my hands should assure me that I am not talking to the air. If you are making a mock of me, you must realize that you are insulting me, and love, I believe, should not be put to the test of insult.'

'Very well! Calm yourself. I am listening to you and not losing a single word; but you must realize too that I cannot in decency permit myself to sit close to you in the dark.'

'So you want me to stay here like this until dawn?'

'Lie down on the bed and sleep.'

'You amaze me – how can you consider that possible, to say nothing of compatible with my passion? Come now! I am going to pretend I'm playing blindman's buff.'

Upon that, I get up and vainly seek her all over the room. I catch someone; but it is always Nanetta or Marta, whose pride makes them name themselves at once; whereupon, stupid Don Quixote that I am, I consider it my duty to let them go. Love and prejudice prevent me from realizing the cowardice of such respect. I had not yet read the anecdotes of Louis XIII, King of France; but I had read Boccaccio. I continue to hunt for her. I reproach her with her cruelty, I put it to her that she ought to let herself be found, and she answers that it is as hard for her to find me as it is for me to find her. The room was not large, and I began to be furious at never managing to catch her.

More disgusted than exhausted, I sit down and spend an hour telling the story of Ruggiero when Angelica disappeared from his sight by means of the magic ring which the lovelorn knight had all too guilelessly given her.

> Così dicendo, intorno a la fontana
> Brancolando n'andava come cieco
> O quante volte abbraciò l'aria vana
> Sperando la donzella abbracciar seco.

> ('So saying he went stumbling around
> the fountain like a blind man. Oh,
> how often he embraced the empty air,
> hoping to embrace the damsel!')

Angela did not know Ariosto, but Nanetta had read him several times. She began defending Angelica and putting the blame on the simplicity of Ruggiero, who, if he had been sensible, should never have entrusted the coquette with the ring. Nanetta enchanted me; but I was too stupid in those days to make reflections which would have led me to change my conduct.

I had only an hour before me; nor could I wait for daylight, since Signora Orio would rather be dead than miss her mass. I spent this last hour talking only to Angela, trying first to persuade her, and then to convince her, that she should come and sit beside me. My soul passed through the whole scale of colors, in a crucible of which the reader can have no idea unless he has been in a similar situation. After using every conceivable argument, I had recourse to prayers, then (*infandum* ['unutterable']) to tears. But when I realized that they were useless, the feeling which took possession of me was *the righteous indignation which ennobles anger*. I believe I should actually have struck the proud creature who had been monster enough to keep me for five whole hours in the most cruel kind of distress, if I had not been in the dark. I showered her with all the insults which a scorned love can suggest to an enraged mind. I hurled fanatical curses at her; I swore that all my love had changed to hate, and ended by warning her to beware of me, for I should certainly kill her as soon as my eyes could see her.

My invectives ended with the darkness of night. At the first glimmerings of dawn and at the noise made by the great key and the bolt when Signora Orio opened the door to go out and put her soul in the state of repose which was a daily necessity to her, I made ready to leave, taking my cloak and hat. But, reader, I cannot depict the consternation of my soul, when, glancing at the faces of the three girls, I saw them melting into tears. In such shame and despair that I felt tempted to kill myself, I sat down again. I reflected that my brutality had driven those three beautiful souls to sobs. I could not speak. Feeling choked me; tears came to my rescue, and I indulged in them with delight. Nanetta rose and told me that her aunt must soon be back. I quickly wiped my eyes, and without looking at them or saying a word, I left and went straight home to bed, where I could not get a wink of sleep.

At noon Signor Malipiero, noticing that I was greatly changed, asked me the reason for it, and, feeling a need to unburden my soul, I told him all. The wise old man did not laugh. His very sensible remarks were balm to my soul. He knew that he was in the same situation in respect to Teresa. But he could not help laughing, nor could I, when he saw me eat with the appetite of a dog. I had not supped; but he complimented me on my excellent constitution.

Resolved not to return to Signora Orio's, about that time I
defended a metaphysical thesis in which I maintained that 'any
being which can be conceived only abstractly can exist only
abstractly.' I was right; but it was easy to make my thesis look
impious, and I was obliged to retract it. I went to Padua, where I
was granted the degree of Doctor *utroque jure*.

On my return to Venice I received a note from Signor Rosa in
which he told me that Signora Orio wished me to come and see
her. I went in the evening, when I was sure that I should not find
Angela, whom I wanted to put out of my mind. Nanetta and Marta
were so gay that they dispelled the shame I felt at appearing before
them after two months; but my thesis and my doctorate sub-
stantiated my excuses to Signora Orio, whose only reason for
wanting to see me was to complain of my never visiting her any
more. As I left, Nanetta handed me a letter containing one from
Angela. 'If you have the courage,' Angela's letter ran, 'to spend
another night with me, you will not have cause to complain, for I
love you. I wish to know from your own lips if you would have
continued to love me if I had consented to dishonor myself.'

Here is the letter from Nanetta, who was the only intelligent one
of the three girls. 'Signor Rosa having undertaken to persuade you
to return to our house, I wrote this letter beforehand to let you
know that Angela is in despair over losing you. The night that you
spent with us was cruel, I admit; but it seems to me that it should
not have made you determine not to come again, at least to see
Signora Orio. I advise you, if you still love Angela, to risk one more
night. She will perhaps be able to justify herself, and you will leave
happy. So come. Adieu.'

These two letters delighted me. I saw that I could now avenge
myself on Angela by treating her with the most open contempt. I
went on the first feast day, with two bottles of Cyprus wine and a
smoked tongue in my pocket, and was surprised not to find the
hardhearted vixen there. Turning the conversation to her, Nanetta
said that Angela had told her that morning at mass that she could

not come until suppertime. I saw no reason to doubt it, so when Signora Orio asked me to stay I did not accept. Just before the supper hour I pretended to leave, as I had the time before, and ensconced myself in the appointed place. I could not wait to play the delightful role I had planned. I felt sure that even if Angela had made up her mind to change her tactics, she would grant me no more than small favors, and these no longer interested me. My only remaining emotion was a great desire for revenge.

Three quarters of an hour later I hear the street door shut, and ten minutes after that I hear footsteps coming up the stairs, and I see before me – Nanetta and Marta.

'But where is Angela?' I ask Nanetta.

'She must have been unable either to come or to send word. Yet she must know that you are here.'

'She thinks she has tricked me, and I admit I did not expect this; now you know her as she is. She is laughing at me in triumph. She used you to make me fall into the snare; and she is better off, for if she had come it would have been I who laughed at her.'

'Permit me to doubt that.'

'Never doubt it, my dear Nanetta; you shall be convinced of it by the delightful time we shall have tonight without her.'

'In other words, as a sensible man you will make the most of second-best; but you shall go to bed here, and we will go and sleep on the couch in the other room.'

'I shall not prevent you; but you would be playing a cruel trick on me, and in any case I should not go to bed.'

'What! You would have the endurance to spend seven hours with us? I am sure that when you run out of things to say you will fall sleep.'

'We shall see. In the meanwhile here is a tongue and here is some Cyprus wine. Can you be cruel enough to let me eat by myself? Have you some bread?'

'Yes, and we will not be cruel. We'll eat a second supper.'

'It is you I ought to be in love with. Tell me, beautiful Nanetta, if you would make me unhappy as Angela does.'

'Do you think I can answer such a question? Only a conceited fool could ask it. All I can tell you is that I haven't the least idea.'

They quickly set three places, brought bread, Parmesan cheese, and water, and, laughing all the while, they ate with me and shared my Cyprus wine, which, as they were not used to it, went to their heads. Their gaiety became delightful. Looking at them, I was surprised at not having realized all their good qualities until that moment.

Sitting between them after our late supper, I took and kissed their hands and asked them if they were truly my friends and if they approved of the contemptible way in which Angela had treated me. They answered together that they had wept for me. 'Then permit me,' I said. 'to feel the fondness of a true brother for you, and do you feel for me as if you were my sisters; let us exchange pledges of our affection in the innocence of our hearts; let us kiss each other and swear eternal fidelity.'

The first kisses I gave them came neither from amorous desire nor from any intention to seduce them, and for their part they swore to me some days later that they returned them only to assure me that they shared my innocent feeling; but these harmless kisses soon became ardent and began to kindle a fire in the three of us which must have taken us aback, for we broke off and then looked at each other in grave astonishment. The two sisters made some excuse to move away, and I remained absorbed in thought. It is not surprising that the fire which these kisses had kindled in my soul, and which was even then creeping through all my limbs, made me fall invincibly in love with the two girls on the instant. They were both of them prettier than Angela, and Nanetta's quick intelligence and Marta's gentle and artless nature made them infinitely superior to her: I felt greatly surprised that I had not recognized their qualities before that moment; but they were well-born and utterly innocent girls, and the chance which had put them into my hands must not prove to be their ruin. Nothing but blind vanity could have made me believe that they loved me; but I could well suppose that the kisses had affected them even as they had me. On this assumption it was plain to me that, in the course of the long night I was to spend with them, I should not find it difficult to bring them to concessions whose consequences would be nothing short of crucial. This thought filled me with horror. I resolved to exercise the severest restraint, and I did not doubt that I should find the strength to observe it.

They reappeared, and when I saw that their faces expressed nothing but trust and contentment, I instantly cast mine in the same mold, firmly resolving that I would not expose myself to the fire of kisses again.

We spent an hour talking of Angela. I told them I was determined not to see her again, since I was convinced that she did not love me. 'She loves you,' said the artless Marta, 'I am sure of it; but if you do not mean to marry her you had better break with her entirely, for she is resolved not to grant you the slightest favor so long as you are only her lover: so you must either leave her or reconcile yourself to her granting you nothing.'

'Your reasoning is perfect; but how can you be sure that she loves me?'

'Nothing is surer. And now that we have promised to love each other like brother and sister, I can frankly tell you why. When Angela sleeps with us, she covers me with kisses and calls me her "dear Abate."'

Nanetta burst out laughing and put a hand over her sister's mouth; but this artlessness so set me on fire that I had the greatest difficulty in controlling myself. Marta said to Nanetta that, since I was so intelligent, I could not fail to know what two girls who were good friends did when they were in bed together.

'Certainly, my dear Nanetta,' I added, 'everyone knows about these little games, and I cannot believe that your sister has been too indiscreet in making this confession.'

'Well, it is done now; but one does not talk about these things. If Angela knew –'

'She would be in despair, I am sure, but Marta has given me such a proof of her friendship that I shall be grateful to her until I die. It is over and done with. I loathe Angela, I shall never speak to her again. She is false-hearted, she wants to destroy me.'

'But if she loves you she has every right to want you to marry her.'

'True enough; but the tactics she employs have no other aim than her own advantage, and since she knows how I suffer she cannot behave as she does unless she does not love me. Meanwhile, by a make-believe as false as it is monstrous, she assuages her beastly desires with this charming Marta, who kindly serves as her husband.'

At this Nanetta's laughter redoubled; but I did not change my serious expression and went on talking to Marta in the same style, praising her admirable sincerity with the most high-flown eloquence.

Finding that the subject was giving me the greatest pleasure, I told Marta that Angela ought to play the part of her husband too; whereupon she laughed and said that she only played husband to Nanetta, which Nanetta was obliged to admit.

'But by what name does Nanetta call her husband,' I asked Marta, 'in her transports?'

'Nobody knows.'

'So then you love someone,' I said to Nanetta.

'Yes, I do, but no one shall ever know my secret.'

At this, I flattered myself that Nanetta might secretly be Angela's rival. But with all this charming talk, I lost any wish to spend the night in idleness with these two girls who were made for love. I said I was very glad that I entertained only friendly feelings toward them, for otherwise I should find it extremely hard to spend the night with them without wishing to give them proofs of my love and to receive proofs of theirs, 'for,' I added coolly, 'you are both ravishingly beautiful and more than capable of turning the head of any man whom you will allow to know you as you are.' After this speech I pretended I wanted to go to sleep. 'Don't stand on ceremony,' Nanetta said, 'get into bed. We will go and sleep on the couch in the other room.'

'If I did that, I should consider myself the most contemptible of men. Let us talk: my sleepiness will pass off. I am only sorry on your account. It is you who should get into bed, and I will go to the other room. If you are afraid of me, lock yourselves in, but you would be wrong, for I love you only with the heart of a brother.'

'We will never do that,' said Nanetta. 'Please do as we say, and go to bed here.'

'If I keep my clothes on, I shan't sleep.'

'Then undress. We won't look at you.'

'That doesn't worry me; but I could never get to sleep, with you obliged to stay up on my account.'

'We'll go to bed too,' said Marta, 'but we won't undress.'

'Such distrust is an insult to my integrity. Tell me, Nanetta, do you consider me a man of honor?'

'Yes, certainly.'

'Well and good. Do you want to convince me of it? You must both lie down beside me completely undressed, and count on my word of honor, which I now give you, that I will not touch you. You are two and I am one – what have you to fear? Won't you be free to leave the bed if I do not behave myself? In short, if you will not promise to show me this proof of your confidence, at least when you see that I have fallen asleep, I will not go to bed.'

I then stopped talking and pretended to fall asleep, and they whispered together; then Marta told me to get into bed and said they would do likewise when they saw that I was asleep. Nanetta made the same promise, whereupon I turned my back to them, took off all my clothes, got into the bed, and wished them good night. I pretended to fall asleep at once, but within a quarter of an hour I was asleep in good earnest. I woke only when they came and got into the bed, but I at once turned away and resumed my sleep, nor did I begin to act until I had reason to suppose that they were sleeping. If they were not, they had only to pretend to be. They had turned their backs to me and we were in darkness. I began with the one toward whom I was turned, not knowing whether it was Nanetta or Marta. I found her curled up and covered by her shift, but by doing nothing to startle her and proceeding step by step as gradually as possible, I soon convinced her that her best course was to pretend to be asleep and let me go on. Little by little I straightened her out, little by little she uncurled, and little by little, with slow, successive, but wonderfully natural movements, she put herself in a position which was the most favorable she could offer me without betraying herself. I set to work, but to crown my labors it was necessary that she should join in them openly and undeniably, and nature finally forced her to do so. I found this first sister beyond suspicion, and suspecting the pain she must have endured, I was surprised. In duty bound religiously to respect a prejudice to which I owed a pleasure the sweetness of which I was tasting for the first time in my life, I let the victim alone and turned the other way to do the same thing with her sister, who must be expecting me to demonstrate the full extent of my gratitude.

I found her motionless, in the position often taken by a person who is lying on his back in deep, untroubled sleep. With the greatest precautions, and every appearance of fearing to waken her, I began by delighting her soul, at the same time assuring myself that she was as untouched as her sister; and I continued the same treatment until, affecting a most natural movement without which I could not have crowned my labors, she helped me to triumph; but at the moment of crisis she no longer had the strength to keep up her pretense. Throwing off the mask, she clasped me in her arms and pressed her mouth on mine. After the act, 'I am sure,' I said, 'that you are Nanetta.'

'Yes, and I consider myself fortunate, as my sister is, if you are honorable and loyal.'

'Even unto death, my angels! All that we have done was the work of love, and let there be no more talk of Angela.'

I then asked her to get up and light some candles, but it was Marta who obliged. When I saw Nanetta in my arms on fire with love, and Marta holding a candle and looking at us, seeming to accuse us of ingratitude for not saying a word to her, when, by having been the first to yield to my caresses, she had encouraged her sister to imitate her, I realized all my good fortune.

'Let us get up,' I said, 'and swear eternal friendship and then refresh ourselves.'

Under my direction the three of us made an improvised toilet in a bucket of water, which set us laughing and renewed all our desires; then, in the costume of the Golden Age, we finished the rest of the tongue and emptied the other bottle. After our state of sensual intoxication had made us say a quantity of those things which only love can interpret, we went back to bed and spent the rest of the night in ever varied skirmishes. It was Nanetta who joined in the last. Signora Orio having gone to mass, I had to leave them without wasting time on words. After swearing that I no longer gave a thought to Angela, I went home and buried myself in sleep until dinnertime.

JAMES BOSWELL

from

The Journals of James Boswell

James Boswell (1740–1795), Dr Johnson's biographer, wrote journals as self-revealing as Pepys's Diary. Boswell writes: 'I thought of my valuable spouse with the highest regard and warmest affection, but had a confused notion that my corporeal connection with whores did not interfere with my love for her.' This is his account of a typically vigorous sexual encounter in December 1762 and January 1763.

I WENT to Love's and drank tea. I had now been some time in town without female sport. I determined to have nothing to do with whores, as my health was of great consequence to me. I went to a girl with whom I had an intrigue at Edinburgh, but my affection cooling, I had left her. I knew she was come up. I waited on her and tried to obtain my former favours, but in vain. She would by no means listen. I was really unhappy for want of women. I thought it hard to be in such a place without them. I picked up a girl in the Strand; went into a court with intention to enjoy her in amour. But she had none. I toyed with her. She wondered at my size, and said if I ever took a girl's maidenhead, I would make her squeak. I gave her a shilling, and had command enough of myself to go without touching her. I afterwards trembled at the danger I had escaped. I resolved to wait cheerfully till I got some safe girl or was liked by some woman of fashion.

TUESDAY 14 DECEMBER. It is very curious to think that I have now been in London several weeks without ever enjoying the delightful sex, although I am surrounded with numbers of free-hearted ladies of all kinds: from the splendid Madam at fifty guineas a night, down to the civil nymph with white-thread stockings who tramps along the Strand and will resign her engaging person to your honour for a pint of wine and a shilling. Manifold are the reasons for this my present wonderful continence. I am upon a plan of economy, and therefore cannot be at the expense of first-rate dames. I have suffered severely from the loathsome distemper, and therefore shudder at the thoughts of running any risk of having it again. Besides, the surgeons' fees in this city come very high. But the greatest reason of all is that fortune, or rather benignant Venus, has smiled upon me and favoured me so far that I have had the most delicious intrigues with women of beauty, sentiment and spirit, perfectly suited to my romantic genius.

Indeed, in my mind, there cannot be higher felicity on earth enjoyed by man than the participation of genuine reciprocal amorous affection with an amiable woman. There he has a full indulgence of all the delicate feelings and pleasures both of body and mind, while at the same time in this enchanting union he exults with a consciousness that he is the superior person. The dignity of his sex is kept up. These paradisial scenes of gallantry have exalted my ideas and refined my taste, so that I really cannot think of stooping so far as to make a most intimate companion of a grovelling-minded, ill-bred, worthless creature, nor can my delicacy be pleased with the gross voluptuousness of the stews. I am therefore walking about with a healthful stout body and a cheerful mind, in search of a woman worthy of my love, and who thinks me worthy of hers, without any interested views, which is the only sure way to find out if a woman really loves a man. If I should be a single man for the whole winter, I will be satisfied. I have had as much elegant pleasure as I could have expected would come to my share in many years.

However, I hope to be more successful. In this view, I had now called several times for a handsome actress of Covent Garden

Theatre, whom I was a little acquainted with, and whom I shall distinguish in this my journal by the name of LOUISA. This lady had been indisposed and saw no company, but today I was admitted. She was in a pleasing undress and looked very pretty. She received me with great politeness. We chatted on the common topics. We were not easy – there was a constraint upon us – we did not sit right on our chairs, and we were unwilling to look at one another. I talked to her on the advantage of having an agreeable acquaintance, and hoped I might see her now and then. She desired me to call in whenever I came that way, without ceremony. 'And pray,' said she, 'when shall I have the pleasure of your company at tea?' I fixed Thursday, and left her, very well satisfied with my first visit.

I then called on Mr Lee, who is a good, agreeable, honest man, and with whom I associate fine gay ideas of the Edinburgh Theatre in my boyish days, when I used to walk down the Canongate and think of players with a mixture of narrow-minded horror and lively-minded pleasure; and used to wonder at painted equipages and powdered ladies, and sing 'The bonny bush aboon Traquair', and admire Mrs Bland in her chair with tassels, and flambeaux before her.

I did not find Lee at home. I then went to Love's. They were just sitting down to a piece of roast beef. I said that was a dish which I never let pass, and so sat down and took a slice of it. I was vexed at myself for doing it, even at the time. Love abused Mr Digges grossly; said he was a worse player than the lowest actor in Covent Garden. Their vulgarity and stupid malevolence (for Mrs Love also joined in the abuse) disgusted me much. I left them, determined scarcely to keep up an acquaintance with them, and in general to keep clear of the players, which indeed I do at present.

THURSDAY 16 DECEMBER. In the afternoon I went to Louisa's. A little black young fellow, her brother, came in. I could have wished him at the Bay of Honduras. However, I found him a good quiet obliging being who gave us no disturbance. She talked on a man's liking a woman's company, and of the injustice people treated them with in suspecting anything bad. This was a fine artful pretty speech. We talked of French manners, and how they studied to make one another happy. 'The English', said I, 'accuse them of being false, because they misunderstand them. When a Frenchman makes warm professions of regard, he does it only to please you for the time. It is words of course. There is no more of it. But the English, who are cold and phlegmatic in their address, take all these fine speeches in earnest, and are confounded to find them otherwise, and exclaim against the perfidious Gaul most unjustly. For when Frenchmen put a thing home seriously and vow fidelity, they have the strictest honour. O they are the people who enjoy time; so lively, pleasant and gay. You never hear of madness or self-murder among them. Heat of fancy evaporates in fine brisk clear vapour with them, but amongst the English often falls heavy upon the brain.'

We chatted pretty easily. We talked of love as a thing that could not be controlled by reason, as a fine passion. I could not clearly discern how she meant to behave to me. She told me that a gentleman had come to her and offered her £50, but that her brother knocked at the door and the man run out of the house without saying a word. I said I wished he had left his money. We joked much about the £50. I said I expected some night to be surprised with such an offer from some decent elderly gentlewoman. I made just a comic parody to her story. I sat till past eight. She said she hoped it would not be long before she had the pleasure of seeing me again.

This night I made no visible progress in my amour, but I in reality was doing a great deal. I was getting well acquainted with her. I was appearing an agreeable companion to her; I was informing her by my looks of my passion for her.

FRIDAY 17 DECEMBER. I engaged in this amour just with a view of convenient pleasure but the god of pleasing anguish now seriously loved my breast. I felt the fine delirium of love. I waited on Louisa at home, found her alone, told her that her goodness in hoping to me *soon* had brought me back: that it appeared long to me since I saw her. I was a little bashful. However, I took a good heart and talked with ease and dignity. 'I hope, Madam, you are at present a single woman.' 'Yes, sir.' 'And your affections are not engaged?' 'They are not, Sir.' 'But this is leading me into a strange confession. I assure you, Madam, my affections are engaged.' 'Are they, Sir?' 'Yes, Madam, they are engaged to you.' (She looked soft and beautiful.) 'I hope we shall be better acquainted and like one another better.' 'Come, Sir, let us talk no more of that now.' 'No, Madam, I will not. It is like giving the book in the preface.' 'Just so, Sir, telling in the preface what should be in the middle of the book.' (I think such conversations are best written in the dialogue way.) 'Madam, I was very happy to find you. From the first time that I saw you, I admired you.' 'O, Sir.' 'I did, indeed. What I like beyond everything is an agreeable female companion, where I can be at home and have tea and genteel conversation. I was quite happy to be here.' 'Sir, you are welcome here as often as you please. Every evening, if you please.' 'Madam, I am infinitely obliged to you.'

[*Boswell is at Sheridan's.*] We talked of Johnson. He told me a story of how 'I was dining', said Johnson, 'with the Mayor of Windsor, who gave me a very hearty dinner; but, not satisfied with feeding my body, he would also feed my understanding. So, after he had spoke a great deal of clumsy nonsense, he told me that at the last Sessions he had transported three people to the Plantations. I was so provoked with the fellow's dullness and impertinence that I exclaimed, "I wish to GOD, Sir, I was the fourth."' Nothing could more strongly express his dissatisfaction.

Mrs Sheridan told me that he was very sober, but would sit up the whole night. He left them once at two in the morning and begged to be excused for going away so soon, as he had another visit to make. I like to mark every anecdote of men of so much genius and literature.

I found out Sheridan's great cause of quarrel with him was that when Johnson heard of his getting a pension, 'What!' said he, 'has *he* got a pension? Then it is time for me to give up mine.' 'Now,' said he, 'here was the greatest ingratitude. For it was I and Wedderburn that first set the thing a-going.' This I believe was true.

SATURDAY 18 DECEMBER. I went to Louisa's. I was really in love. I felt a warmth at my heart which glowed in my face. I attempted to be like Digges, and considered the similarity of our genius and pleasures. I acquired confidence by considering my present character in this light: a young fellow of spirit and fashion, heir to a good fortune, enjoying the pleasures of London, and now making his addresses in order to have an intrigue with that delicious subject of gallantry, an actress.

I talked on love very freely. 'Madam,' said I, 'I can never think of having a connection with women that I don't love.' 'That, Sir,' said she, 'is only having a satisfaction in common with the brutes. But when there is a union of minds, that is indeed estimable. But don't think, Sir, that I am a Platonist. I am not indeed.' (This hint gave me courage.) 'To be sure, Madam, when there is such a connection as you mention, it is the finest thing in the world. I beg you may just show me civility according as you find me deserve it.' 'Such a connection, Sir, requires time to establish it.' (I thought it honest and proper to let her know that she must not depend on me for giving her much money.) 'Madam,' said I, 'don't think too highly of me. Nor give me the respect which men of great fortune get by custom. I am here upon a very moderate allowance. I am upon honour to make it serve me, and I am obliged to live with great economy.' She received this very well.

SUNDAY 19 DECEMBER. I can come home in an evening, put on my old clothes, nightcap and slippers, and sit as contented as a cobbler writing my journal or letters to my friends. While I can thus entertain myself, I must be happy in solitude. Indeed there is a great difference between solitude in the country, where you cannot help it, and in London, where you can in a moment be in the hurry and splendour of life.

MONDAY 20 DECEMBER. I went to Louisa's after breakfast.

'Indeed,' said I, 'it was hard upon me to leave you so soon yester-day. I am quite happy in your company.' 'Sir,' said she, 'you are very obliging. But', said she, 'I am in bad humour this morning. There was a person who professed the greatest friendship for me; I now applied for their assistance, but was shifted. It was such a trifle that I am sure they could have granted it. So I have been railing against my fellow creatures.' 'Nay, dear Madam, don't abuse them all on account of an individual. But pray what was this favour? Might I know?' (She blushed.) 'Why, Sir, there is a person has sent to me for a trifling debt. I sent back word that it was not convenient for me to let them have it just now, but in six weeks I should pay it.'

I was a little confounded and embarrassed here. I dreaded bring-ing myself into a scrape. I did not know what she might call a tri-fling sum. I half-resolved to say no more. However, I thought that she might now be trying my generosity and regard for her, and truly this was the real test. I thought I would see if it was in my power to assist her.

'Pray, Madam, what was the sum?' 'Only two guineas, Sir.' Amazed and pleased, I pulled out my purse. 'Madam,' said I, 'if I can do you any service, you may command me. Two guineas is at present all that I have, but a trifle more. There they are for you. I told you that I had very little, but yet I hope to live. Let us just be honest with one another. Tell me when you are in any little dis-tress, and I will tell you what I can do.' She took the guineas. 'Sir, I am infinitely obliged to you. As soon as it is in my power, I shall return them. Indeed I could not have expected this from you.' Her gratitude warmed my heart. 'Madam! though I have little, yet as far as ten guineas, you may apply to me. I would live upon nothing to serve one that I regarded.'

I did not well know what to think of this scene. Sometimes I thought it artifice, and that I was taken in. And then again, I viewed it just as a circumstance that might very easily happen. Her men-tioning returning the money looked well. My naming the sum of ten guineas was rash; however, I considered that it cost me as much to be cured of what I contracted from a whore, and that ten guineas was but a moderate expense for women during the winter.

I had all along treated her with a distant politeness. On Saturday I just kissed her hand. She now sung to me. I got up in raptures and kissed her with great warmth. She received this very genteelly. I had a delicacy in presuming too far, lest it should look like demanding goods for my money. I resumed the subject of love and gallantry. She said, 'I pay no regard to the opinion in the world so far as contradicts my own sentiments.' 'No, Madam, we are not to mind the arbitrary rules imposed by the multitude.' 'Yet, Sir, there is a decency to be kept with the public. And I must do so, whose bread depends upon them.' 'Certainly, Madam. But when may I wait upon you? Tomorrow evening?' 'Sir, I am obliged to be all day with a lady who is not well.' 'Then next day, Madam.' 'What? to drink a dish of tea, Sir?' 'No, no, not to drink a dish of tea.' (Here I looked sheepish.) 'What time may I wait upon you?' 'Whenever you please, Sir.' I kissed her again, and went away highly pleased with the thoughts of the affair being settled.

WEDNESDAY 22 DECEMBER. This forenoon I went to Louisa's in full expectation of consummate bliss. I was in a strange flutter of feeling. I was ravished at the prospect of joy, and yet I had such an anxiety upon me that I was afraid that my powers would be enervated. I almost wished to be free of this assignation. I entered her apartment in a sort of confusion. She was elegantly dressed in the morning fashion, and looked delightfully well. I felt the tormenting anxiety of serious love. I sat down and I talked with the distance of a new acquaintance and not with the ease and ardour of a lover, or rather a gallant. I talked of her lodgings being neat, opened the door of her bedchamber, looked into it. Then sat down by her in a most melancholy plight. I would have given a good deal to be out of the room.

I then sat near her and began to talk softly, but finding myself quite dejected with love, I really cried out and told her that I was miserable; and as I was stupid, would go away. I rose, but saluting her with warmth, my powers were excited, I felt myself vigorous.

I sat down again. I beseeched her, 'You know, Madam, you said you was not a Platonist. I beg it of you to be so kind. You said you are above the finesse of your sex.' (Be sure always to make a woman better than her sex.) 'I adore you.' 'Nay, dear Sir' (I pressing her to me and kissing her now and then), 'pray be quiet. Such a thing requires time to consider of.' 'Madam, I own this would be necessary for any man but me. But you must take my character from myself. I am very good-tempered, very honest and have little money. I should have some reward for my particular honesty.' 'But, Sir, give me time to recollect myself.' 'Well then, Madam, when shall I see you?' 'On Friday, Sir.' 'A thousand thanks.' I left her and came home and took my bread and cheese with great contentment.

I sat this evening a while with Webster. He entertained me and raised my spirits with military conversation. Yet he sunk them a little; as he brought into my mind some dreary Tolbooth Kirk ideas, than which nothing has given me more gloomy feelings. I shall never forget the dismal hours of apprehension that I have endured in my youth from narrow notions of religion while my tender mind was lacerated with infernal horror. I am surprised how I have got rid of these notions so entirely. Thank GOD, my mind is now clear and elevated. I am serene and happy. I can look up to my Creator with adoration and hope.

THURSDAY 23 DECEMBER. I eat my cold repast today heartily. I have great spirits. I see how little a man can live upon. I find that Fortune cannot get the better of me. I never can come lower than to live on bread and cheese.

FRIDAY 24 DECEMBER. I waited on Louisa. Says she, 'I have been very unhappy since you was here. I have been thinking of what I said to you. I find that such a connection would make me miserable.' 'I hope, Madam, I am not disagreeable to you.' 'No, Sir, you are not. If it was the first duke in England I spoke to, I should just say the same thing.' 'But pray, Madam, what is your objection?' 'Really, Sir, I have many disagreeable apprehensions. It may be known. Circumstances might be very troublesome. I beg it of you,

Sir, consider it. Your own good sense will agree with me. Instead of visiting me as you do now, you would find a discontented, unhappy creature.' I was quite confused. I did not know what to say. At last I agreed to think of it and see her on Sunday. I came home and dined in dejection. Yet I mustered up vivacity, and away I went in full dress to Northumberland House. There was spirit, to lay out a couple of shillings and be a man of fashion in my situation. There was true economy.

SATURDAY 25 DECEMBER. The night before I did not rest well. I was really violently in love with Louisa. I thought she did not care for me. I thought that if I did not gain her affections, I would appear despicable to myself. This day I was in a better frame, being Christmas day, which has always inspired me with most agreeable feelings. I went to St Paul's Church and in that magnificent temple fervently adored the GOD of goodness and mercy, and heard a sermon by the Bishop of Oxford on the publishing of glad tidings of great joy.

SUNDAY 26 DECEMBER. I went to Whitehall Chapel and heard service. I took a whim to go through all the churches and chapels in London, taking one each Sunday.

At one I went to Louisa's. I told her my passion in the warmest terms. I told her that my happiness absolutely depended upon her. She said it was running the greatest risk. 'Then,' said I, 'Madam, you will show the greatest generosity to a most sincere lover.' She said that we should take time to consider of it, and that then we could better determine how to act. We agreed that the time should be a week, and that if I remained of the same opinion, she would then make me blessed. There is no telling how easy it made my mind to be convinced that she did not despise me, but on the contrary had a tender heart and wished to make me easy and happy.

1763

SATURDAY 1 JANUARY. I received for a suit of old clothes 11s, which came to me in good time. I went to Louisa at one. 'Madam, I have been thinking seriously.' 'Well, Sir, I hope you are of my way of thinking.' 'I hope, Madam, you are of mine. I have considered this matter most seriously. The week is now elapsed, and I hope you will not be so cruel as to keep me in misery.' (I then began to take some liberties.) 'Nay, Sir – now – but do consider –' 'Ah, Madam!' 'Nay, but you are an encroaching creature!' (Upon this I advanced to the greatest freedom by a sweet elevation of the charming petticoat.) 'Good heaven, Sir!' 'Madam, I cannot help it. I adore you. Do you like me?' (She answered me with a warm kiss, and pressing me to her bosom, sighed, 'O Mr Boswell!') 'But, my dear Madam! Permit me, I beseech you.' 'Lord, Sir, the people may come in.' 'How then can I be happy? What time? Do tell me.' 'Why, Sir, on Sunday afternoon my landlady, of whom I am most afraid, goes to church, so you may come here a little after three.' 'Madam, I thank you a thousand times.' 'Now, Sir, I have but one favour to ask of you. Whenever you cease to regard me, pray don't use me ill, nor treat me coldly. But inform me by a letter or any other way that it is over.' 'Pray, Madam, don't talk of such a thing. Indeed, we cannot answer for our affections. But you may depend on my behaving with civility and politeness.'

SUNDAY 2 JANUARY. I had George Home at breakfast with me. He is a good honest fellow and applies well to his business as a merchant. He had seen me all giddiness at his father's, and was astonished to find me settled on so prudent a plan. As I have made it a rule to dine every Sunday at home, and have got my landlady to give us regularly on that day a piece of good roast beef with a warm apple-pie, I was a little difficulted today, as our time of dining is three o'clock, just my hour of assignation. However, I got dinner to be at two, and at three I hastened to my charmer.

Here a little speculation on the human mind may well come in. For here was I, a young man full of vigour and vivacity, the favourite lover of a handsome actress and going to enjoy the full possession of my warmest wishes. And yet melancholy threw a cloud over my mind. I could relish nothing. I felt dispirited and languid. I approached Louisa with a kind of an uneasy tremor. I sat down. I toyed with her. Yet I was not inspired by Venus. I felt rather a delicate sensation of love than a violent amorous inclination for her. I was very miserable. I thought myself feeble as a gallant, although I had experienced the reverse many a time. Louisa knew not my powers. She might imagine me impotent. I sweated almost with anxiety, which made me worse. She behaved extremely well; did not seem to remember the occasion of our meeting at all. I told her I was very dull. Said she, 'People cannot always command their spirits.' The time of church was almost elapsed when I began to feel that I was still a man. I fanned the flame by pressing her alabaster breasts and kissing her delicious lips. I then barred the door of her dining-room, led her all fluttering into her bedchamber, and was just making a triumphal entry when we heard her landlady coming up. 'O Fortune, why did it happen thus?' would have been the exclamation of a Roman bard. We were stopped most suddenly and cruelly from the fruition of each other. She ran out and stopped the landlady from coming up. Then returned to me in the dining-room. We fell into each other's arms, sighing and panting, 'O dear, how hard this is.' 'O Madam, see what you can contrive for me.' 'Lord, Sir, I am so frightened.'

Her brother then came in. I recollected that I had been at no place of worship today. I begged pardon for a little and went to Covent Garden Church, where there is evening service between five and six. I heard a few prayers and then returned and drank tea. She entertained us with her adventures when travelling through the country. Some of them were excellent. I told her she might make a novel. She said if I would put them together that she would give me material. I went home at seven. I was unhappy at being prevented from the completion of my wishes, and yet I thought that I had saved my credit for prowess, that I might through anxiety have not acted a vigorous part; and that we might contrive a meeting where I could love with ease and freedom.

MONDAY 3 JANUARY. I begged Louisa to invent some method by which we might meet in security. I insisted that she should go and pass the night with me somewhere. She begged time to think of it.

TUESDAY 4 JANUARY. Louisa told me that she would go with me to pass the night when she was sure that she would not be wanted at the playhouse next day; and she mentioned Saturday as most convenient, being followed by Sunday, on which nothing is done. 'But, Sir,' said she, 'may not this be attended with expense? I hope you'll excuse me.' There was something so kind and so delicate in this hint that it charmed me. 'No, Madam, it cannot be a great expense, and I can save on other articles to have money for this.'

I recollected that when I was in London two years ago I had left a guinea with Mr Meighan, a Roman Catholic bookseller in Drury Lane, of which I had some change to receive. I went to him and got 5s and 6d, which gave me no small consolation. Elated with this new acquisition of pecuniary property, I instantly resolved to eat, drink and be merry. I therefore hied me to a beer-house; called for some bread and cheese and a pint of porter.

I then bethought me of a place to which Louisa and I might safely go. I went to my good friend Hayward's at the Black Lion, told him that I had married, and that I and my wife, who was to be in town on Saturday, would sleep in his house till I got a lodging for her. The King of Prussia says in one of his poems that gallantry comprises every vice. That of lying it certainly does, without which intrigue can never be carried on. But as the proverb says, in love and war all is fair. I who am a lover and hope to be a soldier think so. In this instance we could not be admitted to any decent house except as man and wife. Indeed, we are so if union of hearts be the principal requisite. We are so, at least for a time. How cleverly this can be done here. In Scotland it is impossible. We should be married with a vengeance. I went home and dined. I thought my slender diet weakened me. I resolved to live hearty and be stout. This afternoon I became very low-spirited. I sat in close. I hated all things. I almost hated London. O miserable absurdity! I could see nothing in a good light. I just submitted and hoped to get the better of this.

WEDNESDAY 12 JANUARY. Louisa and I agreed that at eight at night she would meet me in the Piazzas of Covent Garden. I was quite elevated, and felt myself able and undaunted to engage in the wars of the Paphian Queen.

At the appointed hour of eight I went to the Piazzas, where I sauntered up and down for a while in a sort of trembling suspense, I knew not why. At last my charming companion appeared, and I immediately conducted her to a hackney-coach which I had ready waiting, pulled up the blinds, and away we drove to the destined scene of delight. We contrived to seem as if we had come off a journey, and carried in a bundle our night-clothes, hand-kerchiefs, and other little things. We also had with us some almond biscuits, or as they call them in London, macaroons, which looked like provision on the road. On our arrival at Hayward's we were shown into the parlour, in the same manner that any decent couple would be. I here thought proper to conceal my own name (which the people of the house had never heard), and assumed the name of Mr Digges. We were shown up to the very room where he slept. I said my cousin, as I called him, was very well. That Ceres and Bacchus might in moderation lend their assistance to Venus, I ordered a genteel supper and some wine.

We supped cheerfully and agreeably and drank a few glasses, and then the maid came and put the sheets, well aired, upon the bed. I now contemplated my fair prize. Louisa is just twenty-four, of a tall rather than short figure, finely made in person, with a handsome face and an enchanting languish in her eyes. She dresses with taste. She has sense, good humour and vivacity, and looks quite a woman in genteel life. As I mused on this elevating subject, I could not help being somehow pleasingly confounded to think that so fine a woman was at this moment in my possession, that without any motives of interest she had come with me to an inn, agreed to be my intimate companion, as to be my bedfellow all night, and to permit me the full enjoyment of her person.

When the servant left the room, I embraced her warmly and begged that she would not now delay my felicity. She declined to undress before me, and begged I would retire and send her one of the maids. I did so, gravely desiring the girl to go up to Mrs Digges. I then took a candle in my hand and walked out to the yard. The night was very dark and very cold. I experienced for some minutes the rigours of the season, and called into my mind many terrible ideas of hardships, that I might make a transition from such dreary thoughts to the most gay and delicious feelings. I then caused make a bowl of negus, very rich of the fruit, which I caused be set in the room as a reviving cordial.

I came softly into the room, and in a sweet delirium slipped into bed and was immediately clasped in her snowy arms and pressed to her milk-white bosom. Good heavens, what a loose did we give to amorous dalliance! The friendly curtain of darkness concealed our blushes. In a moment I felt myself animated with the strongest powers of love, and, from my dearest creature's kindness, had a most luscious feast. Proud of my godlike vigour, I soon resumed the noble game. I was in full glow of health. Sobriety had preserved me from effeminacy and weakness, and my bounding blood beat quick and high alarms. A more voluptuous night I never enjoyed. Five times was I fairly lost in supreme rapture. Louisa was madly fond of me; she declared I was a prodigy, and asked me if this was not extraordinary for human nature. I said twice as much might be, but this was not, although in my own mind I was somewhat proud of my performance. She said it was what there was no just reason to be proud of. But I told her I could not help it. She said it was what we had in common with the beasts. I said no. For we had it highly improved by the pleasures of sentiment. I asked her what she thought enough. She gently chid me for asking such questions, but said two times. I mentioned the Sunday's assignation, when I was in such bad spirits, told her in what agony of mind I was, and asked her if she would not have despised me for my imbecility. She declared she would not, as it was what people had not in their own power.

She often insisted that we should compose ourselves to sleep before I would consent to it. At last I sunk to rest in her arms and she in mine. I found the negus, which had a fine flavour, very refreshing to me. Louisa had an exquisite mixture of delicacy and wantonness that made me enjoy her with more relish. Indeed I could not help roving in fancy to the embraces of some other ladies which my lively imagination strongly pictured. I don't know if that was altogether fair. However, Louisa had all the advantage. She said she was quite fatigued and could neither stir leg nor arm. She begged I would not despise her, and hoped my love would not be altogether transient. I have painted this night as well as I could. The description is faint; but I surely may be styled a Man of Pleasure.

THURSDAY 13 JANUARY. We awaked from sweet repose after the luscious fatigues of the night. I got up between nine and ten and walked out till Louisa should rise. I patrolled up and down Fleet Street, thinking on London, the seat of Parliament and the seat of pleasure, and seeming to myself as one of the wits in King Charles the Second's time. I then came in and we had an agreeable breakfast, after which we left Hayward's, who said he was sorry he had not more of our company, and calling a hackney-coach, drove to Soho Square, where Louisa had some visits to pay. So we parted. Thus was this conquest completed to my highest satisfaction. I can with pleasure trace the progress of this intrigue to its completion. I am now at ease on that head, having my fair one fixed as my own. As Captain Plume says, the best security for a woman's mind is her body. I really conducted this affair with a manliness and prudence that pleased me very much. The whole expense was just eighteen shillings.

VOLTAIRE

from

Candide

Voltaire (1694–1778) was one of the most influential writers of his day. His real name was Francois-Maria Arouet. His most famous work was Candide, ou L'Optimisme *(1759), an anti-religious, satiric novel which was held to be blasphemous and obscene. Dr Pangloss, the hero's tutor, subscribes to the belief that 'all is for the best in this best of all possible worlds' and holds to it despite the terrible things that befall him. In this tale, Candide is shocked by a woman's story of her abduction by pirates.*

The old woman's story

'MY eyes were not always sore and bloodshot, my nose did not always touch my chin, and I have not always been a servant. I am the daughter of Pope Urban X and the Princess of Palestrina.* Until the age of fourteen I was brought up in a palace whose very stables were grander than all the mansions of your German barons, and any one of my dresses was worth more than all the magnificence of Westphalia. I daily increased in beauty, grace, and accomplishments, and was surrounded by delights of all kinds. I met with tokens of respect and excited expectations wherever I went; and I was already an object of desire. My breast grew shapely,

---

* Notice how exceedingly discreet our author is. There has so far been no Pope called Urban X. He hesitates to ascribe a bastard to an actual Pope. What discretion! What a tender conscience he shows! [*Voltaire's note.*]

and what a lovely breast it was! White as a lily, and as firmly and elegantly moulded as the Venus de Medici's. And when I think of my eyes and those marvellous eyelids and jet-black brows, I remember how our local poets used to tell me that the flames which burned so brightly in those two pupils of mine outshone the twinkling of the stars. The women who dressed and undressed me fell back in ecstasy as they looked at me before and behind; and there was not a man who did not yearn to change places with them.

'I was betrothed to a sovereign prince of Massa-Carrara, assuredly the very pattern of all princes. He was my equal in beauty, a paragon of grace and charm, sparkling with wit, and burning with love. I adored him to distraction, to the point of idolatry: I loved him as one can never love twice. The marriage was to be celebrated with unparalleled pomp and magnificence. It was a continual round of feasting, dancing, and carnival, and the whole of Italy was engaged in writing me sonnets, not one of which was worth reading. The highest point of my happiness was at hand when an old marchioness, who had been my Prince's mistress, invited him to drink chocolate with her. He died less than two hours later in horrible convulsions; but that is a mere trifle. My mother was less afflicted than I was by this blow, yet even her despondency was such that she decided to leave this melancholy scene for a while and visit a beautiful estate which she owned near Gaeta. We set sail in a yacht gilded as richly as the altar of St. Peter's at Rome, but had not gone far when a Moorish pirate bore down upon our ship and attacked us. Our soldiers defended themselves like the Pope's guard: they fell on their knees and threw away their arms, begging the pirates for absolution at the point of death.

'They were immediately stripped stark naked, and so were my mother, our ladies-in-waiting, and I. It is wonderful how quickly these gentlemen can strip people; but what surprised me more was that they put their fingers into a place where we women normally admit nothing but a syringe-tube. This seemed to me an unusual custom, but that is how we regard everything new when we first leave our native country. I soon discovered that they wanted to make sure we had not hidden any diamonds there, a practice dating from time immemorial among civilised seafaring nations. I learnt that the Maltese Knights of St. John never fail to observe it when they capture any Turks and their ladies; and it is, in fact, an established point of international law which has never been called in question.

'I need not tell you what a hardship it was for a young princess and her mother to be carried to Morocco as slaves, and you can readily imagine what we had to suffer on board the pirate ship. My mother was still a beautiful woman, and our ladies-in-waiting, even our chambermaids, had more charms than can be found in the whole of Africa. As for me, I was ravishingly lovely, the pattern of beauty and grace; and I was a virgin – but not for long. That flower of maidenhood, which had been reserved for the handsome Prince of Massa-Carrara, was torn from me by the pirate captain, an odious negro, who even fancied he was doing me an honour. The Princess of Palestrina and I must certainly have been mighty strong to withstand all we had to undergo before reaching Morocco. But that's enough: such experiences are so common that they are not worth the trouble of describing.

'Morocco was swimming in blood when we arrived. The fifty sons of the Emperor Muley Ismael each had his faction, which in effect created fifty civil wars of blacks against blacks, blacks against tawnies, tawnies against tawnies, and mulattoes against mulattoes. It was perpetual massacre throughout the length and breadth of the empire.

'We had scarcely disembarked when some blacks of a hostile faction turned up to carry off my pirate's booty, of which we were the most precious part except for the gold and diamonds. I then witnessed a fight such as you would never see the like of in European climates. Northern races are not sufficiently warm-blooded; their lust for women does not reach the mania that is so common in Africa. It seems that Europeans have milk in their veins, but it's fire and vitriol that runs in the veins of those who live on Mount Atlas and round about. They fought like the lions, tigers, and serpents of their country to decide who should have us. A Moor seized my mother by the right arm, and my captain's lieutenant held her by the left; a Moroccan soldier took her by one leg, while one of our pirates clung to the other. Almost all our women were immediately disputed in the same fashion by four soldiers apiece. My captain kept me hidden behind him, and with his scimitar slew everyone who confronted him. In the end I saw my mother and all our Italian ladies torn limb from limb, slashed, and massacred by the monsters that fought for them. All were killed, both captors and captives, my companions, the soldiers, sailors, blacks, whites, and mulattoes, and finally my pirate chief; and I myself lay dying on a heap of corpses. Scenes such as these took place all over that country, as I know full well – and it is three hundred leagues across. Yet they will not miss one of the five daily prayers prescribed by Mahomet.

'I freed myself with considerable trouble from the pile of bleeding corpses, and managed to crawl to the shade of a large orange tree on the banks of a stream nearby. There I collapsed, exhausted and famished, overcome by fear, horror, and despair; and soon after I fell asleep, if I may so describe what was more like a trance than slumber. I was in this state of weakness and insensibility, hovering between life and death, when I felt myself pressed by something stirring on my body. I opened my eyes and beheld a good-looking man of fair complexion who sighed as he muttered: "*O che sciagura d'essere senza coglioni!*"'

CHARLES DEVEREAUX

from

Venus in India

Venus in India or Love in Hindustan *was first published in Brussels in 1889. Nothing is known about the author, Captain Charles Devereaux (sometimes 'Deveureux'), though there is some evidence he may indeed have been an army officer serving in India.*

IT was in the middle of March, the sun was simply blazing through the day, the crows, fowls, all birds in fact, went about in the shade with their beaks wide open, and wings lifted from their bodies, so much did they feel the blasting heat at this time. I was seated in my long arm chair, dressed only in the thinnest of jerseys, without sleeves, and the slightest of pajamas, in fact, as naked as I could well be, for the clothes I had on hid only the color of my skin, and even that very imperfectly. The punkah slowly swinging from side to side, poured down a breeze of cooling air upon me, and wafted away the smoke of my cheroot. It was midday, frightfully hot, and I could hear the leaves of the trees crackling under the sun's rays, when to my intense astonishment, Mrs. Selwyn and Fanny rushed rather than walked into my room.

Mrs. Selwyn seemed half demented. Fanny looked as if she had been crying and fearfully annoyed. Both looked reproachfully at me. I jumped up, apologized for my state of *déshabille*, for I had not even slippers on, and was in my bare feet, and I got them chairs under the punkah. But before she attempted to sit down, Mrs. Selwyn cried, 'Captain Devereaux, you must, you really must, insist on Dr. Lavie ceasing to annoy us any more! He is killing me! He is mad! I am certain he is not right in his mind! He is killing Fanny too! Oh!' and down she flopped into her chair.

I looked at Fanny but said nothing. Mrs. Selwyn then told me that Lavie had taken to going by at all hours, even at night when everyone had gone to bed, and that he moaned and raved and wept. That Colonel Selwyn had spoken to him kindly, harshly, every way, had ordered him never to come again, and so forth, but it had no effect, and they were at their wits ends, because they feared if they took any other, that is, forcible means, and kept him out of the house, it would only create a scandal, and the people would be dying with laughter over Lavie's miserable courtship.

Whilst she was telling me this, and I was wondering what I could do, in came Lavie, his eyes glaring, his face pale, his lips hard set. He went straight up to Mrs. Selwyn and asked her to go into another room which I had and which was empty.

I begged him to sit down where he was, but he smiled inanely at me, and said he would not keep Mrs. Selwyn two seconds, and she weakly rose and followed him. Fanny drew her chair near mine and begged me to do what I could.

'Oh! dear, dear, Captain Devereaux, do rid us of this monster!' was her cry. I took her hand and assured her that I would; that I had a plan, and that was to get him sent to some other station. I knew the P.M.O. very well indeed, and I would represent the case to him. Poor Fanny was delighted. She gave me one of those looks which meant 'kiss me!' I hesitated a moment, but at last I could resist no longer. Jumping up I seized the willing girl round the waist, lifted her to her feet, and pressing her to me I kissed her red, red mouth, over and over again.

'Oh! my darling Fanny!' I exclaimed in a low tone, quivering with passion that communicated itself to her. 'How I do blame myself for having countenanced that idiot's making love to you!'

'Oh! Charlie! Charlie!' she cried, pressing her swelling bosom to mine, and letting me pull her to me until our bodies seemed to form one, not denying me the thigh I took between mine, nor the motte, the sweet, delicious motte, against which I pressed my own thigh, 'I know now that you love me as I love you! Oh! my darling! darling! so I forgive you! But oh! if it were not for that I would hate you!'

'And do you really and truly love me, Fanny? Oh! my sweetest, own girl, and you must be all mine. Every bit of you! heart, soul, body, all!'

'Oh! I do! I do!' cried the excited girl in an ecstasy of passion. 'Oh! can you not feel that I do?'

'With your heart, my own love!' and I pressed a delicious and firm, round, hard, elastic bubby in my hand.

'Yes! Yes!'

'On your soul?' and I glided a hand swiftly between her thighs and pressed the equally elastic and soft motte with my fingers. For a moment Fanny drew her hips back, but on my again pressing her motte and throbbing cleft with my hands, closing her thighs also on it, and giving me such a kiss as I had never yet had from her. That was her answer. Gods! Gods! I took my hand away. I put my arms round her yielding waist. My shaft mad, raging to get at her, made a perfect tent pole, and stood out my pajamas in front of it. But for the pajamas it would have risen at a bound to an angle much too acute with my body to have enabled me to do what I did, but the pajamas held its head somewhat down, and I pressed the mighty weapon against Fanny's quivering motte with all my force, whilst I kissed her and felt her tumultuous bubbies, which she was pressing against my bosom as though she was trying to flatten them against it. For a moment we stood thus, only that I kept, as it were unconsciously, thrusting at her astonished motte. Then suddenly putting down her hand she said, 'Oh! What is that pressing against me?'

'It is me, my darling!' I whispered in a voice hardly audible or articulate from the excess of passionate emotions, 'it is me! There, take me in your dear hand and take possession of the treasure which is yours henceforth and yours only.'

(Poor Louie! Had she heard those words spoken in a moment of blinding passion!)

'Oh! darling! my darling!' exclaimed Fanny absolutely beside herself with ecstasy. 'My darling! my darling!' and her little hand nervously and excitedly kept clasping my burning member, as if she hardly knew what to say or do, but in delight inexpressible.

'Yes! Yes! Darling Fanny! That is for you! For this! It must be admitted to this abode! To the temple of love!' I again had my hand once more excitedly caressing her now maddened spot, between thighs more than willingly opened to admit it.

Fanny could not stand this caressing. She let go of my yard and tried, clothed as she was, to impale herself on it. It slipped beneath her motte. She felt it do so. She pulled up her dress a little and, suddenly opening her thighs, she closed them, equally suddenly, on my organ, and I acted just as though it had been in her slit! Gods! Gods! I think I should have burst, only nature came to my relief, and I poured forth a torrent of hot, burning spend! This recalled me to my senses.

Gently pushing Fanny away, I begged her to seat herself, whilst I went and changed into trousers. The intelligent and excited girl saw the necessity and reason, as she looked at me in the quite transparent pajamas flooded with spend, and extended in front by my enraged sword, of which the coloring and shape of the head was as clear as if seen in crystal water. But instead of sitting down she came and peeped at me from behind the purdah, as I took off my pajamas and fed her eyes on the galaxy I showed her, with pleasure indescribable. She saw the mighty engine, its ponderous, well-shaped sack, and the forest out of which they grew, and knew that they were now all hers, as she gazed, she tried to quiet the throbbing of the hot little cranny by putting her hand between her lovely thighs. But before I had finished putting these treasures away from sight, some stir made her drop the purdah and flee to a chair, and when

I came out, in shirt, trousers, socks and shoes, she was seated in it. She looked for her new possessions, and with burning eyes asked me where it had gone. For all answer I took her willing hand and slid it on my staff which was buttoned back against my belly. Once more did the excited 'My darling! my darling!' resound, but in whispered tones, and then feeling frightened lest our disordered minds might betray themselves to Mrs. Selwyn who was still talking to Lavie, who might at any moment come into our room, I got a book of views, and opened it so as to look as if Fanny and I had been examining it during their absence.

'You made the wet come in me, as well as yourself, my darling! my darling!' whispered Fanny.

'Did I? Well! my sweet, next time such wet comes it must not be outside of us, but inside you! Inside here! Do you understand?'

For all answer Fanny kissed me, whilst she pressed the hand I had slipped between those thighs, which, if ever opened for man, would first be opened to admit me!

Whilst thus engaged in deliciously feeling one another and talking the language, not the less eloquent because it was dumb, Mrs. Selwyn came almost staggering into the room. She was evidently overcome with emotion, and was far too excited herself to notice any appearance of heat in either Fanny or myself. She managed to reach the chair, to drop into it, but for a moment or two could not speak a word. Fanny and I, both in alarm, were at her side at once, and waited for Mrs. Selwyn to speak.

'Oh! Captain Devereaux!' she whispered, and then paused for breath for she was panting with agitation, 'Go in! go in to that – that – mad man, and for goodness sake, for God's sake, I implore you, calm him, and tell him he must not persecute me in this manner. He talks of cutting his throat if I do not give him Fanny!'

'I will settle him, Mrs. Selwyn,' said I as quietly as I could, 'I will go in now. Fanny, look after your mother, there's a good creature!' and so saying, I made her eyes speak volumes. They said to me, 'Get rid of Lavie and then we will play, my Charlie!'

I went into the next room and there I found the miserable lover, who had, that very morning, been talking, whilst I had been acting! That very morning! Why, it was not yet five minutes since I had had myself, not in Fanny's darling little cranny indeed, but between her thighs, and had spent a perfect flood, and had shown her my lusty treasures naked, and had had her hand caressing me, and herself calling me 'Darling,' and telling me I had made her spend, as she had made me! I must say I felt a considerable amount of contempt for Lavie, and wondered where all that sense had gone to, for which I had once given him so much credit. Poor devil! The fact was, he was quite out of his mind, and his lunacy had taken the form of a passion for Fanny Selwyn. But no one knew or suspected the facts for some days still. No wonder it was no use my speaking to him or advising him to desist from following Fanny, for a time at least. He moaned and groaned, and wept, and behaved in the most extraordinary manner. At least I persuaded him to go home, promising I would see him again the next day. But when he had gone, and when I had ascertained that Fanny and Mrs. Selwyn had gone too, I put on my helmet and went myself to Dr. Bridges, our P.M.O., and put the whole case to him, and begged him to get Lavie removed to some other station. Bridges hemmed and hawed at first, but at last he said that he had noticed that Lavie was not doing his work as well as he used to, and he would see him and come to a conclusion in a day or two. I had to be content with that, but it was something.

That afternoon I got a little note from Fanny saying that Mama had desired her to write and ask me to dine with them unless I had a prior engagement. That was the propriety part, but in the corner, written very small and hurriedly, was, 'Do come, my darling!' I sent reply that I should have much pleasure in accepting the invitation and I went.

As I suspected it was for the sake of a council of war that I was wanted, and I told Colonel and Mrs. Selwyn that I had seen old Bridges, and both thought it was an excellent move. The poor

Colonel was especially anxious to get rid of Lavie, for that fellow used to come in by the most convenient door of my bungalow which happened to suit him, at any time of the day he wanted to see me, and as he used to come some nine or ten times a day, the Colonel was twice nearly caught, in one of my spare rooms having Mrs. Soubratie, and for a week or more he had been entirely without his accustomed greens, and as he never knew when Lavie might perhaps find him partaking of them between Mrs. Soubratie's brown thighs, the Colonel, also, naturally, wanted to put an end to the courtship, which was ridiculous and scandalous, so he determined to see Dr. Bridges himself, and insist on Lavie being sent away.

After dinner we all walked up and down the fine avenue, in the cool evening air, and with the sky lit up by a myriad of lovely stars.

We talked of nothing but Lavie, until Mrs. Selwyn, getting tired took the Colonel in, leaving Fanny, Amy, Mabel and me walking together. Amy got rid of Mabel and I would have been as glad as Fanny if we could have equally got rid of Amy too. Our conversation naturally fell on love and matrimony, and Amy said, 'Well! I only hope nobody will ever ask me to marry him. I will surely say no!'

'Why?' said I laughing.

'Oh! Fancy going to bed with a man! I should die of shame!'

'Your mother goes to bed every night with your father, Amy, and she does not die of shame.'

'Oh! that's different!'

'I don't see it.'

'Well! anyhow I should die of shame. Would not you, Fanny?'

Fanny hesitated. She had hold of my hand and gently squeezing it, she said, 'I think that would depend upon whether I loved the man or not.'

'Exactly,' said I. 'I know my wife was rather ashamed the first night I came to sleep with her, but long before morning she laughed at her foolish fears!'

'Oh! Do tell us all about it!' cried Amy, who seemed to have an eagerness to know how such a change could ever come over my wife in such a short time.

'Well!' I said, 'I will tell you willingly, but mind you, if I do, I shall have to touch on subjects it is not usual to speak of to young virgins.'

'Never mind,' said Amy, 'it is dark and you will not be able to see our blushes.'

I was delighted at the prospect of being able to inflame still more, if possible, the already highly raised passions of Fanny, whose little hand trembled in mine, and I commenced, 'Well! I will tell you all about the marriage ceremony, because you, I dare say, have often seen the open daylight mysteries of marriage. It is of the secret, or real marriage, of the nuptial couch of which I shall speak, and I warn you, if I once begin, I can't leave off. So if I say anything which sounds shocking, you will have to hear it in silence. Do you care?' 'Yes!' cried both girls, and glancing at Amy, I saw her press her hand for a moment between her thighs, for dark as it was, it was not so dark but what I could see that much. I was satisfied. It was evident that her little orifice was tickling and I was determined that it should tickle her a good deal more before I was done. Not that I had any designs on Amy's slit; I aimed at Fanny's rather.

'Well! my bride and I went to Brighton to spend the first night or so of our honeymoon. All the way in the train we had to appear calm, to speak to one another as naturally as could be, but I could see that Louie was not quite the same as she had been before that day. Had we been going to Brighton unmarried, and not as we were, bride and bridegroom. I am sure she would have talked and laughed in a free and open manner, whereas now some thought, which I could easily guess at, was oppressing her. That thought was, of course, that her whole life was going to change now, that I had rights over her body now, which I had never had before, and that, surely, in a very few hours' time I should be exercising them. She told me afterwards she had often longed for that time to come, but now, when it had come, she felt nervous.

'No wonder,' said Amy, again pressing her mound with a trembling hand. I saw the movement, quick as it was and put my searing tool more comfortable under the buttons of my trousers, an act which Fanny saw and which she responded to by a hard squeeze of my hand.

'Ah! no wonder! as you say, Amy. And yet, if our courtships were more natural and less conventional than they are, there would be none of this unnatural restraint. Why, I loved my Louie as I had never loved a girl before. There was not a part of her I did not ardently desire to kiss, to devour! The very ground she stood on, the chairs she sat in, were all sacred to me! In fact, I loved her! I had fancied I had loved others before, but I now knew, for the first time, what love was. Ah! it is not all a matter of the heart alone, but of the body also. I wonder if either of you two girls have any notion of what passion is? When all one's being is stirred up by the thought of the presence of the beloved, of the desired one! I suppose, in fact, I know, that girls do perceive much physical excitement when the passion comes on, but in man the change from quiescence to storm and fury is enormously marked. Yet, in our cold way of making love, which is the conventional way, it would appear to be proper to forget all ideas of knowledge of difference of sex, or even the meaning of marriage. A lover may speak of his Mistress' beautiful face, her beautiful figure, or her beautiful arms, feet, but he must not acknowledge to have even thought of her beautiful bust, her beautiful breasts, her beautiful hips, or her beautiful legs, or thighs, and never, under any circumstances, of that most exquisite and beautiful charm of charms, which, made for him and for him alone, lies between those beautiful thighs.'

'Oh! Captain Deveraux! For shame!' cried out Amy.

'Do be quiet!' exclaimed Fanny. 'Captain Devereaux is quite right Amy, and you know it.'

Amy laughed and seemed uneasy and remained silent.

'Well! I was thinking, thinking, all the way down to Brighton, of all those charming charms, which were now mine, and which I was literally burning to possess myself of, but, ever and anon, would come the thought, how might I do it. How am I to dare to lay a hand on my Louie, which must startle her modesty, even if she has ever let her thoughts run on the consummation of our marriage, a thing I thought not at all unlikely; for modest and virtuous as my Louie was I knew, from her general demeanor, that, although innocent, she could not be ignorant.

'Afterwards Louie told me that similar thoughts had been plaguing her. She longed for me and for my marital and lover's embraces on the nuptial couch with great ardor, but she dreaded the first steps. Oh! she longed to give herself to me, she said, but she feared that in doing so, she might lose something of that valued respect for her which I had so constantly shown. She feared to be immodest. Yet how could she give me her naked charms without doing that which from her babyhood she had learnt to look upon as immodest to a degree. No wonder that we felt an unnatural degree of restraint. A kind of fear of one another, for, believe me, although especially when passion drives hard two lovers can be absolutely naked to one another without a particle of immodesty, yet it is only too possible, without such passion, such nakedness, which ought to be so glorious, and so divine, may be degraded to indecency and nastiness.'

'I cannot imagine it ever being anything else!' exclaimed Amy, vigorously caressing herself between her thighs. 'However –'

'Amy. I wish to goodness you would be quiet, and let Captain Devereaux tell his story!' cried Fanny, petulantly. She had been now walking with her own hand constantly on her thrilling little nook, quite indifferent whether I noticed it or not. I pretended not to do so, however.

'Well!' I resumed, 'at last we arrived at Brighton. Having eaten our dinner, we tried to appear calm to one another. Louie even having ventured to sit on my knees, with her arms round my neck, but careful not to press her bosom against mine; having exhausted every available topic of conversation and, I admit, having behaved like a pair of fools, so terribly afraid were we of one another, I ventured to hint that it was time to go to bed. 'Oh!' said Louie, hiding her hot and blushing face in my neck, 'not yet, Charlie darling! It is not half past ten! I never go to bed so early!' Then for the first time did I pluck up a little courage. I kissed her over her lips and I whispered, 'But this is our wedding night, my darling, darling Louie.'

'She gave me one quick little look, then cast down her eyes, gave me a kiss and whispered, "Well, don't come up too soon, there's a good fellow. Oh! Charlie! I wish it was tomorrow!" she jumped up and ran out of the room.

'Thus, having ventured to hint at what was to follow, and as it was our wedding night, it inspired me with some degree of courage, and with courage came desire, in floods far greater than I had yet experienced with Louie. I literally burned to have her! How long would it be before I might go up? There was a clock on the mantelpiece, and it seemed to take an hour to mark one minute. At the end of ten minutes I could stand it no longer. I was in real pain, for you must know, if passion means pleasure, it means pain too, until it is indulged.

'On going upstairs to our bedroom, I saw Louie's pretty little boots outside the door. I hailed this as a good omen. I picked them up and kissed them, and then, giving a little warning knock, and without waiting to be told to come in, I turned the handle and entered. Louie was in her nightdress just getting into bed. She gave a little cry. 'Oh! you have come sooner than I expected!' and she huddled herself under the clothes, showing only the upper part of her face. Oh! once she was in bed, I seemed to shake off my most unnatural cowardice. I closed the door and running over to her, I turned the clothes off her face and neck, and I put one arm round her shoulders, and rained the most burning and ardent kisses on her sweet lips, at the same time I slipped my hand into her bosom, and for the first time took possession of the two most beautiful globes which adorned it. Louie did not draw back. She in no way tried to prevent my caressing her there. I was more than tempted to let my hand stray much lower, and to seek for the temple of love of which the closely barred door is to be found at the foot of the forested hill, sacred to the goddess of love!'

'Gracious!' cried Amy, 'where and what is that?'

'As if you did not know, Amy,' said I. 'Well! I did not do so. Louie had both her arms around me and held me tight but I should have liked to have undone the front of her nightdress altogether, and to have kissed the beautiful breasts I had found there, but poor Louie, who would have liked me to have done that too, was still a prey to the struggles of her dying modesty. At last I slipped my hand under her armpit and tickled her. With a little shriek she let me go, but she did not cover herself up any more. She lay looking at me with really longing eyes whilst I rapidly undressed. I put my watch on the table. I managed to get off my clothes, to put on my nightshirt, without offending modesty very much, and I was just going round to the other side of the bed to get in, when Louie told me I had not wound my watch, and that she had not wound hers either. "Oh!" I cried, "let them go down, my Louie, never mind now!" "No!" said she, "Charlie, darling, don't let us begin our married life by leaving undone anything which we ought to do." "Oh! bother!" To please her I wound up both watches with a hand trembling with excitement and then jumped into bed.'

'Did you not blow out the candle?' asked Amy.

'Amy, if you interrupt any more,' cried Fanny, angrily, 'I will ask Captain Devereaux not to let you know what happened next.'

'No, I did not blow out the candle, Amy. Louie said something about it, but I pretended not to hear. I jumped into bed, and put my arms around her, and I hugged her to me. For just a moment she resisted a little stiffly, but the next moment she yielded, she hid her face, which was all on fire, in my neck and whilst I kissed her frantically, I put down my hand and gently drew up the veil, which interposed itself between me and those glorious charms, which could not much longer be kept from me or remain virgin. With as much delicacy as possible I passed my trembling hand over the smooth surface of her exquisite thighs, until I reached the "Bush with frizzed hair, implicit," as Milton says.'

'Captain Devereaux!' shrieked Amy.

'And finding the sweet entrance to the temple, I caressed it with an ardor which Louie could feel pouring in burning flames from my fingers. All she did, or said, was to hug me closer and murmur, "Oh! Charlie! Oh! Charlie!" Finding her so quiet, I –'

'What?' cried both girls in suffocating tones.

'I begged her to make place for me, and let me worship her with my body, as I promised to do in my marriage vows. Gently she turned on her back, and putting one knee first, and then the other, between hers, I gently but in the greatest excitement, lowered myself on to her beautiful body, and then awoke every hidden source of pleasure and passion in her as I made the High Priest enter the Holy of Holies. Oh! dear girls, the rapture of that moment! To feel that I really and truly was now the husband of my Louie! That I was, really and truly joined to her, and that the same throb which pulsated in and through her, equally pulsated in and through me! It was a glimpse of heaven! It was love! Love in its very highest fulfillment! Louie gave herself to me without further restraint – all fear was gone – all ill-placed modesty was banished, and before morning light had come, to take the place of that still yielded by the nearly burnt-out candles, my Louie lay, perfectly naked, but not red with shame, in my equally perfectly naked embrace. There was not a part of our bodies which we hadn't mutually caressed and gazed upon, and eaten up with kisses, ardent and plentiful! Our sacrifices were without number! We kept no count! But the entire night was spent in revels, which the angels, sexless and passionless, must have envied had they the means of realizing, even in imagination, what they were like!' Neither Fanny nor Amy had done more than breathe during the last part of this recital, and their steps had grown so short that we hardly moved over the ground. It was evident to me what constrained them moving, was owing to the fact that each of them was trying to control the powerful throbbing of her little slit by squeezing her thighs tightly. We were near the front of the bungalow and Amy, without a word, but with her hand still pressed between her thighs, suddenly darted into the house. Fanny remained with me. I took and put her hand on my burning and terribly stiff joint, whilst I at the same time kissed her and caressed her delicious little cleft.

'Come! Oh! come! quickly!' said she.

I felt her draw me quickly towards the lawn on one side of the house, where some thick shrubs grew. I guessed her intention. Arrived at the edge of the grove, I unbuttoned my trousers, and taking her hand, slipped it in. Fanny eagerly seized the tremendous weapon she felt, but alas, my shirt was still in the way, and so excited was she that all she could do was to exclaim, 'My darling! My darling!' as her little hand nervously clutched and grasped my burning tool, in alternate tightening and loosening of her fingers. Not apprehending that Amy would return, that she had gone in to solace her little moist cave there with the help of a finger or a plantain, or anything which could imitate the 'high priest,' I had spoken of, I stood, and enjoyed to the fullest Fanny's excitement and the pleasure her hand gave me, yet while so standing, I suddenly and luckily saw Amy coming. I whispered to Fanny, 'Take care! Here is Amy!'

'Ho! ho! There you are!' she cried, 'kissing I do declare.'

'No,' said Fanny in muffled tone, 'I have sprained my ankle!'

'Yes!' said I immediately, glad and delighted to find Fanny so quick witted as to invent a reason on the spur of the moment for not moving on. I had my rod right out, sticking out from my trousers, covered still by my shirt indeed, which had interfered with poor Fanny's endeavors to feel it naked in her hand, and it would have been instantly seen by Amy, only that Fanny leant against me, as it were for support, whilst I did my best to push back the most unruly and raging member.

'Yes!' I repeated, 'poor Fanny somehow turned her ankle, and I am afraid it is hurting her very much, poor girl!' Then addressing Fanny, I said, 'If you will let me apply my Grandmother's remedy, I am sure I can relieve the pain, even if I cannot take it away altogether. But the sooner you let me do so, the more certain the result.'

Fanny gave a kind of groan as she said, 'Oh! do whatever you like, and quickly, for it is hurting me so!'

I knelt on one hand, keeping myself close to Fanny's petticoat, whilst, with rapid fingers I managed to fasten a couple of the more important buttons, so as to keep my beast of a pole a tight prisoner. Then taking hold of her right ankle with my left hand, I pretended to press it with my other, but the temptation to do more was too strong, and Fanny felt, with delight, my wicked, delicious hand rapidly mount her well-turned and beautiful leg, pressing her calf most voluptuously and amorously, as it got higher and higher. She bent a little more over me, resting her hands on my shoulders, and gave a little groan from time to time.

'It will be better soon, I think,' said I, as my hand reached her smooth, warm, polished and plump thigh. Fanny had really beautiful legs and thighs. My tool bounded and throbbed.

'Yes! I think it will!' gasped Fanny, 'if you continue as you are doing now.'

Amy stood by, looking on and sympathizing, but quite unable to see what I was doing.

I rapidly moved my hand up that glorious virgin thigh, pressing it and feeling it delightedly as I mounted, until I arrived at the spot between the delicious columns of ivory. I turned my hand back down, and gently seizing the two soft full lips of her plump little prize, I pressed them together by alternate squeezes, so as to tickle and excite the clitty until Fanny could hardly stand still. Then slipping my big middle finger in, up to the knuckles, and using my other finger as a fulcrum against her swelling and bushy motte, I imitated what my throbbing manhood would have done, had it had a fair chance, until almost expiring with pleasure, Fanny deluged my exciting and lascivious hand with a perfect torrent of hot spend, which ran down my wrist and arm. I caressed the sweet, responsive motte with my most voluptuous touches and then, hardly able to keep a steady face, I asked her, 'Well, how does it feel now Fanny?'

'It is all right! Oh! thanks – that was nice! Now that the pain is gone!'

'Did what he did really do you any good?' asked Amy wonderingly.

'Of course it did, you silly girl!' cried Fanny, 'or I shouldn't have said so!'

'Well! That is wonderful!' said Amy. 'I'll tell Mama!'

'Don't do anything of the sort!' exclaimed Fanny, 'you would only frighten her. I dare say it was nothing but a sprain. At any rate, I'm all right now.'

'Mama told me to tell you to come in,' said Amy.

'Oh! bother!' cried Fanny. 'Amy! there's a good girl, go and ask her to let me stay out a little longer.'

Amy was not inclined to do so, and, much to Fanny's and my dissatisfaction, we had to go in. Before we did enter the house, however, Fanny managed to throw both her arms round my neck and give me two most ardent kisses, without being seen by Amy. Gods! how my groin did nearly split with aching.

After I got home I had the inevitable visit from poor Lavie. What a terrible plague he was! I did my best, as usual, to try and reconcile him to his fate, and I strongly urged him to do as much whoring as he could.

He said he had been doing this regularly and irregularly every night but could not work off his passion for Fanny, and I resolved to do my best to get him removed. Before going to bed I wrote to Dr. Bridges and I told him that I feared that Miss Selwyn was not safe. That Lavie prowled about all night, round her house, and that he had a perfect lust for her, which might induce him to attempt to rape her. I really believed this, for Lavie was like one mad for Fanny. He had begun a habit of muttering to himself, and I over-heard a semi-threat to have Fanny whether she liked it or not. Calling up Soubratie from his slumbers, I told him to take the letter, first thing in the morning, to Dr. Bridges, and the results will be seen in the actions of that never to be forgotten day, the seven-teenth of March, the very next day, the day on which Fanny Selwyn attained the double dignity of seventeen years of age and womanhood, the day I, at last took her most charming maiden-head, ravishing her, both to her and my hearts' content, relieving her sweet cranny and my groin of the load which had oppressed it since we had declared our mutual passion.

I knew the seventeenth was Fanny's birthday, but I had no idea I should be invited to assist at keeping the feast. However, after breakfast I had two very agreeable visits. As usual I was very much undressed, having nothing on me but my short-sleeved jersey and pajamas, for it was much too hot, and there was far too blazing a sun outside, for me to expect visitors. The first who came to see me was old Bridges, our P.M.O., who seemed very anxious about Lavie. He said he had lately noticed a considerable alteration in him, a laxity in the way he carried out his duties, which he could not account for, until he heard of his unfortunate love affair. He now wanted to know about the subject of my last letter, because it was of a very serious nature, and, if I did think there was any danger, he would telegraph to Simla for permission to send Lavie to Benares, where, he understood, there was room for another doctor. I easily satisfied Bridges on this head. During our conversa-tion I noticed his eyes constantly directed at the still blue and red looking scars on my left arm, caused by the knife of the brutal Afghan who had buggered poor Amy, and after he had finished speaking about poor Lavie, the good doctor went in for a complete history of the scars.

I showed him the rose looking ones on my chest, and Bridges exclaimed that I ought to consider myself the chosen of

Providence, for I had had the most extraordinary escape he had ever heard of. Of course I did not tell him about poor Amy's catastrophe, but he had heard the rumour that she had been buggered. I lied to him, I told him the rumour was false, and I was glad to be able to do so, although I had to tell a lie, because I knew that Bridges would talk, and would look upon any one who persisted in believing in the buggery as a slanderer who he must at once put down.

Hardly had he gone and I resumed my book and cheroot, than in ran Mabel, in a real hot haste. She sprang into my arms, and gave me a number of hearty kisses, and then looked over her shoulder, to be sure that no one had come yet, she pulled at the strings of my pajamas before I knew what she was up to, and had my member in her hands as stiff as a poker. As I have before said, I should never at any time object to so great a pleasure as having my tool and sack handled by a very pretty girl, whom I knew to be capable, but Mabel was so frightfully daring. I guessed she was not coming alone and asked her. To my horror she said that her Mama with Fanny and Amy were on their way over, and she had run ahead to peep at her 'pet' if she could manage it before they came into the house. As she spoke I heard Mrs. Selwyn's voice and the footsteps of the three coming along the verandah. Hastily pushing Mabel to one side I ran into my bathroom, where I at once splashed myself with water, as though I had been bathing my face and neck, and then fastening my towel around my waist so as to hang down in front and hide the tent formed by my terribly excited ramrod, I came into the sitting room and, as if quite surprised, greeted the ladies and begged them to excuse my *déshabille*.

My jersey, still open, showed the really terrible looking scars, and then Mrs. Selwyn and Amy, who had never seen them since the bandages had been taken off, for Mrs. Selwyn had been too much agitated when she came and found me in the same dress, or undress rather, to notice anything, gave little cries of horror and sympathy, which did me good to hear. All three inspected them, and Mrs.

Selwyn laid her finger on one, on my chest, and asked was it still
tender. I said not there, and then my darling Fanny pretending to
feel one also, took as much of my left breast as she could gather in
her hand, and gave me such a tender little squeeze, as I should have
done to one of her own sweet, pretty bubbies had I had the chance.
Amy exclaimed at the thick hair between my breasts, and I made
her blush by saying, *sotte voce*, to her and Fanny:

'Ah! Amy, you are as beautiful as could be!

You've Jacob's beauty in your face;

And Esau's – where it should be!

Whereas I am Esau all over!'

'For shame!' said Amy.

Fanny only smiled and reddened, and I knew longed to let me
see that she, too, had Esau's beauty covering the moon above her
lovely moist little nether mouth.

Well, the visitors having talked the whole story of the attack on
their house at Cherat over again, now declared the object of their
visit, which was to invite me to dinner that evening. They were
not going to ask anyone else, but Mrs. Selwyn said she had looked
upon me so much at one time as quite one of the family, that she
hoped I would let myself be prevailed upon to come and see them
very much more frequently than I had recently done. Fanny
looked at me with imploring eyes, full of passion and desire, and
she looked so lovely, so delicious, so voluptuously tempting, that
I could not have declined, even had my old virtuous (?) intentions
returned again. Ah! no! Those virtuous intentions had altogether
died away, and my weapon stood upon them, stiff and erect, and
swollen with pride, as a perfect conqueror naturally feels when he
has overcome his foe. I therefore accepted, with every manifesta-
tion of real and unmistakable pleasure, and as I escorted Fanny out
of the house, following her mother and sisters, I took the opportunity of letting her judge of the sincerity and strength of my
passion by the relative force and intense stiffness of my manhood.
But for the friendly towel I could have given another view, that

is sure, and I felt thankful to Mabel after all, though at first I was vexed at her insane liberties taken with me under such dangerous circumstances.

Fanny, seventeen years old, was this day promoted to the dignity of low dress, and when she welcomed me that evening I found her as proud as a peacock, in all the glory, not of extended tail, but of a very lovely exposed bosom. The two darling little breasts were indeed more hidden than I could approve of, but I could see some small portions of their smooth and polished globes, and my delighted eye gazed on the sweet path between them which followed lower, would end in her exquisite little prize. Alas! the presence of her father, mother, sisters and little brother Harry, prevented me taking my privileges, as her lover, and once more feeling those beautiful bubbies, but I gave my eyes such a feasting that I found it necessary to be very careful how I moved, for fear of displacing my terrible engine, which had, as usual, become unmanageable. I sat next to Fanny at dinner, and whenever occasion offered gently pressed her thigh, a compliment she returned as often as she could. Oh! if chance was but a little favorable. It was in the hands of that most revered and beloved Goddess Venus, and it was most favorable.

After dinner, we all walked up and down the avenue, where in the semi-darkness, caused by a sky only lighted by the stars, I was enabled to let Fanny judge of my feelings by the never-failing stiffness of my gender. I could, however, take no freedom with her. Mabel, whether suspicious or not, was too attentive an observer, but though she could not see what I did with Fanny's hand when we turned in our walk, any movement of mine towards Fanny's mossy down would certainly have been detected by her. I was on thorns, and also in real pain, for my groin pained me from the overstocked fullness of the reservoirs, the magazines of spend which had been storing up, waiting for an opportunity to be unloaded.

At length Mrs. Selwyn proposed that we should all go in and play a round of cards and, once it was set going, Fanny and I very quickly managed to lose all our cards, and pretended to watch the game very eagerly. In reality I had one of her legs on my knee, her foot hanging between my calves, where I pressed it. I whispered to her to come out, but she seemed afraid to attract attention and did not stir. We were near the corner of the table, which was a long rectangular one.

Everybody else was deep in the game going on. I became desperate. We were losing an opportunity which might not recur that evening. I unbuttoned my trousers and getting my staff out, free from my shirt, I took Fanny's hand and put it on it. She gave a perfect jump! Her hand tightened on the subject of her delightful thoughts and wishes, and her bosom rose and fell to such a degree that, together with her intense color, made me fear she would burst! But in a moment or two she got up and said she would go out for a moment, it was so hot.

'Do, darling,' said her mother, 'I dare say Captain Devereaux will go with you.'

Fanny went at once, and I, rising quickly and turning my back on the company, walked with rapid strides after her, my prick completely out and pointing like a bow-sprit at the ceiling. Oh! that walk across the room! How I dreaded anyone calling me back! But Venus, dear Venus, protected her servants, and I joined Fanny in the verandah safe and unsuspected. Neither of us spoke a word to the other; our feelings were too intense; and hers altogether too agitated.

Quietly and swiftly we made for the friendly shrubs, of which I have spoken before. Arrived on the grass between them, I put my cracking yard again into Fanny's trembling hand, whilst I rapidly undid my braces and unbuttoned the rest of my trousers; for though poor Fanny tried her utmost to manage these, she was in such a state of nervous excitement that her strength seemed to fail her. However, all strength did not fail me. I soon had the pleasure of putting my heavy and painfully swollen sack into Fanny's curious and eager hands, and she, with the instinct of pleasure and extreme tenderness, felt and touched them as though the slightest rough handling would surely destroy such delicate jewels. All this was delicious to me, but I was all the same in a desperate hurry to get our first coupling over for fear of interruption. I rolled my shirt up, so as to leave as much as possible of my belly naked, and then pushing my trousers a little down off my hips, I took the sweet and eagerly longing Fanny round the waist and laid the willing girl on the ground. Not one single attempt at playing false modesty did the dearest girl make. She allowed me to lift the front of her dress well up and lay it carefully back upon her, so as to crease it as little as possible, and next to do the same with her petticoats, and last of all to take up her chemise, so as to leave her lovely, sweet, dimpled belly as naked as mine; for Fanny, as I had discovered the evening before, wore no drawers, and from her waist to her knees, she was quite and sweetly naked. Dim as was the light, there was enough to show me her beautiful thighs, shining white, and the dark triangle of her bush; yes, even the soft line of her delightful little slit was apparent! I gave it one burning kiss, which made the excited Fanny jump, and then, without further delay, I took my position between her thighs, put my left hand under her head to give it support, to raise it above the rather harsh and rough grass beneath it, whilst I pressed my lips to hers, and adjusted the point of my eager pike against the soft portals of her equally excited grotto!

Glory! glory! I am in.

As he entered that beautiful temple of heat and passion my proud man doffed his head dress and did not stay his progress till pulled up by the virgin veil of Fanny's maidenhead! Whispering to her to 'Raise your hips a little, my darling, to let me put my hand under you,' she did so at once, and then, having a firm grip, I drew back for a strong forward thrust. I had not time to spare her. Fanny did not require to be educated up to that point, which makes the rending in twain of the maidenhead a less timorous thing for the sweet victim. She wanted all of me in, and showed it by the firm way she pushed up against me and the frank manner with which she gave me her delicious little sheath. I made the thrust. For one hardly appreciably little space of time the doomed maidenhead resisted. There was a little check, a sudden yielding, accompanied by a slight tremor of Fanny's form, and a very, very slight little cry, and I was in the Holy of Holies. God! but I acted as I always have done. I remembered that, whatever my pleasure might be, my chief object in having a girl must be to give her pleasure. So it was when by rapid movements, backwards and forwards, by thrilling sweeps of my burning stallion, commencing at the very outside of her, and only ending with the feeling of resistance to further progress, that I finally succeeded in being buried up to my motte in the slit of the exquisite and passionate girl, who helped me all she could! I felt as if I had never taken a maidenhead before. As if this was my first conquest of a maiden! – delightful love which can make even old pleasure appear new! – long before I came to the thrilling and maddening short digs, I had Fanny hardly able to keep from crying out loud, with the hitherto unknown rapture of being taken! Of an ardent and generous temperament, she 'came' frequently and always with a thrilling tremor which shook her from head to foot, and she spent abundantly and copiously. As long as possible I kept back my offering, for once in Fanny, I did not care who came. Not that it was so in reality, but my blood was up, my ram was up, and nothing now should interfere with the bliss I found I enjoyed. So that I made this first poking of Fanny last as long as I could. But alas; how short! how much too short is even the longest poking a man can make! I could not restrain the lava torrents very long, and amidst a chorus, or rather a duet of sighs, voluptuous groans and little cries, and at the rushing end of the maddening short digs, at last came that burst of spend which makes a man drive in his lance as though he would send it through his lovely comrade, and press his motte to hers as though to flatten it forever. Certainly Fanny was well anointed with the holy oil that first time. I had only spent once, or at most twice, since I had last had Lizzie Wilson. The first time was when I had the wet dream at Nowshera, and the last time was when I had sham poked Fanny yesterday in my bungalow, and I was boiling over. But all things come to an end, and after enjoying for a while the leaps of Fanny's motte and the compressions of her lovely little tunnel I withdrew my still iron-stiff pike and wiped the sweet girl between the thighs with my handkerchief. Fanny lay still on the ground, her eyes turned up to the stars, and her thighs open, in the most voluptuous attitude, whilst I was rapidly restoring the disorder of my attire. She seemed like one in an ecstasy. At length I roused her, and assisted her to rise to her feet. For a moment she seemed hardly able to stand without support, and then she threw her lovely arms around me, and pressing me to her, she gave me a shower of kisses which I returned with interest.

'Oh! my darling!' she cried, 'at last you have loved me as I have so longed, longed to be loved! But, oh! I am all wet down my legs!'

Of course. Her filled grotto was overflowing and that reminded me that I must take care of Fanny. Kneeling down and telling her to let me do what I liked, I passed my hand up her thighs, and introduced two fingers, as far as they would go into her hot, soft little place. I used them like glove stretchers and succeeded in bringing another flow of imprisoned spend down my hand and wrist, and so relieved Fanny of what might otherwise have proved a dangerous burden.

WALTER

from

My Secret Life

My Secret Life by Walter is the best known of the underground classics of the Victorian period. It is not known who 'Walter' was or when My Secret Life was first circulated but it was probably first published in France in the 1880s.

ONE night, I met at the Argyle rooms Helen M and was struck with her instantly. My experienced eye and well trained judgment in women, as well as my instincts told me what was beneath her petticoats and I was not deceived. I have had many splendid women in my time, but never a more splendid perfect beauty, in all respects.

Of full but not great height, with the loveliest shade of chestnut hair of great growth, she had eyes in which grey, green and hazel were indescribably blended with an expression of supreme voluptuousness in them, yet without bawdiness or salacity, and capable of any play of expression. A delicate, slightly retroussé nose, the face a pure oval, a skin and complexion of a most perfect tint and transparency, such was Helen M. Nothing was more exquisite than her whole head, tho her teeth were wanting in brilliancy – but they were fairly good and not discoloured.

She had lovely cambered feet, perfect to their toes; thighs meeting from her cunt to knees and exquisite in their columnar beauty; big, dimpled haunches, a small waist, full firm breasts, small hands, arms of perfect shape in their full roundness. Everywhere

her flesh was of a very delicate creamy tint, and was smooth to perfection. Alabaster or ivory, were not more delicious to the touch
than her flesh was everywhere from her cheeks to her toes.

Short, thick, crisp yet silky brown hair covered the lower part of
her motte, at that time only creeping down by the side of the cunt
lips, but leaving the lips free, near to at her bumhole, a lovely little
clitoris, a mere button, topped her belly rift, the nymphae were
thin, small, and delicate. The mouth of the vulva was small, the
avenue tight yet exquisitely elastic, and as she laid on her back and
opened her thighs, it was an exquisite, youthful, pink cunt, a
voluptuous sight which would have stiffened the prick of a dying
man.

Her deportment was good, her carriage upright but easy, the
undulations of her body in movement voluptuous, and fascinating;
every thing, every movement was graceful; even when she sat
down to piss it was so – and taking her altogether, she was one of
the most exquisite creatures God ever created to give enjoyment to
man. – With all this grace, and rich, full, yet delicate of frame, she
was a strong, powerful woman, and had the sweetest voice – it was
music.

I saw much of this in her at a glance, and more completely as she
undressed. Then the sweetest smell as if of new milk, or of almonds
escaped from her, and the instant she laid down I rushed lascivi-
ously on her cunt, licked and sucked it with a delight that was maddening. I could have eaten it. Never had I experienced such
exquisite delight in gamahuching a woman. Scarcely ever have I
gamahuched a gay woman on first acquaintance, and generally
never gamahuched them at all.

As I went home with her in a cab I had attempted a few liberties, but she repulsed them. – 'Wait till we get home, I won't have
them in the cab.' – Directly we arrived I asked what her compliment was to be. – No she had never less than a fiver. – 'Why did
you not tell me so, and I would not have brought you away. – What
I give is two sovereigns, here is the money, I am sorry I have wasted

your time' – and was going. – 'Stop,' said she – 'don't go yet!' – I looked in my purse and gave her what I could – it was a little more than the sum I'd named – and promised to bring her the remainder of a fiver another day. Then I fucked her. – 'Don't be in such a hurry,' I said, for she moved her cunt as women either do when very randy, or wishing to get rid of a man. That annoyed me, but oh my God my delight as I shed my sperm into that beautiful cunt, and kissed and smelt that divine body, and looked into those voluptuous eyes. I had at once a love as well as lust for her, as my prick throbbed out its essence against her womb. – But *she* had no pleasure with *me*. – She was annoyed and in a hurry, she had another man waiting in another room in the house to have her – as she has told me since.

What was in this woman – what the specific attractions, I cannot say, but she made me desire to open my heart to her, and I told rapidly of my amatory tricks, my most erotic letches, my most blamable (if any be so) lusts; things I had kept to myself, things never yet disclosed to other women, I told *her* rapidly. I felt as if I must, as if it were my destiny to tell her all, all I had done with women and men, all I wished to do with *her*, it was a vomit of lascivious disclosures. I emptied myself body and soul into her. She listened and seemed annoyed. She did not like me.

Nor did she believe me. Two days afterwards, I took her the promised money, she had not expected it, and then designed to ask if she should see me again. No. She was far too expensive for me – not that she was not worth it all. – Yea more – but blood could not be got out of a stone. – I had not the money and could see her no more. – 'All right,' she replied very composedly and we parted. As I tore myself away, my heart ached for that beautiful form, again to see, smell, to kiss, and suck, and fuck that delicious cunt, to give *her* pleasure if I could. Tho I saw her afterwards at the Argyle rooms – even went to look at her there, I resisted. – What helped me was the belief that I was distasteful to her, why I could not tell, and a year elapsed before I clasped her charms again.

On leaving her that day, I could think of nothing but *her*, went
to a woman I knew, and shut my eyes whilst I fucked her, fancy-
ing she was Helen M. – 'You call me Helen,' said she. 'You know
a woman of that name I suppose,' – I told her it was the name of
my sister. Not the only time the same thing has happened to me,
and in exactly the same manner with other ladies when fucking
them, but thinking of *another*.

One night at the Argyle rooms, Helen spoke to me. I had several
times been there solely to look at her, each time she seemed more
beautiful than ever, yet beyond nodding or saying, 'How do you
do,' we held no conversation, for she was always surrounded by
men. I used to sit thinking of her charms with swollen pego, then
either found outside a lady, or once or twice selected one in the
room, so that Helen could see, and ostentatiously quitted the salon
with her. I felt a savage pleasure in doing so. – A species of sense-
less revenge.

Sitting by my side, 'You've not been to see me again.' – 'No.' –
'Why?' – 'I'm not rich enough.' – 'Nonsense, you've got some
other woman.' – 'None.' – 'Come up.' – 'No, I'll let no woman
ruin me.' – We conversed further, she got close to me, her sweet
smell penetrated me, and in spite of myself I promised to see her
next day.

She had changed her abode, had a larger house, three servants
and a brougham. I had a sleepless night thinking of coming felicity, and on a lovely spring afternoon, hot as if in the midst of
summer, she was awaiting me with an open silk wrapper on,
beneath it but a laced chemise so diaphanous, that I could see her
flesh and the colour of her motte through it. Her exquisite legs
were in white silk, and she'd the nattiest kid boots on her pretty
little, well cambered feet. She was a delicious spectacle in her
rooms, through the windows of which both back and front were
green trees and gardens.

'Say I'm not at home to any one,' said she to the maid. Then to
me, 'So you have come.' – 'Did you doubt me?' – 'No, I think

you're a man who keeps his word.' Then on the sofa we sat, and too happy for words I kissed her incessantly. She got my rampant cock out and laughing said, 'It's quite stiff enough.' – 'Let me feel *you* love,' said I putting my hand between her thighs. – 'Why don't you say, cunt?' – again I was silent in my voluptuous amusement, kissing and twiddling the surface of her adorable cleft. 'Oh let us poke.' – 'Why do you say poke – say fuck,' said she moving to the bed and lying down.

'Let me look at your lovely cunt.' She moved her haunches to the bedside and pulled her chemise well up, proud of her beauty. Dropping on my knees I looked at the exquisite temple of pleasure, it was perfection, and in a second my mouth was glued to it. I licked and sucked it, I smelt it and swallowed its juice, I could have bitten and eaten it, had none of dislike to the saline taste which I've had with some women, no desire to wipe the waste saliva from my mouth as it covered the broad surface of the vulva in quantity, but swallowed all, it was nectar to me, and sucked rapturously till, 'That will do, I won't spend so – fuck me' – said she jutting her cunt back from my mouth.

Quickly I arose and was getting on the bed when, 'No – take your things off – all off, – be naked, it's quite hot – I'll shut the window,' which she did, and throwing off her chemise sat herself at the edge of the bed till I was ready. – 'Take off your shirt.' – As I removed it, she laid on the bed with thighs apart, the next second my pego was buried in her, and our naked bodies with limbs entwined were in the fascinating movements of fucking. What heaven, – what paradise! – but alas, how evanescent. In a minute with tongues joined, I shed my seed into that lovely avenue, which tightened and spent its juices with me. She enjoyed it, for she was a woman voluptuous to her marrow, my naked form had pleased her I was sure, not that she said that *then*, she was too clever a Paphian for that.

We lay tranquilly in each other's arms till our fleshy union was dissolved. She then – as she washed – 'Aren't you going to wash?'

– 'I'll never wash away anything which has come out of your cunt you beautiful devil, let it dry on, I wish I could lick it off.' – 'You should have licked me before I washed my cunt, you bawdy beast,' – she rejoined, laughing.

She then came and stood naked by the bedside. – 'Aren't you going to get up?' – fearing her reply. 'Let me have you again,' I said. – She laughed and gave me a towel – 'Dry your prick – you can't do it again.' – 'Can't I, – look?' My pego was nearly full size. She got on to the bed, laid hold of it, and passed one thigh over my haunch, my fingers titilated her clitoris for a minute, and so we lay lewdly handling each other. Then our bodies were one again, and a fuck longer, more intense in its mental pleasure, more full of idealities, more complete in its physical enjoyment to me, was over within a quarter of an hour after I had had her the first time. – Nor did she hurry me, but we lay naked, with my prick in her lovely body, in the somnolence of pleasure and voluptuous fatigue, a long time, speechless.

Both washed, she piddled (how lovely she looked doing it), put on her chemise and I my shirt. Recollecting my first visit and her hurry, 'Now I suppose you want your fiver and me to clear out' – said I bitterly and taking hold of my drawers, for I felt a love almost for *her* and sad that I was only so much money in her eyes. – 'I didn't say so, lie down with me.' – Side by side on the bed we lay again.

She was not inquisitive. Hadn't I really a lady whom I visited, she knew that I'd had Miss — and Polly — I had had, she'd spoken about me to them. – Why didn't I see *her*. Hadn't I a lady, now tell her – I only repeated what's already told. – Then the vulgar money business cropped up. – No, she never had and never would let a man have her, for less than a fiver. Going to a drawer, she showed me a cheque for thirty pounds and a letter of endearments. 'That's come today, and he only slept with me two nights.'

She'd soon again my soft yet swollen cunt stretcher in her hand, and fingered it deliciously, never a woman more deliciously. I felt her clitoris, and kissed her lovely neck and cheeks almost unceasingly. – 'Give me a bottle of phiz,' said she after a minute's silence – I complied. – 'It's a guinea mind.' – 'Preposterous, I'm not in a bawdy house.' – 'It's my price, my own wine, and splendid.' – Of course I yielded, who would not when such a divinity was fingering and soothing his prick? It was excellent, we drank most of it soon, and then she gratified me after much solicitation, by lifting her chemise up to her armpits and standing in front of a cheval glass for my inspection, pleased I fancied by my rapturous eulogiums of her loveliness – and exquisite she was. – 'You know a well made woman when you see one,' she remarked. – Then quickly she dropped her chemise, – she'd not held it up a minute, – it seemed but an instant, – and refused in spite of my entreaties to raise it again. 'You have seen quite enough.' – Again on the bed we sat, again our hands crossed and fingers played on prick and cunt, – silent, with voluptuous thoughts and lewd sensations.

Then came the letch – 'Let me gamahuche you.' – 'I won't you beast.' – 'You did the other day.' – 'Be content then, I won't now' – and she would not. But I kissed her thighs, buried my nose in the curls of her motte, begging, entreating her, till at length she fell back, saying, 'I don't like it, you beast.' – Her thighs opened and crossed my arms, whilst clasping her ivory buttocks my mouth sought her delicious scented furrow, and licked it with exquisite delight. She at first cried out often, 'Leave off, you beast.' Then suddenly she submitted. I heard a sigh, she clutched the hair of my head – 'Beast – Aha – leave off – beast – aherr' – she sobbed out. A gentle tremulous motion of her belly and thighs, then they closed so violently on my head, pinching and almost hurting me, – she tore at my hair, then opened wide her thighs – a deep sigh escaped her, and she had spent with intense pleasure. (That vibratory motion of her thighs and belly, increasing in force as her pleasure crisis came. I have never noticed in any other women, when gamahuching them, tho most quiver their bellies and thighs a little as their cunt exudes its juices.)

With cock stiff as a rod of iron, with delight at having voluptuously gratified her, wild almost with erotic excitement, – 'I've licked your cunt dry – I've swallowed your spending my darling' (it was true). I cried rapturously. 'Let me lick your cunt again.' – 'You beast, you shan't.' – But as she denied it, lustful pleasure was still in her eyes. – 'Let me.' – 'No, fuck me.' – At once I laid by her side, at once she turned to me – grasped my pego and in soft voice said, 'Fuck me.' – 'You've just spent.' – 'Yes – fuck me – go on.' – 'You can't want it.' – 'Yes, I do, fuck me, fuck me,' – she said imperiously. I didn't then know her sexual force, her voluptuous capabilities, did not believe her. But I wanted *her*, and she was ready. On to her sweet belly I put mine, plunged my pego up her soft, smooth cunt, and we fucked again a long delicious fuck, long yet furious, for though my balls were not so full, I felt mad for her, talked about her beauty whilst I thrust, and thrust, and cried our bawdy words, till I felt her cunt grip and she, 'You beast, – beast, – Oh – fuck me – you beast – aher' – all was done, I'd spent and she with me.

And as she spent, I noticed for the first time on her face, an expression so exquisite, so soft in its voluptuous delight, that angelic is the only term I can apply to it. It was so serene, so complete in its felicity, and her frame became so tranquil, that I could almost fancy her soul was departing to the mansions of the blest, happy in its escape from the world of troubles amidst the sublime delights of fucking.

Then she wished me to go. But only after a long chat, during which she laid all the time in her chemise, her lovely legs, her exquisite breasts showing, she was curious and I told her more about myself than I'd ever told a Paphian.* 'When shall I see you again?' – 'Most likely never.' – 'Yes I shall.' – I told her it was impossible. 'Yes, come and sleep with me some night.' – Laughing, I said, – 'I can't do it more than three times.' – 'I'll bet I'll make you.' – Then with sad heart, and almost tears in my eyes, I repeated that I should not see her again. – 'Yes – you will – look – I'm going to

* Paphian – prostitute

the races tomorrow' – and she showed me a splendid dress. – 'I'm going with — of the 40th.' How I envied him, how sad I felt when I thought of the man who would pass a day and night with that glorious beauty, that exquisite cunt at hand for a day and night.

Helen and I now began to understand each other (tho not yet perfectly). She knew I was not easily humbugged, so abandoned largely Paphian devices, treated me as a friend, and her circumstances compelling her to avoid male friends, and not liking females much, and it being a human necessity to tell someone about oneself, I became to some extent her confidante. She then had a charming, well furnished little house, replete with comfort, and her own. I have eaten off her kitchen boards, and the same throughout the house. She was an excellent cook, cooked generally herself and liked it, was a gourmet. It was delightful to see her sitting at table, dressed all but a gown, with naked arms and breasts showing fully over a laced chemise, with her lovely skin and complexion, eating, and drinking my own wine, she passing down at intervals to the kitchen. We ate and drank with joy and bawdy expectation, both of us – for she wanted fucking. – Every now and then I felt her thighs and quim, kissing her, showing my prick, anxious to begin work even during our dinner.

Afterwards adjourning to her bedroom, we passed the evening in voluptuous amusements – we had then but *few* scruples in satisfying our erotic wishes. – Soon after had *none*. – How she used to enjoy my gamahuching, and after a time abandoning herself to her sensations she'd cry out, 'Aha – my – God – aha – fuck spunk' and whatever else came into her mind, quivering her delicious belly and thighs, squeezing my head with them, clutching my hair, as her sweet cunt heaved against my mouth when spending, till I ceased from tongue weariness. Sometimes this with my thumb gently pressing her bum hole, which after a time she liked much. Then what heavenly pleasure as I put my prick up her, and grasping her ivory buttocks, meeting her tongue with mine, mixing our salivas,

I deluged her cunt with sperm. – Never have I had more pleasure with any woman, with few so much.

Resting, we talked of *her* bawdy doings and mine – of the tricks of women. – We imagined bawdy possibilities, planned voluptuous attitudes, disclosed letches, suggested combinations of pleasure between men and women, and woman with woman – for Eros claimed us both. In salacity we were fit companions, all pleasures were soon to be to us legitimate, we had no scruples, no prejudices, were philosophers in lust, and gratified it without a dream of modesty.

One day I told her again of the sensitiveness of my pego, that with a dry cunt the friction of fucking sometimes hurt me, that my prick at times looked swollen and very red, unnaturally so. – French harlots – more than others – I found washed their cunts with astringents, which my prick detected in them directly, so when I was expected, I wished H not to wash *hers* after the morning, her natural moisture then being so much pleasanter to my penis. – No saliva put there, is equal to the natural viscosity, mucosity of the surface of a vagina. – But from her scrupulously cleanly habits, I had great difficulty in getting her to attend to this.

That led one day to her asking, If I had ever had a woman who had not washed her quim after a previous fucking. She then knew my adventure with the sailor, that at Lord A's, and at Sarah Frazer's – but not the recent one at Nelly L's. – I told her that I had not with those exceptions. – 'I'll bet you have without knowing.' She told me of women where she had lived, merely wiping their cunts after a poke, and having at once another man and of its not being discovered; of she herself once having had a man fuck her, and his friend who came with him, insisting on poking her instantly afterwards.

We talked soon after about the pleasure of fucking in a well buttered cunt, and agreed that the second fuck was nicer if the cunt was unwashed. I racked my memory, and recollected cases where I had had suspicions of having done so. Helen who always then washed her quim, again said it was beastly. – I said that if more agreeable to me and the woman, there was nothing beastly in it; nor cared I if there was, fucking being in its nature a mere animal function, tho in human beings augmented in pleasure, by the human brain. 'So why wash after, if the two like it otherwise?'

About that time I found I had not quite as much sperm as in early middle age, testing that by frigging myself over a sheet of white paper, and wished to see what a young man spent both in quality and quantity. We chatted about this at times, and one day she told me she had a man about thirty-five years old, who visited her on the sly, but very occasionally; a former lover who had spent a fortune on her (I know since his name, his family, and that what she told me was true). She let him have her still, for gratitude. He was very poor but a gentleman, and now he helped her in various ways. It struck me she liked him also, because he had as she told, a large prick. I found she had a taste for large pricks, and described those of her former friends who possessed such, in rapturous terms. This man spent much, I expressed a desire to see it, and after a time it was arranged that I should see this cunt prober, him using it, and her cunt afterwards, but this took some time to bring about. In many conversations, she admitted that she had not more physical pleasure from a great prick, than from an average size one. 'But it's the idea of it you know, the idea of its being big, and it's so nice to handle it.'

I was in her bedroom as arranged, he was to have her in the adjoining room. She placed the bed there, so that when the door was very slightly opened I could see perfectly thro the hinge side. We were both undressed, she with delight describing his prick, repeating her cautions to be quiet, and so on. – A knock at the street door was heard. 'It's his,' said she, and went downstairs. – Some time passed, during which I stood on the stair landing listening, till I heard a cough, – her signal – then going back and closing my door, I waited till they were upstairs and I heard them in the back room. Opening mine ajar again I waited till a second cough. Then in shirt and without shoes, I crept to their door which was slightly open.

They were sitting on the edge of the bed, she in chemise, he in shirt, feeling each other's privates. His back was half towards me, her hand was holding his large tool not yet quite stiff; but soon it grew to noble size under her handling. Then he wanted to gamahuche her, she complied, being fond of that pleasure as a preliminary. He knelt on the bed to do it, tho he'd wished to kneel on the floor. – She insisted on *her* way, to keep his back to me. So engrossed was he with the exercise, that when her pleasure was coming on, I pushed further open the door (hinges oiled) and peeping round and under, saw his balls, and that his prick was big and stiff – I was within a foot of him. – But he noticed nothing, all was silent but the plap of his tongue on her cunt, and her murmurs. When she had spent once, he laid himself by her side, kissing her and feeling her cunt, his stiff, noble pego standing against her thigh, – she pulling the prepuce up and down, and looking at the door crack. After dalliance prolonged for my gratification, he fucked her. She pulled his shirt up to his waist when he was on her, so that I might contemplate their movements. I heard every sigh and murmur, saw every thrust and heave, a delicious sight; but he was hairy arsed, which I did not like.

Then said she, 'Pull it out, he'll wonder why I have been away so long; you go downstairs quietly, and I'll come soon.' He uncunted, they rose, I went back to my room. He had been told that she was tricking the man then keeping her, and knew that a man was then in the house. and *he* there on the sly was happy to fuck her without pay – for he loved her deeply – and not at all expecting or knowing that his fornicating pleasures, were ministering to the pleasure of another man.

Then on the bedside she displayed her lovely secret charms – a cunt overflowing with his libation. – It delighted me, my pego had been standing long, I seemed to have almost had the pleasure of fucking her as I witnessed him, and now to fuck her, to leave my sperm with his in her, came over me with almost delirious lust. 'I'll fuck you, I'll fuck in it,' I cried trembling with concupiscent desire. – 'You beast – you shan't.' – 'I will.' – 'You shan't.' But she never moved, and kept her thighs wide apart whilst still saying, – 'No, no.' – I looked in her face, saw that overpowering voluptuousness, saw that she lusted for it, ashamed to say it. 'Did *you* spend?' – 'Yes.' – 'I will fuck.' – 'You beast.' – Up plunged my prick in her. 'Ahaa' sighed she voluptuously as my balls closed on her bum. I lifted up her thighs which I clasped, and fucked quickly for my letch was strong. 'Ain't we beasts,' she sighed again. – 'I'm in his sperm, dear.' – 'Y – hes, we're beasts.' The lubricity was delicious to my prick. 'Can you feel his spunk?' – 'Yes dear, my prick's in it. I'll spend in his spunk.' – 'Y – hes – his spunk. – Aha – beasts.' – All I had just seen flashed thro my brain. – His prick, his balls, her lovely thighs, made me delirious with sexual pleasure. – 'I'm coming – shall you spend, Helen?' – 'Y – hes – push – hard – ahar.' – 'Cunt – fuck – spunk,' we cried together in bawdy duet – her cunt gripped – my prick wriggled, shot out its sperm, and I sank on her breast, still holding her thighs and kissing her.

When we came to, we were both pleased. – 'Never mind Helen if we are beasts – why say that if you like it?' – 'I don't.' – 'You fib, you do.' – After a time she admitted that the lasciviousness of the act, had added to the pleasure of coition greatly – to me the smoothness of her vagina seemed heaven. – I was wild to see all again, but circumstances did not admit of it then, yet in time I did, and one day after he and I had had her, 'Go down to him,' said I, 'don't wash, and let him have you again on the sofa.' – The letch pleased her, he fucked her again, and thought he was going into his own leavings. When she came up, I had her again, I was in force that day. – Her taste for his lubricity then set in, and stirred her lust strongly, – she was in full rut – I gamahuched her after she had washed, thinking where two pricks had been, and half an hour after she frigged herself. Whilst frigging, 'Ah! I wish there had been a third man's spunk in it.' – 'You beast – ah – so – do I.' – She rejoined as she spent, looking at me with voluptuous eyes.

We often talked of this afterwards, and agreed that the pleasure of coition was increased by poking after another man, and we did so when we could afterwards with her friend and others. Sometimes it is true she shammed that she allowed it only to please *me*, but *her* excitement when fucking told me to the contrary. She liked it as much as I did, and it became an enduring letch with her.

Whether Helen or any other woman – I've known several who liked it – had increased physical pleasure by being fucked under such pudendal condition, it's not possible to say. – With me owing to the state of my gland, no doubt it did. But imagination is a great factor in human coition, and by its aid, the sexual pleasure is increased to something much higher than mere animalism. It is by the brain that fucking becomes ethereal, divine, it being in the highest state of excitement and activity during this sexual exercise. It is the brain which evokes letches, suggests amatory preliminaries, prolongs and intensifies the pleasure of an act, which mere animals – called 'beasts' – begin and finish in a few minutes. Human beings who copulate without thought and rapidly *are like beasts*, for with them it is a mere animal act. – Not so those who delay, prolong, vary, refine, and intensify their pleasures – *therein is their superiority to the beasts* – the animals. What people do in their privacy is their affair alone. A couple or more together, may have pleasure in that which *others* might call *beastly* – although *beasts* do nothing of the sort – but which to them is the highest enjoyment, physical and mental. It is probable that every man and woman, has some letch which they gratify but don't disclose, yet who would nevertheless call it *beastly*, if told that others did it, and would according to the accepted notions – or rather professions – on such matters, call all sexual performance or amusements *beastly*, except quick, animal fucking. But really it is those who copulate without variety, thought, sentiment or soul, who are the *beasts* – because they pro-create exactly as *beasts* do, and nothing more. – With animals, fucking is done *without brains* – among the higher organised human beings, fucking is done *with brains* – yet this exercise of the intel-

lect in coition is called *beastly* by the ignorant, who have invented
a series of offensive terms, to express their objections. – Their
opinion of the sweet congress of man and woman – which is love
– is, that it should be a feel, a look, a sniff at the cunt, and a rapid
coupling – *very like beasts that!!!*

ANONYMOUS

from

Eveline

Eveline is classic Victorian erotica. Nothing is known of its author or when it was first published.

I had been at home three weeks. Lady L— kept to her own apartments upstairs. I saw very little of her, except only when I paid my dutiful morning visit. Sunday is not a lively or convivial day in London. Not in a general way. I lunched alone on this Sunday. Sir Edward was to return in a week's time. I was thinking his advent would be a change for me and a relief. I sat before my empty plate.

'Will you take some more sweetbread, miss?'

'No, thank you, John. You may take it away, and bring me some seed cake. Who is Lady L— entertaining upstairs, John?'

'The Reverend Mr. Doubletree, miss. He is the Honourable and Reverend Trestleton-Doubletree. He belongs to the church they call the Sepulchre, miss, round in the square.'

'Was that he who arrived an hour and a half ago in our carriage, John?'

'Yes, miss, my lady always sends it after the service on Sunday mornings to bring him round from the Sepulchre.'

'He does not look as if he required much bringing round; he does not strike me in any way as resembling a ghost.'

'Oh, no, miss, he's in very good condition. He knows how to keep it up too; I never knew such a particular gent. He can't eat any soup but real turtle, miss – except on Fridays when he says he tries to digest mock. He must have his grouse with a nice bit of red in the breast. He says there's only one cook in London who can do quail proper, miss, and that's ours. Yes, he's a funny gentleman for a parson. He's so particular about his stomach – says common food doesn't agree with him. Can't digest it, miss – comical stomach, very. He's funny in other ways too, miss, when he likes.'

'How so, John?'

'Why, one day he caught my lady's own maid, Sippett, on the stairs, miss, and chucked her under the chin, quite familiar-like.'

'Dear me, John! And what did Sippett do?'

'Oh, she just did nothing, miss, till he was gone. Then she up and told my lady. Not that she got much by that, for my lady told her not to mind. That it was only his kindness; for he was like a good pastor to his flock, and he considered her like one of his lambs.'

'What did she say to that, John?'

'Oh, she kept her mouth shut, as was her duty, miss, but when she came downstairs, she let out. She said that if he tried on any more of his pastoral tricks, he would find she was no lamb, but a ravenin' wolf, miss – there's the drawing-room bell, miss!'

'The Honourable and Reverend Trestleton-Doubletree would like to know, miss, if you will see him in the drawing room.'

'Say I will follow you immediately, John.'

I took just one look in the glass. I tripped lightly upstairs. John opened the door. The reverend gentleman came forward with an air of ineffable tenderness and condescension. I took him in at a glance. I mistrusted those roving dark eyes; that anxious smile on the broad sensual lips of a man about forty years of age.

'So glad, my dear Miss Eveline, to make your acquaintance. They told me you were at home; your lady mother has commissioned me, my dear girl –'

My baptismal name! My dear girl! What did he take me for? I cut him short.

'Have you lunched? I trust they have taken care of you? I fear Lady L— is too great an invalid to receive you properly.'

'Oh, yes, a thousand thanks, we lunched together. Had I known –'

'Oh, thank you, I took my little meal alone. It is a very simple one – a cutlet, or a sweetbread – a slice of seed cake – that usually comprised all I care for alone.'

'*Côtelletes à la Nesselrode* – *riz de veau à la sauce blanche* are things not to be lightly denied; or perhaps you prefer than *à la sauce financière?*'

'How did you find Lady L— today?'

'She is suffering. She confided to me her wish that we should meet, that we should confer – ahem, that I should endeavour to impress upon you the advantages of attending divine service at our church of St. Sepulchre at least once on the Sunday.'

'My mother is very considerate towards me. She has never yet mentioned the subject to me herself.'

'Oh! Possibly not – possibly not. Oh, no – no – quite likely! She is so nervous, you know, such an invalid – still, if you will allow me to suggest –'

He began to see it might be dangerous to persist.

'It is a subject on which I have formed my own judgment.'

'What? Already? So young too! Well, well; we will not pursue the subject further now. The young nowadays desire a large degree of latitude – a very large degree of latitude. I am always disposed to grant it them. I approve of freedom of thought; of individual responsibility. There are those who in their weakness require spiritual guidance. You are not one of those, my dear – my dear young friend. But you are too young, and permit me, too beautiful – far too superbly beautiful to altogether emerge from the cocoon of childhood into the full-blown perfection of womanhood without advice, without some sort of tuition. The world is deceitful – very much so.'

I listened with patient wonder. I saw at once that my reverend visitor had lunched perhaps not wisely, but too well. As he spoke, he drew his chair towards mine quite confidentially. His breath was redolent of wine. He leered into my face with an expression that reminded me of my old friend the teapot.

'But you forget that before I can emerge as a moth to flutter round the candles of society, I must have been a grub!'

'A grub – but what a grub! And now a butterfly. Ah! Ah!'

The whole manner of the man had undergone a change. He was no longer the reverend incumbent of St. Sepulchre endeavouring in his choicest inflection of pulpit eloquence to win a lamb to his fold. He was the man of the world – the would be lover of one he took for an inexperienced schoolgirl. One who in her ignorance would be flattered by the gross and too palpable insinuations of his honeyed words.

'A butterfly – ah! Such a beautiful, beautiful butterfly, whose golden wings, softly perfumed with the choicest scents of Araby, waft their sweet fragrance to the inmost follicles of my manly heart!'

He spoke in a purring whisper. I felt that his eyes were fixed upon my face. My own gaze rested on the pattern of the carpet. I waited for what was to come next. He moved nearer. His arm passed behind me. It dropped from the back of the chair in a half unconscious way upon my dress.

'You will not deny me the delight and the privilege of being your friend – your guide – your protector in this mad society of London?'

I made him no reply. My foot beat a warning tattoo, and my breath came in an angry flutter from my lungs.

He misinterpreted my agitation. He altogether delighted in my emotion. He counted already on his easy victory. He drew his arm closely round my waist. He advanced his thick and sensual lips. He actually imprinted a kiss upon my right cheek.

'Thus, my dear child, do we seal our compact!'

I snatched myself away. The blood of my ancient race rushed furiously through every vein.

'Then take *that* from the butterfly!'

A sounding crack, like the sharp report of a pistol. A moment's silence. The reverend incumbent of the Sepulchre had risen from his seat with a savage glare in his dark eyes. His hand covered a very distinct outline of my palm upon his left cheek. A study in red and white.

The door opened. It was John.

'Did you ring, miss?'

'No – yes, John. Show this – this *gentleman* to the front door.'

I ran upstairs. I entered my lady's room. I found her in her easy chair. She was apparently asleep or unconscious. Sippett was agitating a Japanese fan before her flushed face. I took in the situation at a glance. On the table were the remains of the luncheon; two empty champagne bottles among them.

'Quick, Sippett, open her stays – give her air.'

I rushed to the window. I threw it open. As I passed behind the heavy curtain to do so, I kicked over another empty champagne bottle. A second, half full, stood beside it. Two or three empty sodawater bottles rolled upon the floor.

Sippett had opened the front of Lady L—'s morning wrapper. She was fumbling over the laces of her corset.

'Scissors! Sippett – cut them! Let her breathe freely.'

I remained just long enough to see that Lady L— was recovering.

'Sippett, you will not leave your mistress for a moment on any account.'

I had been only just in time. She had been as near an attack of apoplexy as a stout and inebriated woman of her age could be without incurring the full penalty of her conduct. Then I left the room. Vexed, humiliated, degraded, all the angry contempt which had culminated within me during the past twenty minutes gave way to a feeling of passionate despair.

I felt at that moment the 'little devil' my friend the fair young man of Soho had called me. I slowly descended the broad stairs. John was in the dining room. He was employed in clearing away the lunch things.

'Where are the maids, John?'

'Sippett is upstairs, miss, the others are both gone out. It is their turn out, Sunday afternoon.'

'Where is the butler – and the cook?'

'Cook is preparing for the dinner in the kitchen, miss. The butler is asleep before the kitchen fire.'

'Make haste. Clear the things away. I want you, John.'

'Yes, miss.'

I threw myself into an easy chair. I waited. Presently John returned.

'Oh, Miss Eveline! How you did give it to him!'

'No more than he deserved, John.'

'Anyway he got it very hot, miss. I doubt if he'll ever come back.'

'I have hurt my hand very much. It aches, John.'

I held it up. My little palm was all red, and tingled dreadfully.

'So you have, miss. You're still all of a tremble.'

'Only wait, John, until Sir Edward comes home.'

'Well, miss, of course it is not my place to say so, but if I was you, miss, I should say nothing about it. My lady has been going on for nearly a year now like that. Sir Edward knows it, miss. But he can't stop it. No one can stop a woman, miss, once she takes to *that*.'

I held up my hand to show him. It stung and burnt. John took it respectfully in his big paw. He carried it to his lips as if I was a child.

'Poor little hand! Kiss it to make it well!'

It only wanted that. I broke into a flood of tears. One touch of sympathy is worth a sack of gold sometimes. How lonely I was! Why was I thrown into this man's arms?

I leant my head on his shoulder. John's attention was divided. A great part no doubt was full of sympathy for me. The rest was centred in an effort to protect his best livery.

'Don't take on, missy. It's all right – I knew how it would be. I was near by. When I heard the sound of that smack, miss, why – I was in it too. I would have knocked him silly, if you hadn't.'

I kissed John on the mouth. John kissed me back. I dried my tears and saved his Sunday livery.

'Are you sure the butler is fast asleep, John?'

'Well, miss, he always takes an hour after his dinner, Sundays, and he's only begun snoring about five minutes ago.'

'John, you're a good fellow and I like you very much.'

I smiled up at him through my tears. I put on the air of a spoilt child.

'I want to feel that thing again, John.'

He looked right and left – then he listened.

'There's no one about now, miss.'

I had suited the action to the word. My hand was on his plush breeches.

'Oh, John! How stiff it is! My hand can't get round it.'

His eyes glistened. He got more at home.

'Put it in here, miss.'

He undid a couple of buttons. I plunged my hand down. I grasped his huge limb. Only his shirt covered it now. It was hot and throbbing. I pressed it. I pinched it. I tried to get my hand under the shirt.

'Wait a minute, miss. If you must, you know, you must.'

He undid the other buttons. His limb was now free with only his linen over it. It stuck up in front of him like a great peg to hang dresses on.

'What a beauty he looks, John!'

'He is that, miss. My mother found that out when I was a little 'un, miss. She used to show him to the neighbours. One old single lady used to bring him biscuits.'

'Biscuits – John – why? How could he swallow biscuits?'

'I ate 'em for him, miss. They went down to him that way, I suppose. They were ginger nuts, miss. Anyhow, he got fine and large.'

'You ought to give him a name, John. I shall call him Robin, because of his red breast. Come here, Robin.'

I had released the prisoner from his confinement. I beheld the man's nudity erect in all its glorious proportions. How shall I describe the thing which reared its noble crest close under my nose as I sat in the low chair, its huge white shaft standing out against the curling black hair of John's belly? The blue veins coursing over the pale waxy surface; the big bell-shaped top – dark, menacing, its knob descending until a little slit-like aperture terminated its broad surface, which pouted on either side like ripe cherries.

'What a beauty he looks, John, my Robin!'

The man's lust, however, was rising furiously all this time. It was no child's play for him. I had excited the lion. It wanted flesh. He lost much of his subservient manner – his respect. He knelt down and pushed his hand up under my clothes. His cheek flushed and his breath came hot and fast.

'My good Lord, miss, how beautifully made your legs are! What lovely stockings – oh, what a soft thigh! Ah! Oh! How delicious it is! It's like so much velvet!'

The last exclamation was called forth by his touching a certain central portion of my person, the moist and hot reception with which his finger was regaled giving him evidently the liveliest pleasure.

'That's where Robin wants to go. That's where he'd like to hide his head, miss. Just in there!'

He slipped his finger in and tickled by button acutely – deliciously. I retained my hold of his thing. I gently moved the loose skin up and down.

'I am afraid he would not be content only to hide his head there, John.'

'He can be very soft and gentle when he likes, miss.'

'He may go wherever he likes, John. Only be careful and quiet.'

He now lost what little self-restraint was left to him. He caught me in his strong arms. He rubbed his body against mine. He kissed me on the mouth. Our tongues met — my eyes looked into his. He read desire — hot, voluptuous desire, there. We both groaned to indulge it — to enjoy — to satisfy it. We were mad, but there was method in our madness. John glanced all round. The armchairs and sofa were tempting, but then it was just possible we might be interrupted. Suddenly an inspiration came to him. By the door he could hear all approaching footsteps. The case was desperate. There was no time to be lost. He pushed me roughly with my back against the door. His breeches' flap was already unbuttoned. His nakedness was in full evidence. I assisted him to raise my clothes in front. He pressed his belly against me. He stooped. He thrust his hot, long limb between my legs. I opened them to make way.

'You must be quick, John. Listen! Do you hear anything?'

'No, no, all is quiet. It is the only chance. Let me do it. I am bound to get into you now, miss.'

With my own hand I guided the red head to my slit. I rubbed it between the lips of my orbit. He bore forward. It slipped in. In and up me half its length at least. I put my hands on his broad shoulders. I raised myself to meet his fierce thrusts. With each strong effort he almost lifted me off my legs. I moaned faintly. The pleasure mounted quickly. John hissed his ecstasy in short gasps.

'Good Lord! I'm in now — it's — it's — oh! Oh! I'm nearly coming!'

He gripped me round the haunches with an iron hold. He moved in quick, short jerks. His limb grew hard and even stiffer. He pressed me to him. I felt his discharge. I knew he was flooding my interior with his sperm. I cared for nothing but to receive all, *all*. He withdrew in haste. My parts were swimming. My thighs were slippery with the thick warm seed. A pool of it lay on the carpet between my feet.

'Oh, John, you have nearly killed me. You must never do that again.'

I ran upstairs to my own chamber. I made liberal use of my toilet appliances. I neither cared, nor feared, for the results of my imprudence.

Twenty minutes later, John came to announce the carriage at the door. He assisted me into it with the most respectful and matter-of-fact air in the world.

ANONYMOUS

from

The Adventures of a School-boy

The Adventures of a School-boy *is another classic of Victorian erotica. The narrator – the school-boy of the title – is an orphan as is his friend George Vivian. To cement their intimacy he helps George lose his virginity.*

WE used often to talk about our previous histories and compare our thoughts and feelings. He had lost his parents at an early age, and had been brought up by his grandmother – a stern, though not unkind old lady. She resided in a curious old mansion which had formerly been an Abbey, and the only inmates of the family were a maiden daughter, approaching fifty years of age, and two young ladies, one a year and the other a few months younger than George.

Those young ladies were not related to him, being relatives of his grandmother's second husband. They were both well provided for, but being without any near relations they had lived under the charge of his grandmother as long as he could recollect.

Of these girls he would never tire of speaking, and he soon gave me the details of everything that had passed with them. He had no companions of his own sex, and his whole time was spent with them. They shared the lessons in Greek and Latin which he received from the curate of the parish, and he, in turn, participated in their French, Italian, music and dancing lessons, for which masters attended from a neighbouring town.

Their schoolroom was a large apartment, somewhat detached from the house, which had formerly been the chapel of the Abbey. As from its situation any noise they made there did not disturb the inhabitants of the rest of the house, this apartment gradually came to be their usual resort and the scene of all their indoor amusements. The greater part of the walls were covered with book presses, which were kept locked and from which they occasionally persuaded their aunt to allow them to take a few books, such as she approved of. As they grew older, however, and became fond of reading, they longed to become better acquainted with the contents of the bookshelves.

Luckily George discovered a key which opened the presses and enabled them to gratify their curiosity. For some time they indulged themselves, to their great delight, with the perusal of *Tom Jones*, *Peregrine Pickle*, and some other works of the old school which had been carefully concealed from them, but with which they were highly diverted.

One day they made a discovery which, at first, startled them not a little. While replacing some books on an upper shelf, George allowed one to get behind the others, and leaning forward to pick it up, his foot slipped, and he nearly fell from the chair. This made him press forcibly against the bookshelf, and in doing so he touched a secret spring, upon which the shelf started forward and disclosed a small recess behind.

Their curiosity was of course excited to ascertain what the hiding place contained, and they discovered two or three old books, which, from the dust on them, had evidently not been touched for many years. They turned out on inspection to be some collections of erotic plates from the Académie des Dames, Aretino, and other works of a similar description.

Their astonishment on seeing these may be imagined; George was delighted with them, and attracted by the sight of the naked figures and the strange attitudes, he wished to examine them minutely; but the girls said they were not proper to be looked at,

and insisted on putting them back. George, however, was not satisfied with this hasty glance, but used often to return to them by
himself and pore over them wondering what their meaning could
be.

Before long, too, he became aware, from noticing that the position of the books was sometimes changed that, though the girls had
professed to him their dislike to look at them, they also were in the
habit of amusing themselves with them in secret. To make certain
of this, he one day concealed himself beneath the sofa, and when
he found them employed in examining the plates, he made his
appearance and, somewhat to their confusion, rallied them upon
their pretended modesty, which he now found was no greater safe-
guard against their curiosity than his own.

After this there could be no further disguise on the subject
amongst them, and they used often to take the books down,
examine the pictures, and discuss their different ideas and conjec-
tures as to the purposes and meanings of the various attitudes. This
led before long to a comparison between the beauties of the figures
thus represented, and those of the similar parts which they themselves possessed. George vowed that he was certain the girls were
much handsomer than any of the personages represented on the
plates, and insisted on satisfying himself on the point, but they at
first resisted his attempts to gratify this very natural curiosity.

One day, when they were discussing the strange appearance of
the virile member as represented in a state of erection, George took
courage and, letting down his trousers, exhibited to them his little
bijou, with all its surrounding attributes, that they might compare
it with the representation.

They pretended at first to be shocked, but curiosity and desire
soon got the better of every other feeling, so that, after he had
induced them to explore all his secret charms, he had not much
difficulty in persuading them to gratify him by exposing in turn all
the beauties they had to show.

The ice having been once broken, this soon became their constant amusement when they had a safe opportunity for indulging in it. But at this time they were all too young to be able to comprehend, and still less to put in practice, the lessons which were thus exhibited to them.

In imitation of the scenes depicted in the plates, George would get between their thighs and endeavour to introduce his little member, which their caresses had made quite stiff, within their secret recesses; but as the attempt to insert it always occasioned pain to them, and was not accompanied by any corresponding increase of pleasure to George, they soon gave up attempting what appeared to them to be something preposterous, and contented themselves with toying with and kissing and caressing each other's secret charms.

At first the total absence of hair from the parts of their own bodies,which they saw depicted in the engravings as surrounded with curly locks, occasioned them some amazement; but in the course of time it became evident that Eliza, the elder of the cousins, was beginning to give proof positive that this was not an exaggeration of the artist, as they had at first supposed. Her bubbies too began to swell out, and her mount to increase in size, and George found that when he tickled and played with her little secret part, she now exhibited more evident tokens of pleasure and enjoyment.

His own pretty jewel too was now becoming more and more excited, and was increasing considerably in size, while the two little appendages began to show themselves more prominently depending from the belly, and hanging down as he saw them represented in the pictures.

In short, matters were fast progressing in the natural train, so as to bring on with them the age of puberty, and a very short time longer would no doubt have sufficed not only to render them capable, but to supply the desires which would induce them to carry out experiments far enough to initiate them into the whole secret; but to their infinite sorrow and regret, their pleasant party was suddenly dispersed.

George's grandmother, Mrs Montague, had another daughter who had been for some time residing abroad. She had recently been attacked with a dangerous illness, which threatened to be of long continuance; and at her urgent request, Mrs Montague had been induced to break up her establishment at the Abbey, and proceed with her unmarried daughter to join the invalid in Italy. This, of course, involved a complete separation between George and his fair companions. After a sorrowful parting, the girls went to a boarding school, and George was also sent to a school, where he was so uncomfortable that at length he petitioned to be removed. To his great joy this was agreed to; and he went to the Doctor's, where he had only been for a few months when I joined him.

When we became intimate, nothing rejoiced him so much as to talk of the girls, and many a long conversation we had regarding them, when he would detail to me all the minute particulars of what had passed between them, and bitterly regret his own ignorance and want of ability to avail himself of the pleasure which he now thought he might have enjoyed; and he looked forward with the greatest eagerness to the enjoyment he anticipated when he should again have the happiness of meeting them.

It was some years before he was to have that joy. One day towards the end of our schooldays together, he gleefully handed me an open letter. It was from his grandmother, who a short time previously had returned to the Abbey, and contained an invitation for him to spend the summer holidays with her. She mentioned that he would meet his old friends Eliza and Maria, who had again come to reside with her, and told him that if he wished he might bring one of his school-fellows with him as a companion. His object was now to induce me to accompany him on this visit, and to participate with him in all the enjoyments he anticipated on meeting his two old friends.

Although I was by no means quite so sanguine as he was of our being at once admitted to all his previous intimacy, still I was very anxious to see the girls of whom I had heard so much and readily agreed to his proposal, thinking that what had previously happened gave us a fair reason to hope that even all his anticipation might be realised.

Accordingly, on the appointed day, having made ourselves as smart as possible, we arrived at the Abbey. It was near the dinner hour when we reached it, and we were received by his grandmother – a stately though by no means disagreeable dame – who told us that we had just time to get ready for dinner.

We proceeded to decorate ourselves as quickly as possible; and like young fools, as we then were, we fancied that we would be most likely to make an impression by affecting as much as possible the appearance and manners of the man. When we met the family party in the drawing room, I was greatly struck with the beauty of the two girls, and could not help acknowledging that the glowing description George had so often given of them was by no means an exaggeration of the reality.

The impression made upon me by our reception was of the most favourable description; but with poor George it was quite the reverse. Being an utter stranger I could expect nothing beyond civility, and I was not at all surprised at the coldness with which the girls received me. George, whose impressions of their former intimacy were just as vivid as if they had only separated the day previously, had calculated upon being received exactly on the same footing as that on which they had parted. And on going up to them with open arms, he was horrified to find that he was received upon the same cold and frigid terms which were accorded to me.

He was sadly mortified at this cool treatment and at finding that all his advances were met with the utmost reserve, while he was addressed as Mr. George and I as Sir Francis, on every occasion.

Poor George could not conceal his mortification, and with difficulty prevented the tears from gushing from his eyes at the sad contrast which this reception presented to the delightful interview he had pictured to himself. I, of course, had never anticipated anything else so far as I was concerned but I was more at my ease, and consequently able to observe matters more calmly. It struck me that there was something forced and overdone in the manner in which the girls were acting; and that it looked rather as if they were afraid of themselves and were obliged to resort to all this formality to prevent their showing their real feelings.

While, therefore, I was polite and attentive to them, I devoted myself almost exclusively to the old ladies, upon whom I was desirous to produce a good impression, directing my conversations chiefly to them and avoiding in this manner any appearance of being too anxious to make myself agreeable to the young ladies.

In this way I was enabled to make my observations on their demeanour more easily and without attracting attention. As the evening wore on, matters did not improve so far as George was concerned. The same cold and formal stiffness was still kept up towards him. Once, when we were left alone with the young ladies he summoned up courage, and on some pretext took an opportunity of passing his arm round Maria's waist, but he was instantly met with a sharp 'Come, come, behave yourself, sir; we must not have any of your school-boy tricks here.'

Poor George was quite abashed at such an unexpected rejoinder, and hardly ventured to open his mouth again during the evening. I, however, rattled away as well as I could, and did my best to amuse the old ladies, and made things pass off pleasantly.

At George's suggestion we had been accommodated in two adjoining apartments, which he had formerly occupied, and which were situated in a semidetached wing abutting on the library.

When we had retired to our rooms for the night, George was quite frantic at the manner in which he had been treated, and was half inclined to be angry with me for taking the matter so coolly as I did; and now, when he could freely give way to his feelings, the tears which he had hitherto had some difficulty in suppressing rolled down his cheeks. I had been disposed to rally him a little on his disappointment, but when I saw how seriously he took it to heart, I had not the cruelty to add to his annoyance, and proceeded to try to console him a little. I reminded him that now more than five years had elapsed since he and his fair friends had met.

During that period he had acquired a good deal of experience and knowledge of the world, and it was only reasonable to suppose that the girls also must have made similar progress. That during all this time they had had no opportunity of ascertaining what his views and feelings were, beyond the exchange of a few formal letters which were necessarily very guarded on both sides; and that it was hardly reasonable to expect that they should at once throw themselves into his arms – a proceeding which they might naturally suppose would appear to him more like the conduct of two prostitutes than anything else, and more likely to disgust him than otherwise.

He admitted that there was some truth in this, and that he had expected too much at first. But he was much more relieved when I proceeded to tell him the opinion I had formed, that in their conduct this evening the girls were only acting a part. I related to him some observations I had made, which led me to think that my first supposition to this effect was correct.

What chiefly satisfied him was one circumstance I had remarked while I was playing chess with Miss Vivian, and they thought I was not observing them. George was standing opposite us, looking over a portfolio of engravings which his grandmother had brought from the Continent. While turning them over he raised his foot upon a chair to support the portfolio, the light was shining strong upon his figure, and the proportions of his manly appendage were plainly exhibited.

Poor George was thinking less of engravings he was turning over, than of those he had been accustomed in former days to amuse himself with, along with his fair companions, and this caused the unruly member to be in rather an excited state. Its full development attracted the attention of Maria, who, with a smile, pointed it out to Eliza, and a meaningful look passed between them as if they were well pleased to see such a change upon it.

All this byplay did not escape my observation, though they thought I was too intent on my game to observe it, and from George's position he could not be at all conscious that he was the object of their attention.

What I thus told George comforted him very much, and with some anxiety he asked my advice as to what we ought to do in the circumstances in which we found ourselves, so different from what he had expected. I told him I was afraid we had made a mistake in trying, as we had done, to play the young gentlemen, and that we had thereby given them too good an opportunity of keeping us at a distance, which they would hardly have been able to do if we had come down upon them in the character of two riotous school-boys. I said that it was perhaps not yet too late to rectify the error, and that as Miss Maria had chosen to refer to school-boy tricks, it was worth while to try, at least, whether we could not play some upon them to good effect. He said he was willing to do anything I thought best, as nothing could be more unsatisfactory than our present position. We therefore determined on our course, and after consoling one another in the best way we could for our present disappointment, we fell asleep.

The next morning, discarding broadcloth and silks, jewellery and French polish, we made our appearance at breakfast in short jackets, trousers of plain woollen stuff, fitting close to our waist and haunches, open breasted waist coats, and our necks merely encircled with a light handkerchief loosely tied in front. I cannot so well say what this effect had upon myself, though I had no reason to suppose from George's compliments on my appearance that it was unfavourable. But in so far as he was concerned, I could not help thinking that it was a great improvement, and that he now looked to be much more likely to captivate a girl's fancy than he had appeared to be on the previous evening, when dressed up to the highest pitch of the then youthful fashion. Like myself he had rather a young appearance for his age. This suited our purpose well, and I had little doubt we should be able to pass ourselves off in the character we had assumed.

Perhaps a closer observer would have remarked that our forms were more rounded, and our muscles more prominent than was reconcilable with our assumed youthful appearance; but this was not likely to be much noticed in the quarter where alone we cared about making a good impression. Our only fear was that our thin, tight-fitting trousers might betray to the elder ladies the secret of our manly organs having arrived at a size and proportion likely to render us dangerous companions for two young girls.

But we resolved to be cautious in our movements and proceedings before them, for there had been an object in our purposely selecting these garments – in order that without appearing to make any display, we might have an opportunity of exhibiting to the young ladies, as if accidentally, on every possible occasion that there was something beneath them which was likely to prove an agreeable and satisfactory plaything, if they would only throw off their reserve and give us an excuse for producing them for their amusement.

During breakfast, George and I talked of nothing but the sporting amusements which we looked forward to enjoying in the country; and as soon as the meal was over he insisted on carrying me off to the river to fish, where we remained all day till dinner time.

I thought I observed some slight indications of disappointment at our course of procedure; but as this was exactly what we wished, we were encouraged to pursue our plan.

During the evening I devoted myself as before, almost exclusively to the old ladies; and George who had somewhat recovered his spirits, amused himself with occasionally teasing the younger ones a little, at the same time taking every opportunity he could find of allowing them, as if accidentally, to catch a glimpse of the proportions of a certain weapon, which he eagerly longed to make use of, and which every now and then he made to erect itself and, as if unconsciously on his part, to appear prominently beneath his trousers.

On more than one occasion, when he contrived to do this in such a position that they thought he could not observe them, I noticed the same meaningful look of satisfaction pass between the girls which I had observed the previous evening. Upon the whole, we were convinced that everything was now proceeding as satisfactorily as we could expect.

The next morning at breakfast we continued the same game, and George again proposed some expedition which would occupy the whole day; but here his grandmother interfered and said, 'Come, come, George, this will never do. You must not engross Sir Francis so entirely, you see enough of him at school, and you must allow us to have a little of his company while he is here. Why, here are the two young ladies who have been putting off any distant excursion all the summer, until they should have somebody to escort them about.'

George and I exchanged a quiet look of satisfaction at this exposé, and at once said that if the ladies would accept of our services, we were quite at their command whenever they chose.

They, on their part, disclaimed any wish to interfere with our amusements, but Mrs Montague again struck in and said, 'Well, George you and Sir Francis can occupy yourselves in any way you like till lunch time. After that I shall order the horses to be at the door, and you can take him to see the old castle. If you have forgot the way, the ladies will be able to show it to you.'

After lunch, we accordingly set off on an expedition to some ruins about ten miles off. As it was by no means our plan to remain on a distant footing with our friends, when we had them by ourselves we both endeavoured by all means in our power, when thus thrown into close contact with them, to make ourselves as agreeable as possible.

Before long we separated into two pairs, George taking Maria who was just of his own age, and leaving Eliza for me. I believe we both at first took the same mode of proceeding – that of praising each other, being pretty well assured that what we said of one another would not fail to be repeated by the listener to her friend.

I soon found myself rapidly improving my intimacy with Eliza, who was not only an extremely handsome, but an accomplished girl; and I strove, not without some success, to make myself as agreeable as possible to her, though of course I at first preserved the utmost respect in my manner so as not to alarm her.

When we reached the ruins we put up our horses and walked about, in order to inspect them, thoroughly. George and Maria soon separated from us. Eliza sat down to take a sketch of the ruins, and after sitting talking to her for a while, I also drew out my sketchbook, and took up my position a little behind her, imitating her example.

While thus occupied, I could occasionally hear from the merry tones they made use of that George and Maria were getting on at a most satisfactory rate. At length, when I had nearly completed my sketch, and was filling in the foreground with the outline of Eliza's figure, they came up behind us, and looking over my shoulder, Maria exclaimed, 'Oh, Sir Francis, how beautiful that is! I should so like to have it, it is such a capital likeness of Eliza. Oh, pray, do give it to me.'

I answered, 'By all means! But upon one condition, and that is that you will persuade Miss Eliza to give me in exchange her sketch, as a remembrance of the place.'

Having heard what passed, Eliza now turned round to us, and on looking at my drawing, she said that Maria might do anything she liked with hers as it was not good for anything, and she would make a much better one by copying mine. The exchange was accordingly made.

Seeing that there were some other sketches in my book, they asked to be allowed to look at them. I appeared to hesitate and said that I was not quite sure I could permit this, that they must recollect a school-boy's sketchbook was generally filled with everything that came in his way which struck his fancy, sometimes without much regard to propriety.

In fact, the very reason why I had selected this book was that among other things, it contained several sketches of George and myself, taken when we were bathing, and exhibiting our naked figures at full length. There was nothing absolutely indecent in them, either in the attitudes or even in the form and position of the Priapean member, but there was no attempt to conceal it, and it was exhibited in its full natural proportions when in a state of rest, with its shading of foliage, as yet but scanty, around it. My hesitation only excited their curiosity the more; and though Eliza said little, Maria pressed me to show them anything I thought I could.

I then turned over the leaves, allowing them to look at some of the other sketches, and when I came to those of ourselves, I at first folded down part of the leaf and only exhibited the upper portion of our persons naked as far as the navel.

Though they made no observation, I saw from their flushed cheeks how much they were affected by the sight; and when they came to one or two sketches where our virile members were not so prominently displayed, although sufficiently indicated, I allowed them to see them, affecting to do so through awkwardness in turning over the leaves. When they had gone over the whole they expressed their admiration and their thanks; and we soon after mounted our horses to return home.

While getting the horses out, George found an opportunity to tell me what I had already guessed from the expression on his face, that he had got on even better than he had expected with Maria. That though she would not allow him to take any serious liberty, he thought this arose more from the fear of being observed than from unwillingness on her part; and he had even been able more than once to place his hand upon his old darling friend, now clothed in a new dress; and had made her grasp and feel the increased proportions of his throbbing weapon.

This was as much as we could possibly expect and emboldened by what he told me, I ventured while raising Eliza into the saddle and adjusting her dress, to press her leg and bottom, and even to insinuate my hand under the riding habit and touch the naked, soft, smooth skin of her thigh, without meeting with either rebuke or resistance.

We had a merry ride home, and during dinner all were in high spirits. George, especially, was so much so that it attracted the observation of his grandmother, who made some remark upon it; to which he replied that he had formerly been so scolded for being a madcap, that he had been trying for the last two days to see if he could not gain a better character, but that he found it was of no use to make the attempt, and he must just submit to the reproach.

This produced a smile, and the evening passed on very pleasantly. For the first time since our arrival, the piano was opened, and the young ladies gave us some music. They both had good voices, and sang well; but they wanted that taste and polish which can only be acquired by hearing first-rate performers. I had had great advantages in that way in consequence of my mother's fondness for music, which was almost the only amusement she ever indulged in. During our visits to London, she was not only a regular attendant at the Opera, but was in the constant habit of having at her house all the highest talent of musical celebrity. George, too, had one of the finest voices I have ever heard, and latterly, at least, he had had the advantage of a most excellent master.

I was engaged with Miss Vivian in a game of chess, when I heard Maria say to George, 'Well, George, I suppose you have entirely forgotten all the lessons in music I used to take so much pains to give you.'

George laughed, but I answered for him, 'No, indeed, Miss Maria, I can assure you he has not at all forgotten them, and I am quite sure you will find you have no reason to be ashamed of your pupil.'

She insisted that from the way in which I spoke, I must be musical myself, and that she must get me to sing to her, as she was sure I was a much better performer than George. I replied that I would not at all deny that I was fond of music, and would be glad to do anything I could to contribute to their amusement, more especially as I saw it was useless to struggle any longer with Miss Vivian, who was just about to checkmate me, but that I must make one condition, which was that I was to be allowed to make my exhibition first, as I was quite sure that after they had heard George they would never have patience to listen to me.

I had by this time learned that it was sometimes politic to allow one's self to be occasionally beaten, even at chess, and I very soon allowed Miss Vivian to win the game, and then joined the musical party.

I selected a song that had Eliza's name upon it. Maria smiled, and called to Eliza that it was one of her songs and she must come and play it, which she accordingly did. I tried to do my best, and certainly had no reason to be dissatisfied with the commendations which I received and, at their request, I gave them two or three more, which they suggested. I then resigned my place to George.

Maria offered to play for him, but he said he would rather accompany himself, and took his seat at the piano. He played the prelude to the beautiful air 'Una furtiva Lagrima', and then commenced to sing. For the first few notes his voice rather wavered, but he soon regained his confidence, and poured out a strain of exquisite music in the most charming manner. Even I, who had been in the constant habit of hearing him sing, was surprised at the manner in which he acquitted himself, but animated by the presence of those he loved, he was evidently induced to exert himself to the utmost, and certainly he did succeed in creating a most powerful sensation. Long before he had finished, there was not a dry eye in the room. Even Mrs Montague, usually so impassive, was roused from her imposing gravity. She first laid down her book to listen, and then rose from her seat and came and stood behind George.

When he had finished, there was perfect silence, for a minute or two, and then his grandmother, who was the first to recover herself, said, 'George, my dear boy, I knew you had a fine voice, but I had no idea it would have improved so greatly. You must have practised a great deal to have become so perfect. I hope it has not been at the expense of your other studies.'

I here struck in, 'No, indeed, Mrs Montague. I can assure you that it has not, and I am certain if you apply to the Doctor, he will tell you the same thing. I know some people think a taste for music is a dangerous one and likely to lead one into bad society, and it may be so with some, but I am quite sure it has had quite a different effect with us; it has often amused us, and kept us out of company where we might not have been so well employed.'

'I am very glad to hear it,' she replied, 'and I hope this will always be the case. But where did you contrive to improve yourself so much, George? I was not aware you had taken lessons in music.'

'Why,' answered George, 'my two first instructors, to whom I owe most, are both present.'

'Indeed,' said I, 'you owe everything to Miss Maria. At one time, I certainly had the presumption to fancy I could give you some instruction, but I soon found that the pupil was far before the master, though I suspect that neither of us would have made much progress latterly, had it not been for the kindness of the worthy signor.'

'And pray who is the signor?' asked Maria.

'Why, he is an Italian nobleman – a refugee, whose acquaintance I made some time ago. His story is too long to detail here, though I shall give it you some day for it is a very curious one; but he considered he was under some obligation to me for getting my uncle to use his interest with some influential people in his favour, so as to save the remnant of his property, and he took a great fancy to George, which has induced him to devote a good deal of time and trouble to our instruction.'

George was then requested to give them another song, which he did at once, and we continued the musical entertainment during the evening, taking care to make the young ladies join with us, so as to avoid any appearance of wishing to show off.

At the end of one of George's songs, I heard Maria say in a low tone, 'Oh, George! George! How could you be here for two whole days without giving us this pleasure?'

'It is all your own fault,' retorted he. 'You snubbed me so much the first night I came, that I have been afraid ever since even to open my mouth.'

When we retired to bed in the evening we congratulated ourselves on the success of our plan, feeling satisfied that we had made as much progress as we could have expected under the circumstances. In the morning, too, we had another proof of the effect we had produced on the girls. On returning from our ride the previous afternoon, I had pretended to hide my sketchbook in the pocket of my overcoat, which was hanging up in the hall, taking care that Maria should see where I put it. On looking at it in the morning, we found that it was not only quite apparent that it had been inspected, but that two of the sketches – those which gave the most complete and perfect representations of our organs of manhood – were wanting, and had evidently been cut out by our young friends. As a good many other pages had been taken out in the same manner, they probably thought the theft would never have been discovered, but I knew quite well what was there, and could not be mistaken on the subject.

We of course took no notice of this, but we thought it was a complete demonstration of their inclinations, and we determined that we should now take the first opportunity in our power to bring them to such terms as would enable us to procure the pleasure we desired to share with them.

The day turned out to be very wet, and we made an excuse of this to remain in the house and cultivate our intimacy with the girls. After breakfast, Maria said, 'Well, George, will you come to the drawing room, and pay me back some of the music lessons I used to give you?'

'With all my heart,' said George. 'There is nothing would give me greater pleasure than to practise *all* the lessons you used to teach me.'

She blushed and seemed a little confused, but immediately led the way to the drawing room, where we spent a couple of hours practising over all the old songs they had been accustomed to sing together. At last I said, 'Why, George, this will never do. If we continue at this rate we shall exhaust all our stores, and shall never be able to create a sensation again.'

George, however, did not seem disposed to leave the piano, apparently thinking that his position, bending over Maria, gave him a favourable opportunity for a little fingering upon a still more delicate instrument than the one she was performing on.

I wished to leave the field there clear for him and therefore turned to Eliza, who was sitting with her back turned to them, netting a purse.

'Oh, this is exactly what I wanted,' said I. 'I want to make a landing net, but I am afraid I have quite forgotten how to form the meshes. Perhaps you will be good enough to give me a lesson.'

She at once assented. I brought my materials and sat down beside her. She soon discovered that I knew quite as much on the subject as she did, but she said nothing, and continued to give me all the instruction I applied for, apparently not objecting to the use I made of the opportunity afforded me of pressing her hand and taking a few other liberties with her person.

In the meantime I kept up the conversation, which soon turned upon the subject of the Abbey. I said I felt myself quite at home there and could hardly persuade myself that I had entered it for the first time only three days before; I told her that George had been so fond of talking of it, and of describing everything that had occurred to him in it, that I believed I was almost as well acquainted with it as himself, for I was quite sure there was not a room in the house he had been in, not a book he had read, not a picture he had looked at, which he had not described over and over again.

As I said this in rather a marked tone, I saw Eliza's cheeks become suffused with a deep blush, and heard Maria whisper to George, 'Oh, George! George! How could you?'

'Never do you mind,' was his reply. 'He is quite safe: you need not be afraid of him.'

I took no notice of this, and soon changed the subject, adverting to our school days, and to all we had done for one another. Among other things I told them the only time we had ever got into a regular scrape was because we had refused to tell upon each other, and preferred to submit to a flogging rather than bring each other into disgrace.

At the mention of flogging they seemed greatly interested, and Maria especially pricked up her ears and put some questions on the subject as to how often we had been subjected to it and how we liked it. Seeing that they were amused with what I told them, I continued, greatly to George's diversion, to entertain them with sundry accounts of floggings, some of which were purely imaginary and the others improvements upon scenes that had actually occurred, not with ourselves, but with some of our acquaintances.

I gradually wound up their curiosity to a high pitch and Maria especially seemed to take a great interest in the subject. Observing this, I went on to say that it was a matter which one could convey no adequate idea of by mere description, and that to understand it properly it was necessary to have gone through it, or at least to have witnessed the operation itself. 'I only wish,' said I, 'that I had you at school some day when it was going on, that you might see the thing regularly carried through.'

Maria here burst out with 'Oh! it would be so funny to see it.'

'Well,' said I, 'I am afraid there is no possibility of conveying you to school for that purpose, but here is George, who is such a perfect ladies' man, that I am quite sure if he thought it would afford you any amusement he would at once submit to undergo the operation, in order merely to give you an idea of how it is done, and for my part, I shall be quite willing to act the part of the school-master, and apply the birch in a satisfactory manner.'

'Speak for yourself,' said George, 'I am not a bit fonder of it than you are.'

The girls burst out in a fit of laughter, and I gave George a look which he at once understood as a hint to keep up the joke. I continued to banter him, alleging that he was afraid of the pain and that he had not courage enough to stand the punishment.

Maria chimed in, and encouraged me to go on. After some little jesting on the subject, George appeared to come round, and at length agreed that he would submit to go through the ceremony of being flogged in their presence, exactly as the operation would be performed at school. He said the only thing he did not like about the punishment was the being kept in suspense, and he therefore stipulated that there should be no delay, and that the affair should be brought to a conclusion at once. I said there was but one objection to this, which was that as the punishment was to be a bona fide and not in joke, there was a risk that he might make an outcry which would disturb the house and get us into a scrape.

He affected to take this in high dudgeon, and to be greatly offended at the idea that he would cry out for such a trifle, and made an excuse of it for insisting that the affair should go on, in order to prove that he did not care in the least for the pain. At length he said that if we had any apprehension on this account it might easily be obviated by our going to the old schoolroom, where any noise that might be made could not be heard in the rest of the house.

At this allusion to the schoolroom, the girls exchanged a glance of alarm, and I hastened to remove any suspicion by saying it would be better to delay until the weather improved, when the scene could take place in the open air, at a distance from the house. George, however, insisted that there should be no delay, and at length a compromise was made by which it was arranged that if the rain ceased after luncheon we should go into the park, and if not, the ceremony should take place in the schoolroom.

As the day wore on without any symptom of improvement,

George and I made all the necessary preparations. After lunch, we sat for some time with the girls without referring to the subject, which occupied all our thoughts. At length Maria made an allusion to it, upon which George started up and insisted on its being got over at once.

The so-called schoolroom – or rather library – was a large oblong apartment, which had formerly been the chapel of the Abbey. At one end was the principal entrance, and at the other a large bay window, which occupied the whole of that end of the room, with the exception of a closet on each side. The portion within the recess was elevated by two steps from the rest of the floor, and the window, though on the ground floor, was thus so high that no one the outside could look into the room without getting up on to the window sill, which, though not impossible, as George and I had already ascertained, was not an easy matter without some assistance. In the centre of the room was a long library table. A great portion of one side was taken up with a large fireplace; the remainder, and the whole of the opposite side, was occupied by bookshelves, while beside the table and opposite the fireplace, was a large old-fashioned sofa, more like a bed than a sofa of modern times.

When we reached the room I at once took upon myself the character of schoolmaster, and George assumed that of the pert school-boy. I placed the girls on the sofa, and drew a large stand for holding maps across the space between the sofa and the table, thus cutting off the communication between them and the door.

I then told George to prepare for punishment. He inquired, in a flippant tone, if he was to strip entirely naked. I pretended to be shocked, and answered with a serious air, 'No, sir; you know quite well that if I were about to punish you in a severe manner I should not expose you before your companions; but take care, sir, and do not provoke me too far; for though kissing a pretty girl is a grave fault and deserves the punishment you are about to undergo, still, disrespect to your master is a much greater crime, and if you continue to show it in this manner, I shall be obliged, however unwillingly, to resort to the severest punishment in my power to inflict.'

I then made him take off his coat and waistcoat, and pretended to fasten his hands above his head to the roller from which the maps depended. I then turned his handsome bottom to the girls, and taking up a birch rod which I had provided, I affected to flog his posteriors severely. He writhed and twisted his body in the most ridiculous manner, as if he was suffering greatly from the infliction of the blows, but at the same time he turned round his head, made wry faces, put out his tongue, and made fun to the girls, who were in fits of laughter and heartily enjoying the whole scene.

I rebuked him for his improper conduct, and told him that if it was continued, I must resort to severer measures with him. The more I appeared to get angry, the more he made game of me and the more outrageous he became. At length I approached him, and took hold of one hand, as if for the purpose of restraining his antics, and making him keep still, in order that I might be better able to apply the rod; but my object was of a totally different nature. I had taken care that he should have no braces on, and his trousers were merely fastened in front by two or three buttons. These I secretly unloosened, and having satisfied myself that his beautiful organ of manhood was in a sufficiently imposing state for the exhibition I meditated, I suddenly slipped down his trousers, raised up his shirt and inflicted two or three sharp blows on his naked posteriors, pure and white as snow, saying, 'There sir, since you will have it in this manner, how do you like it so?'

I had no sooner finished than he turned round, and as I took good care to hold his shirt well up, he exhibited to the astonished eyes of the two girls an object which they have often contemplated before, but certainly never in such a beautiful or satisfactory state. There it stood bolt upright, issuing from the tender curls which had begun to adorn it, with the curious little balls, as yet unshaded with hair, but of a slightly darker colour than the rest of his person, which made them show off in contrast with the pure white of his thighs, the pillar rearing itself proudly up towards his navel, surmounted with its lovely coral head.

The whole proceeding only occupied a few seconds, and took the girls entirely by surprise. Uttering a shriek, they started up, and endeavoured to reach the door. This movement, however, had been foreseen, and as in order to arrive at it they had to round the table, George was enabled to reach it before them. He hastily locked it, took out the key, and then planted himself before it, with his shirt tucked up round his waist, and his trousers down to his knees, exhibiting his flaming priapus as a formidable bar to their exit, while he exclaimed, 'No, no! You shan't escape in this manner. You have all had your share in the amusement, and it is now my turn to have mine, and not one of you shall leave the room till you have all undergone the same punishment as I have been subjected to. Come, Frank, this is all your doing, so I must begin with you.'

'By all means,' replied I, 'it shall never be said that I proposed to any one else what I was afraid to undergo myself.'

Prepared as I was for the scene, not a moment was lost. In a trice, my jacket and waistcoat were off, my trousers were down at my heels, and my shirt tucked up round my waist like George's, presenting, I flattered myself, as favourable a proof of my manly prowess as he had done. Taking up the rod, he applied a few stripes to my naked posteriors, while we watched the proceedings of the girls.

Finding their escape by the principal door barred by the flaming falchion which George brandished in their faces, they made an attempt to escape by the side door. This also had been guarded against. Ascertaining that it was locked, and now catching a glimpse of the new formidable weapon, which I disclosed to their sight, and which George took care should be presented in full view, they retreated to the sofa, covered their faces with their hands, and kneeling down, ensconced themselves in each corner, burying their heads in the cushions.

In this position, though they secured the main approach to the principal scene of pleasure which they probably supposed would be the first object of attack, they forgot that the back entrance was left quite open to assault. Nor were we now all disposed to give them quarter. While George threw himself upon Maria, I made an attack on Eliza.

Before they were aware what we are about their petticoats were turned up and their lovely bottoms exposed to our delighted gaze. Although we did not profane with the rod, a few slaps of our hands upon the polished ivory surfaces made them glow with a beauteous rosy tint. Ashamed of this exposure, they struggled to replace their petticoats. Nor was I at all unwilling to change the mode of attack. Throwing one arm round Eliza's waist to keep her down, and pressing my lips between her cheek, I inserted my hand beneath her petticoats as she attempted to pull them down, and gliding it up between her legs, I brought it by one rapid and decisive sweep fairly between her thighs to the very entrance, and even insinuated one finger within the lips, of the centre of attraction, before she was in the least aware of the change in my tactics.

She struggled at first, and endeavoured to rise up and get away from me. But I had secured my advantage too well to be easily defeated, and after a few unavailing attempts she gave up the contest, and seemed to resign herself to her fate.

I was not slow to avail myself of the advantage I had thus gained and, after kissing away a few tears, I contrived to insert the hand, with which I did not now find it necessary to hold her down, within the front of her gown, and proceeded to handle and toy with a most lovely pair of little, smooth, firm bubbies, which seemed to grow harder under my burning touches.

All this time I continued to move my finger up and down in the most lascivious manner within the narrow entrance of the charming grotto into which I had managed to insert it, and the double action soon began to produce an evident effect upon her. The tears ceased to flow, and my ardent kisses, if not returned, were at least

received with tokens of approbation and pleasure. Presently I felt
the tips of her delicious recess contract and close upon my lascivious finger, and after a little apparent hesitation the buttocks began
to move gently backwards and forwards in unison with the stimu-
lating motions of the provoking intruder. Encouraged by this and
feeling convinced that her voluptuous sensations were now carrying her onward in the path of pleasure in spite of herself, I took
hold of her hand and placed it upon my burning weapon. At first
she attempted to withdraw it, but I held it firmly upon the throbbing and palpitating object; and after a little struggle I prevailed
upon her not only to grasp it, but also to humour the wanton
movements which I made with it backwards and forwards within
the grasp of her soft fingers. This delightful amusement occupied
us for some little time, and I was in no hurry to bring it to a close,
for I found Eliza was every moment getting more and more
excited, and her actions becoming freer and less embarrassed. But
I felt that if I continued it longer we must both inevitably bring on
the final crisis. Having already succeeded so well in my under-
taking, I was anxious that she should enjoy the supreme happiness
in the most complete manner possible, and I had little doubt that
her excited passions would now induce her to give every facility to
my proceedings. Changing her position a little to favour my object,
I abandoned the advantage I enjoyed in the rear for the purpose of
obtaining a more convenient lodgement in front. Inserting one
knee under her thigh, I turned her over on her back, and throwing myself upon her to prevent her from rising, though to tell the
truth, she did not appear to dislike the change of position, I again
tickled her up with my finger for a minute or two. Then withdrawing it from the delicious cavity and pressing her closely to my
bosom and stifling her remonstrances with kisses and caresses, I
endeavoured to replace the fortunate finger with the more
appropriate organ, which was now fierce with desire, and burning
to attain its proper position and deposit its luscious treasures within
the delicious receptacle. The head was already at the entrance, and

I was just flattering myself that another push or two would attain my object and complete our mutual happiness, when a confounded bell rang out loudly.

I at once foreboded that it sounded the knell of all my hopes, for that opportunity at least, nor was I far wrong. However, I took no notice of it, but continued my efforts to effect the much desired penetration. But starting up with a strength and energy she had not previously exhibited, Eliza exclaimed, 'Oh, Sir Francis, you must let me go! It is the visitor's bell, and we shall be wanted immediately.'

I was extremely loth to lose the opportunity, and at first was disposed to try to retain the advantage I had already gained until I had secured the victory. But the evident distress she displayed affected me. I could not help feeling from the sudden change in her manner that it was urgent necessity, and not want of inclination, that forced her to put a stop to our proceedings. When she exclaimed, 'Oh, do have mercy on us! Think what would be the consequence if we were to be found in this state!' I could not resist the appeal, and allowing her to rise,I said that however greatly disappointed I might be at such an untoward termination to our amusements, I could not think of putting any contemplated enjoyment on my own part in competition with what might prove injurious to her, and that I should make no opposition to their leaving us at once, trusting that I should meet with the reward for my forbearance on some future more favourable occasion.

She thanked me warmly, and would doubtless have promised anything in order to get away, but I was not disposed to place much value upon any promises made in such a situation, and therefore did not attempt to extort any. She hastily began to arrange her dress, which had been not a little disarranged in the amorous struggle, and we then turned our glances towards George and Maria.

Whether it was that he had been more enterprising than I had been, or had met with less opposition, I know not, but when our attention was drawn to them we found Maria extended on her back on the sofa, with her legs spread wide out, and her petticoats above her waist, and George, with his trousers down about his heels and his plump white posteriors exposed to view quite bare, extended on the top of her, his legs between hers, clasping her tightly round the waist, and planting fiery kisses upon her lips, which were returned with interest. His buttocks were moving up and down with fierce heaves, and he endeavoured to effect his object and obtain admission to the virgin fortress.

At first I thought he had been more successful than I had been, but on a closer inspection, I found he was still beating about the bush, and that his weapon was still wandering in wild and hurried movements around the entrance without having yet hit upon the right spot, or managed to get within the secluded avenue of pleasure. Eliza spoke to them without producing any effect, and I was obliged to lay my hand on George's shoulder, and make him listen while I explained to him the state of matters. His answer was 'Oh goodness, I can't stop now, I must get it in.'

At this moment another bell rang, which Eliza told me was a signal they were wanted. There was now no help for it. I was forced to remind George that we should not only ruin the girls, but also lose all chance of having any future enjoyment with them if we allowed ourselves to be surprised on this occasion. It was with difficulty I could persuade him to get up and permit Maria to rise. He wished to keep the girls until they promised to come back to us; but as the thing must be done, I thought the sooner the better, and I therefore opened the side door and enabled them to escape to their own room where they hastened to repair the disorder in their hair and dress, which might have led to suspicion. Fortunately they were able to accomplish this and to make their appearance in the drawing room without their absence having attracted attention.

George had managed to extort a promise from Maria that they would return when the visitors departed; but not putting much faith in this, we dressed ourselves and proceeded to join them, hoping that we might be able to induce them to give us another opportunity when they were left alone. In this, however, we were disappointed. Being obliged to attend some ladies to their carriage, we found on our return that the birds had flown, nor did they make their appearance again till dinner time.

We were greatly annoyed at this unfortunate issue of our first attempt, just when it was on the very point of complete success; more especially, as every effort we could make to persuade them to give us another opportunity to accomplish our object was unavailing. It is true that all restraint among us was now removed. They laughed and joked with us, and did not take amiss the minor liberties we sometimes contrived to take with their persons. Nay, they even seemed to enjoy the fun, when occasionally, on a safe opportunity, we would produce our inflamed weapons and exhibit them in the imposing condition which their presence never failed to produce, in order to try to tempt them and to excite them to comply with our desires. Occasionally they would even allow us to place their hands upon them and make them toy and play with them; but still they took good care never to accompany us alone to any place where our efforts might be successfully renewed to accomplish the great object of our wishes.

One very hot day we took our books to enjoy the fresh air under the shade of a tree on the lawn in the front of the Abbey. We were quite near enough to the house to be visible from the window, and the place was so exposed that it was out of the question to think of attempting the full gratification of our desires.

Nevertheless, we were so far off that our proceedings could not be distinctly observed, and there were a few low shrubs around which entirely concealed the lower parts of our persons, but still not so high as to prevent us from easily discovering if anyone approached us.

There was thus a fair opportunity afforded us for indulging in minor species of amusement for which we might feel inclined. Our desires, kept constantly on the stretch as they had been, were too potent to permit us to let such an opportunity escape us. George's trousers were soon unbuttoned, and his beautiful article, starting out in all its glory, was placed in Maria's hand.

After a little pretended hesitation and bashfulness, she began to get excited and interested in the lovely object, twisting her fingers among the scanty curls which adorned its root and toying with the little balls puckered up beneath, all which were freely exposed to her inspection.

For my part, I had laid my head on Eliza's lap and, slipping my hand under her petticoats, had insinuated a finger within her delicious aperture, playing with it, and tickling it, in the most wanton manner I could devise. The effects of both these operations were soon quite apparent on the lovely girls. Their eyes sparkled, and their faces became flushed, and I had very little doubt that could it have been safely done, they would have consented to gratify our fondest desires. I knew that some visitors were expected to spend the afternoon with us, who would occupy the girls and prevent any chance of further amusement for that day at least; and it occurred to me that though it would be too rash to attempt the perfect consummation of our happiness, we might at least indulge ourselves by carrying our gratification as far as we could safely venture to do so, and at all events thoroughly enjoy all the minor pleasures which were within our power. I therefore made a sign to George, which he at once understood. Following my example and getting his finger within Maria's centre of pleasure, he operated upon it in such an agreeable manner that she became excited beyond measure. Stretching herself beside him, she convulsively grasped the ivory pillar which she held in her hand, hugging and squeezing it and indulging in every variety of tender pressure. George instantly took advantage of her excitement, and while he continued to move his finger rapidly in and out of her lovely grotto, he agitated his own body so as to make his throbbing member slip backwards and forwards in the fond grasp which she maintained upon it. His involuntary exclamations of rapture and delight appeared to touch and affect Maria, and seeing how much pleasure she was giving him, as well as receiving herself, she could not refrain from trying to do everything in her power to increase his enjoyment. A word or two from him, every now and then, regulated the rapidity of their movements, and I soon saw that they were on the high road to attain that degree of bliss to which alone we could aspire under present circumstances.

Finding them so well employed, I hastened to follow their example. Unloosening my trousers, I set at liberty my champion, which was burning with impatience to join in the sport. Taking Eliza's hand, I placed it upon the throbbing object. She started with surprise and pleasure, on feeling its hot inflamed state, but did not attempt to remove her hand from where I placed it. She was sitting on the ground, with her back leaning against a tree. I gently raised up her petticoats and slipping my hand beneath them, separated her thighs, and pressed my lips upon her spongy mount and kissed it fondly. Searching out with my finger the most sensitive part, I played with it and tickled it until it swelled out and became inflamed to the utmost degree.

I soon ascertained the successful effect of my operations by the delightful manner in which she rewarded me, compressing my organ of manhood in her charming grasp in the most delicious manner possible and meeting and humouring the hurried and frantic thrusts with which I made it move to and fro between her fingers.

Finding that she was quite willing to continue the operations, which afforded us both so much enjoyment, I raised myself up on my knees, and while I gazed in her lovely countenance, sparkling with all the fires of luxurious delight, I exhibited to her the full proportions of my foaming champion as it bounded up and down under the fierce excitement of the delicious pressure she exercised upon it. I had intended to have made her witness the final out-bursts of the tide of pleasure. And, therefore, while I kept up the pleasing irritation with my finger, I purposely delayed bringing on with her the final crisis. But as I felt the flood of rapture ready to pour from me, I could restrain myself no longer, and hastily drawing up her petticoats before she could make any opposition, I bent forward and threw myself down across her. My stiff and bursting instrument penetrated between her thighs, and deposited its boiling treasure at the very mouth of the abode of bliss. As the stream of pleasure continued to flow out from me in successive jets, I felt Eliza's body give a gentle shiver under me. We lay wrapt in bliss for some minutes, during which she made no attempt to dislodge me from my situation. I guessed what had happened to her; but to make certain, I again placed my finger within her aperture and found the interior quite moist with a liquid which I knew had not issued from me.

When I put the question to her, she acknowledged with burning blushes that from the excited state she had been in, the touch of my burning weapon so near the critical spot had applied the torch to the fuel ready to burst into flame, and had brought on with her the final bliss at the very same time with me.

As I wiped away the dewy effusion from her thighs, I tenderly reproached her with having allowed it to be wasted in such an unsatisfactory manner, when it might have afforded so much greater gratification to us both. I could read in the pleased and yet longing expression of her lovely eyes that such a consummation would have been no less agreeable to her than to me; and I could fancy that were a favourable opportunity to offer itself, there would now be no great objection on her part to allow the wondrous instrument of pleasure, on which she again gazed with surprise and admiration as it throbbed and beat in her fond grasp, to take the necessary measures to procure for us both the highest gratification of which human nature is susceptible.

On casting my eyes around to where George and Maria were placed, I saw that we were still in time to enjoy a delightful spectacle to which I hastened to call the attention of my companion. George was stretched at full length on his back on the ground. The front of his trousers was quite open, disclosing all the lower part of his belly and his thighs. His charming weapon protruded stiff and erect up from the few short curls which had begun to adorn it. Maria was kneeling astride him, grasping in her hand the instrument of bliss, and urging her fingers up and down upon it with an impetuosity that betokened the fierce fire that was raging within her. George's operations upon her we could not discern, for his head was buried between her thighs, and was entirely concealed by her petticoats, which fell over it. But that he was employed on a similar operation was quite evident from the short hurried movements which her posteriors kept up, no doubt in response to the luxurious and provoking touches of his penetrating finger. Maria's face was bent down within a few inches of the object of her adoration, upon which she was too intent to take any notice of us.

We enjoyed for a minute or two the pleasing contemplation of her delightful occupation and of the libidinous heaves of George's buttocks, which increased in strength and rapidity as the critical moment began with him. At length it arrived, and accompanied with an exclamation of rapture, the creamy jet issued forth from him with an energy that made it fly up, and bedew the countenance of the astonished Maria. Retaining her grasp, she gazed for an instant with rapture on this unexpected phenomenon; but her time was to come too, and almost before George's tide had ceased to flow, she sank down upon him, pressing his still stiff and erect weapon to her lips, and showering kisses upon it while, as we soon found, she repaid George's exertions with a tender effusion from her own private resources, which somewhat calmed her senses and restored her to reason.

When we had a little recovered ourselves, the girls appeared to be rather ashamed of the excesses which they had committed. And as George continued to tease them not a little, regarding the sacrilege they had been guilty of in thus wastefully pouring out both their own and our treasures, they soon took refuge in the house to hide their blushes and confusion.

We soon found, however, that though still too frightened to

allow us to proceed to the last extremity, they would have no objection to a renewal of our late exploit. But this did not suit the purpose of George and myself, and we were determined not to allow them thus to tantalize us and slip through our fingers, now that we had obtained such a hold over them.

After some days' fruitless endeavours to effect our object, we became aware that we must again resort to stratagem for success. But the difficulty was how to accomplish it, for after having been once entrapped, they were now upon their guard with us.

We had taken down with us some of the best amatory pictures we could procure, and on the night of the flogging scene, when we found we could not prevail on them to return with us to the library, George had told them that we were not going to imitate their cruelty but would do all in our power to amuse them, and that he would accordingly deposit the pictures in the old hiding place that they might inspect them whenever they felt disposed. We kept a watch upon them, but without any great hope of immediate success from the stratagem, as we were aware they would suspect us and would take care not to be caught looking at them. We soon discovered however, from the marks we placed, that they were in the habit of amusing themselves with those pictures when they were certain we were out of the way, and we laid our plans accordingly.

One morning it was announced at breakfast time that the old ladies were going to dine that day at the house of a friend some miles off, so that the young people would be left quite alone for the whole evening. Although we were perfectly aware of this, and had founded our scheme upon it, we affected not to have known it. George turning to me said, 'Oh Frank, this will suit us nicely. Mrs Montague will perhaps be good enough to allow us to dine at luncheon time, and by that hour the river will be in prime fishing order after the rain, and we shall have a good afternoon's sport.' Mrs Montague at once agreed and gave orders accordingly. I thought the young ladies looked rather blank at this announcement, and I told George to whisper to Maria that if they would promise to be kind to us, we would return at seven o'clock to take tea with them when we would have the house all to ourselves. This satisfied them and put them off their guard.

All proceeded as we hoped. After luncheon we started for the river, and plied our rods as effectually as we could, in order that we might have something to show on our return. When the time approached at which the old ladies were to leave the Abbey, we returned to it; and hiding our fishing apparatus in one of the plantations, we made our way into the library by the window which we had purposely left open. We then concealed ourselves in a large closet of which there were two, one on each side of the window. We knew we could accomplish this without discovery as the girls would then be engaged assisting the old ladies to dress.

Having safely ensconced ourselves in our hiding place, we waited patiently at first for the departure of the old people. In a short time the carriage came to the door, and soon after we heard it drive off. We now became very impatient, for we confidently trusted that the girls would take advantage of such a favourable opportunity of being left entirely to themselves to derive some amusement from an inspection of the pictures, to which George had told them the night before that he had added some new ones, and we had taken care that they should have no opportunity of looking at them that day. Imagine therefore our dismay when we heard them leave their own room, proceed to the front door, and issue forth, closing it after them somewhat loudly.

George was in a sad state of vexation, and proposed that we should follow them, but this I objected to, saying that we should have plenty of time if we were obliged to go to work openly, and it was well worth while to wait patiently for some time longer for the chance of taking them at such advantage as would place them entirely in our power. George acquiesced and agreed to remain quiet. But his patience had nearly forsaken him when he heard the side door, which gave access to the library from the garden, gently open. We were in a state of anxious suspense until we heard it close, and beheld Maria's face peep through the door of the library. Finding all apparently safe, she came into the room and was immediately followed by Eliza.

They closed the door softly, and we at once anticipated complete success as soon as we saw them draw the bolts of both it and the principal door. Our patience was now extreme, but seeing everything proceeding so favourably, so resolved to curb it until we were in a situation to make the most of the advantage we had calculated on gaining. We therefore remained perfectly quiet, watching their proceedings.

Apparently satisfied that there was no occasion for any restraint upon their actions, they threw off all disguise and, removing their bonnets, proceeded to open the secret place and take out the pictures. They inspected them for some minutes, evidently with great pleasure, and the luscious details of the libidinous scenes they saw there depicted soon produced their natural effect upon them. After some little preliminaries, Maria laid herself back at full length upon the sofa, stretching out her legs before her, and drew up her petticoats as far as they would go; and at the same time pulled up the petticoats of Eliza, who was sitting beside her turning over the pictures, in such a manner to exhibit her thighs, belly, and the beautiful cleft with its surrounding fringe of curly hair. She inserted a finger into it and proceeded to titillate it, while with her other hand, she operated a similar diversion on her own charming aperture.

This was too much for us to view, and stand longer inactive. We had quite divested ourselves of the whole of our clothes, and softly opening the door, we rushed out perfectly naked, and with splendidly erected weapons threw ourselves at once upon our defenceless prey. They were so utterly taken by surprise, and so confounded at the state in which we appeared before them and the situation in which they themselves had been discovered, that they were perfectly unable to stir, and remained motionless in the same attitudes until we had clasped them in our arms and pressed them to our breasts, without their having the power to make the slightest resistance.

Maria's position, stretched at full length on the sofa, with her legs hanging down and wide apart, was too tempting to be resisted. In an instant George was between her thighs, his arms clasped around her waist, his naked belly rubbing against hers, and his fiery champion pressed against the lower part of her belly, endeavouring to find an entrance to that abode of bliss from which he had just snatched her finger, with the intention to replace it with a more satisfactory and appropriate organ.

For my part, though equally desirous to profit by the occasion, I was still cool enough to decide upon the best course of procedure. There was only one sofa in the room, so that only one pair could, with comfort and satisfaction, proceed with the pleasing operation. George was so maddened with excitement that I saw he could brook no delay, and I resolved that I should allow him to accomplish without hindrance his first victory in the field of Venus. I was the more induced to do this from the consideration that the exploration my finger had already made on the former occasions had convinced me that the fortress I had to attack was to be approached by an entrance so straight and narrow that the passage of my battering ram into the breach was not likely to be effected without considerable difficulty, and some suffering on the part of the besieged party. From George's account, there was not likely to be the same difficulty with regard to Maria, partly because her entrance was more open and partly because his member had not yet attained the same size as mine.

All these considerations made me think it advisable to secure every advantage by having Eliza favourably placed in a convenient position on the sofa before I attempted the assault; and I thought likewise that the previous sight of the raptures, which I was certain George and Maria would experience and exhibit before her, would encourage her and reconcile her to any little suffering she might undergo in becoming qualified to enjoy a similar bliss. I therefore sat down on the sofa, and keeping her petticoats still raised up, I made Eliza sit down, with her naked bottom on my knees, and slipped my instrument between her thighs, so as to make it rub against the lips of her lovely aperture. At the same time I whispered to her that I thought we had better allow George and Maria to enjoy themselves in the first place, as there was not room for us all on the sofa at the same time.

She was in such a state of confusion and distraction, arising from the shame of having been detected in her previous occupation, as well as from the exciting nature of the novel scene now presented before her eyes of two handsome youths exhibiting all their naked charms, that she was in no condition to resist anything I required. But wishing to keep up her excitement to the utmost, I now directed her attention to the proceedings of our companions.

Maria apparently now thought that it was no use to mince matters, and that as the operation must be gone through, she might as well enjoy it thoroughly. Accordingly, instead of making any resistance, she had clasped her arms round George's naked body, and with burning kisses was animating him to his task, while the forward movements of her buttocks to meet his thrusts, showed that her anxiety was fully equal to his that they should effect an immediate and pleasing conjunction. I saw, however, that in their inexperience they were still beating about the bush, and had not yet taken the proper means to introduce the impatient stallion into the opening that was thus left quite free for his reception. I said to George, 'Wait a minute, my boy, I think I could manage to place you in a more satisfactory position.'

Throwing my arms round the legs of both, I lifted them up and placed them in an advantageous position on the sofa. Then inserting my hand between their bellies, I laid hold of George's fiery weapon, and keeping it directed right upon the proper spot, I told him to thrust away now. This he did with hearty good will. The first thrust he was within the lips, the second he was half way in, and the third he was so fairly engulfed, that I had to let go my hold, and withdraw my hand, so as to admit of their perfect conjunction.

At the first thrust Maria met him with a bound of her buttocks, at the second she uttered a scream, and as he penetrated her interior at the third, she beseeched him to stop, saying that he was killing her. George, however, was not now in a state to be able to listen to her remonstrances. Satisfied that the worst was over and his object fully gained, as much to her benefit as his own, he merely replied with repeated fierce heaves and thrusts, while his fiery kisses seemed intended to stifle her complaints. A very few movements of his weapon, driven in as it was from point to hilt within her, were sufficient to drown all sense of suffering, and to rekindle the flame of desire which had previously animated her. Very soon her impetuous and lascivious motions rivalled his own in force and activity, as straining each other in their close embrace they strove to drive the newly-inserted wedge still further and further into the abode of bliss. Maria's upward heaves and the impetuous motions of George's bounding buttocks, as they kept time together at each luscious thrust, soon produced their pleasing effect, and with a cry of rapture, the enamoured boy, drowned in a sea of delight, poured forth his blissful treasures, while the no less enchanted girl, wrought up to an equal pitch of boundless pleasure, responded to his maiden tribute by shedding forth the first effusion every drawn from her by manly vigour, a happy consummation which was accompanied on both sides with the most lively demonstrations of perfect delight.

BRAM STOKER

from

Dracula

Dracula, *the most famous of all vampire stories, was published in 1897. The author, Bram Stoker (1847–1912), was English and for some years the business manager of the actor, Sir Henry Irving. The story is told through the diaries of a young solicitor, Jonathan Harker.*

WHEN I had written in my diary and had fortunately replaced the book and pen in my pocket, I felt sleepy. The Count's warning came into my mind, but I took a pleasure in disobeying it. The sense of sleep was upon me, and with it the obstinacy which sleep brings as outrider. The soft moonlight soothed, and the wide expanse without gave a sense of freedom which refreshed me. I determined not to return to-night to the gloom-haunted rooms, but to sleep here, where of old ladies had sat and sung and lived sweet lives whilst their gentle breasts were sad for their menfolk away in the midst of remorseless wars. I drew a great couch out of its place near the corner, so that, as I lay, I could look at the lovely view to east and south, and unthinking of and uncaring for the dust, composed myself for sleep.

I suppose I must have fallen asleep; I hope so, but I fear, for all that followed was startlingly real – so real that now, sitting here in the broad, full sunlight of the morning, I cannot in the least believe that it was all sleep.

I was not alone. The room was the same, unchanged in any way since I came into it; I could see along the floor, in the brilliant moonlight, my own footsteps marked where I had disturbed the long accumulation of dust. In the moonlight opposite me were three young women, ladies by their dress and manner. I thought at the time that I must be dreaming when I saw them, for, though the moonlight was behind them, they threw no shadow on the floor. They came close to me and looked at me for some time and then whispered together. Two were dark, and had high aquiline noses, like the Count's, and great dark, piercing eyes, that seemed to be almost red when contrasted with the pale yellow moon. The other was fair, as fair as can be, with great, wavy masses of golden hair and eyes like pale sapphires. I seemed somehow to know her face, and to know it in connection with some dreamy fear, but I could not recollect at the moment how or where. All three had brilliant white teeth, that shone like pearls against the ruby of their voluptuous lips. There was something about them that made me uneasy, some longing and at the same time some deadly fear. I felt in my heart a wicked, burning desire that they would kiss me with those red lips. It is not good to note this down, lest some day it should meet Mina's eyes and cause her pain; but it is the truth. They whispered together, and then they all three laughed – such a silvery, musical laugh, but as hard as though the sound never could have come through the softness of human lips. It was like the intolerable, tingling sweetness of water-glasses when played on by a cunning hand. The fair girl shook her head coquettishly, and the other two urged her on. One said:–

'Go on! You are first, and we shall follow; yours is the right to begin.' The other added:–

'He is young and strong; there are kisses for us all.' I lay quiet, looking out under my eyelashes in an agony of delightful anticipation. The fair girl advanced and bent over me till I could feel the movement of her breath upon me. Sweet it was in one sense, honey-sweet, and sent the same tingling through the nerves as her voice, but with a bitter underlying the sweet, a bitter offensiveness, as one smells in blood.

I was afraid to raise my eyelids, but looked out and saw perfectly under the lashes. The fair girl went on her knees and bent over me, fairly gloating. There was a deliberate voluptuousness which was both thrilling and repulsive, and as she arched her neck she actually licked her lips like an animal, till I could see in the moonlight the moisture shining on the scarlet lips and on the red tongue as it lapped the white sharp teeth. Lower and lower went her head as the lips went below the range of my mouth and chin and seemed about to fasten on my throat. Then she paused, and I could hear the churning sound of her tongue as it licked her teeth and lips, and could feel the hot breath on my neck. Then the skin of my throat began to tingle as one's flesh does when the hand that is to tickle it approaches nearer – nearer. I could feel the soft, shivering touch of the lips on the supersensitive skin of my throat, and the hard dents of two sharp teeth, just touching and pausing there. I closed my eyes in a languorous ecstasy and waited – waited with beating heart.

But at that instant another sensation swept through me as quick as lightning. I was conscious of the presence of the Count, and of his being as if lapped in a storm of fury. As my eyes opened involuntarily I saw his strong hand grasp the slender neck of the fair woman and with giant's power draw it back, the blue eyes transformed with fury, the white teeth champing with rage, and the fair cheeks blazing red with passion. But the Count! Never did I imagine such wrath and fury, even in the demons of the pit. His eyes were positively blazing. The red light in them was lurid, as if the flames of hell-fire blazed behind them. His face was deathly pale, and the lines of it were hard like drawn wires; the thick eyebrows that met over the nose now seemed like a heaving bar of white-hot metal. With a fierce sweep of his arm, he hurled the woman from him, and then motioned to the others, as though he were beating them back; it was the same imperious gesture that I had seen used to the wolves. In a voice which, though low and almost a whisper, seemed to cut through the air and then ring round the room, he exclaimed:–

'How dare you touch him, any of you? How dare you cast eyes on him when I had forbidden it? Back, I tell you all! This man belongs to me! Beware how you meddle with him, or you'll have to deal with me.' The fair girl, with laugh of ribald coquetry, turned to answer him:–

'You yourself never loved; you never love!' On this the other woman joined, and such a mirthless, hard, soulless laughter rang through the room that it almost made me faint to hear; it seemed like the pleasure of fiends. Then the Count turned, after looking at my face attentively, and said in a soft whisper:–

'Yes, I too can love; you yourselves can tell it from the past. Is it not so? Well, now I promise you that when I am done with him, you shall kiss him at your will. Now go! go! I must awaken him, for there is work to be done.'

'Are we to have nothing to-night?' said one of them, with a low laugh, as she pointed to the bag which he had thrown upon the floor, and which moved as though there were some living thing within it. For answer he nodded his head. One of the women jumped forward and opened it. If my ears did not deceive me there was a gasp and a low wail, as of a half-smothered child. The women closed round, whilst I was aghast with horror; but as I looked they disappeared, and with them the dreadful bag. There was no door near them, and they could not have passed me without my noticing. They simply seemed to fade into the rays of the moonlight and pass out through the window, for I could see outside the dim, shadowy forms for a moment before they entirely faded away.

Then the horror overcame me, and I sank down unconscious.

ANONYMOUS

from

The Lustful Memoirs
of a Young and Passionate Girl

The Lustful Memoirs of a Young and Passionate Girl *was printed for private circulation in 1904 and is a good example of early Edwardian erotica.*

I NEXT lived with a family named Manus. There were two girls, young women in the family. I began to get some light, on the many things that had puzzled me by listening to them when they did not suppose I was paying any attention. I got an idea of the difference in the sexes, and some confused ideas about sexual intercourse. The girls each had a beau. They used to tell each other about them, but they said many things I didn't understand. In the next place that I lived were two girls orphans, one about my own age, the other about two years older. I lived there about three years. The girls were both well informed in regard to sexual matters and they soon imparted their knowledge to me. Not far from where we lived was a neighbour who had a dairy. Among other employees were a couple of boys, two or three years older than we were. We were quite intimate with them but there had been no grievous improprieties when I again had to change my residence, this time to live with an old couple who lived adjoining the dairyman. The girls used to visit me quite often and we almost always managed to meet the boys when we were together. Julia was almost old enough now to put in long dresses while Lizzie and I began to feel a strong attraction for the male sex. Julia was really the most amorous, but

Lizzie was the most reckless in words and acts. One day we girls were out in the barn where we had had an exciting conversation, so that we felt in a mood for any thing almost. Julia had taken off her drawers and pulling up her skirts to show that the hair was beginning to grow on her's. Lizzie took her's off then, and was diligently hunting for some sign of hair when the barn door opened and in came one of the boys. We had spread some blankets on the floor and had been laying on them. Julia jumped up when she heard the door open, but Lizzie and I remained on the blanket. Abner came in and seeing us on the blanket he got down with us. Julia too did the same. I know we were all glad he had come in. Lizzie soon got astradle of him and when he rolled her off, she exposed her legs so much that I said, 'Why Lizzie! pull your clothes,' but she only rolled over two or three times with her legs bare. Then Julia began to scold her, but Lizzie only laughed and said she didn't care if he wanted to. Abner, however, seemed to care more for Julia than either Lizzie or I. For something she said or did he caught hold of her and held her fast. In her struggles she exposed her legs nearly as much as Lizzie had, but she could not get her clothes down, she was helpless. Then Lizzie began – 'Why Julia! ain't you ashamed to show your legs so. I am shocked that you would do such a thing.' Julia squirmed and asked me to pull her clothes down, but Abner said: 'Don't you do it,' and we didn't while he was trying to get her clothes up still higher. She finally got loose from him and jumped to her feet.

He grabbed her by the ankle and over she went again and up her clothes went too. Lizzie was so pleased that she kicked up her heels as she lay on her back making no effort to hide anything. Abner got Julia's skirts up so that her thighs were naked and he got his hand up on her belly or somewhere under her skirts. Julia fairly squeeled out and tried to get his hand away but didn't succeed. Instead of helping Julia, Lizzie caught hold of one of her feet and helped him get her legs separated so that he got his hand on her nest. Then Julia just threw her arms across her face to hide it, and made no further objections. Lizzie and I looked on very much interested. Indeed there was a place between my own thighs that was burning and throbbing with amorous excitement and Lizzie felt much as I did. When Abner unbuttoned his pants and took out his staff, Lizzie at once took hold of it. He seemed to like it, for he rolled over partly on his back so we could get a better view of it. Julia took a look at it too, then put her hand on it. I felt of it also, – ah, how nice it felt in my hand. While we were feeling of it and commenting on it we heard a dog bark not far away. We all jumped to our feet and on going to the door saw a man coming towards the barn. Abner got away without being seen and we girls got to the house. I must now tell you of some other persons before I tell you more about the boys. Immediately after going to live with the old folks, (I call them old folks because both were past sixty. Mrs. Hall was not a bad looking woman for her age and had evidently been a fine looking woman in her younger days.) I discovered that a Mr. Brown was quite intimate with Mr. and Mrs. H. He was not more than 28 or 30 and he used to be there sometimes two or three times a week. I noticed right away that if Mrs. H. was alone when he called, I was at once sent out of doors or some where, so that Mr. Brown and Mrs. H were left together. Of course, I was curious to know why they wanted to be alone, so I began to watch and soon managed to find a way to listen to what they said. They related to each other all the scandal they heard and did it too in plain language that showed they were accustomed to it. At that time there was a rape trial going on in town. A Mr. Hay, who lived some 8 or 10 miles from town in a lone some place near the mountains hired a girl who lived a mile or two away to help in the house as his wife was about to be confined. The girl went with Mr. Hay to town to do some shopping one day, and on their way home the girl said he drove away from the road to a secluded place, then got her down in the bed of the wagon and raped her, after which they went on to Mr. Hay's house. Some time afterwards Mr. H. was arrested for rape and the trial excited considerable interest. Before a verdict had been rendered Mr. Brown called on Mrs. Hall. I was sent out as usual, but was soon where I could hear every word said.

After a few unimportant remarks Mrs. H. asked if the rape case was over yet. Brown said the jury were still out. 'Well,' said Mrs. H. 'I'll tell you what I think of the matter. There was no rape about it. Hay was getting all he wanted of the girl and her mother found it out and she put up the job on him.' Brown asked why she thought so. 'Why,' said she, 'If the girl had not been willing she wouldn't have gone back home with Hay and staid a week or two before making any fuss about it.'

Another time they talked about married women taking means to avoid getting in the family way. They spoke of it in a way to show that it could be prevented, but din't tell what the way was. I was anxious to hear that but was doomed to disappointment. This last conversation I heard just after Abner was with us in the barn. The next time I saw the girls I told them what I had heard. Julia said she was sure there was some way it could be done but she was at a loss to know how to ascertain it. Lizzie asked me why I didn't ask Mrs. Hall. 'I did rather ask Mr. Brown,' said I dubiously. 'Oh, that's it,' said Julia, 'ask Mr. Brown then,' and Lizzie joined her in urging me to ask Mr. Brown and both said they would if they had a chance. Every time I saw Mr. Brown after that I thought of the request I wanted to make and feared I'd not have courage if I had a chance. One day Mr. et Mrs. Hall went to town to be gone all day. I was all excited at once. He knocked and when I opened the door he came in and enquired for Mrs. H. 'It came into my mind at once that if I told him she was going to be gone all day he would go right away, so I said she is out just now. Won't you sit down and wait? So he sat down and soon picked up a paper and began to read. I was anxious to ask him, and when he laid the paper down I was afraid he was going. Without stopping to choose my words I blurted out – 'Mr. Brown won't you tell me how to keep from getting in the family way?' He looked up astonished at my question, and some how my courage came back to me at once, so when he asked what I knew about getting in the family way, I said, 'I know about screwing.' Catching me by the arm he drew me up to him and placed me on his knees. 'Now tell me,' said he, 'What you know about screwing.' He kept questioning me till I told him about Julia and Lizzie and about my hearing him and Mrs. Hall talk. While talking he felt of my bosom, then put his hand under my skirts. I didn't try to hinder him at all. When he said we must keep a look out for Mrs. Hall I told him she would be gone all day and explained why I had lied to him. At his request I took off my drawers. While doing that he unbuttoned his pants and pulled his shirt up. My goodness! his jock was as big 3 or 4 like Abners. I was so much interested in it I forgot he had not answered my question. As I had hold of his staff of life he asked how I'd like to have that in my belly. I said I was afraid I was not big enough for it yet. 'No, you are not old enough nor large enough now, but it won't be long,' said he, 'before your pussy will be able to take in one as big as that.' He placed me astraddle his legs and then put the big red head between the lips of my pussy and rubbed it about making me feel pleasure in every nerve. He enquired about Julia and Lizzie. I told him all about them except that I didn't tell about Abner. It was yet early in the forenoon. He said if I would go over and get the girls he would tell us all about getting in the family way. Without stopping to put on my drawers I ran across the field and met Julia some distance from the house. I quickly told her that Mr. B. was waiting for her and Lizzie to tell what we were so anxious to know. Lizzie was absent so Julia went back with me. Julia was eager, but a little shamefaced when we went in where he was. He had his charmer fully exposed to view, standing stiffly and rampant.

Julia fixed her eyes on it, and as if strongly attracted by it she slowly approached Mr. Brown, he said not a word till she had come near enough for him to take her arm. He drew her right up in front of him when she at once took his stiff prick in her hand. She seemed surprised at its size and magnificent appearance. After she had handled it a few minutes he seated himself and took her on his lap. He first felt of her bosom as he had mine, then he pulled her skirts up and finding she had drawers on he asked her to take them off. When she had done so she seated herself on his lap again. He laid her over on his arm and slid his hand up to her pussy. He spread her legs and he began to titillate her clitoris and the surrounding parts till she could not keep from moving her bottom. He asked her if it felt good. 'Yes, yes,' said she, 'I feels so good.' After getting her passions all excited he said: 'You would enjoy it much better if I put this in there' and he put her hand on his cock. 'Shall we try it?' said he. Julia was too happy just then to refuse anything. Indeed he had to carry her to the bed where he quickly got her placed to suit him, then got between her legs, and carefully placing the head of his charmer between the lips of her pussy, he moved it about a little, the contact even in this manner giving her exquisite pleasure. But soon he began to push. At once I saw her countenance change. 'It is going to hurt you somewhat,' said he, 'but don't be afraid, it will soon be over.' She began to struggle but he had her so she could not avoid his thrusts, but as he shoved she exclaimed: 'Oh don't, it hurts,' her voice rising almost to a shriek as the obstruction gave way and his rod was buried in her belly. As soon as he had over-come the obstacles and effected a complete entrance he remained motionless telling her it was all over now, that she would only feel pleasure hereafter. She soon dried her tears and in answer to his question said it didn't hurt any more, only smarted a little. He kept very quiet for quite a while, but when he saw by her countenance that she was beginning to feel some pleasure he began slowly to move his sweetener out and in 'Don't it begin to feel good?' he asked. 'Yes,' she replied, 'it does feel good!' The pleasure soon became so great that she began to heave her bottom in response to his shoves. He somehow, was not disposed to hurry matters. He would stop shoving occasionally, letting his charmer remain buried in her. While letting it soak in this way he turned to me, who was looking on a much interested spectator and asked what I thought of screwing now.

I think it is good. I wish I was big enough, I replied. 'Well, it won't be many months before your pussy can take it in too,' said he. 'You won't have to wait very long.' But after awhile he began to shove quite regularly. Julia quite as actively responding, then he moved faster and faster and soon he began to breath loud and to shove furiously, just as Mr. Amberg did when he was screwing my poor mama. All at once Mr. Brown ceased shoving, except an occasional, spasmatic shove, his head dropped and he seemed to become limp and lifeless, except his breathing. After he had remained quiet some time he got off of Julia, his yeard still large but hanging his head, which was not of such a deep red as before, while drops of a queer looking stuff dropped from it. Julia was going to get up but he told her to lay still. I could not help noticing the change in her pussy too, as he took his handkerchief and carefully wiped it, for I could see some of that queer looking stuff running out of it. He then carefully wiped his rod but didn't button his pants and so hide it from our sight. When Julia got up she looked at his ram rod and seemed surprised to see its head dropping.

She began to handle it and the bag beneath and asking questions about them. It was not many minutes before he was preparing for another engagement. 'Would you like to try it again?' he asked. 'I'm afraid it will hurt,' said Julia. 'Suppose we try and see,' said he. Without any further urging she got on the bed and pulled up her clothing.

He got between her legs again and surprised Julia by easily shoving his charger into her without hurting her any. 'It don't hurt a bit this time,' said she, 'and it feels so nice.' After he had got his stiff one embedded in her body, he let it remain there quietly while he said 'Well girls, I promised to tell you how to avoid getting in the family way. There is one way,' said he, 'I have never known to fail.' 'What is it,' I asked. 'Keep your legs together and you will never get in the family way,' he said laughing. 'Oh!' said I, 'that ain't what we mean. Men screw their wives – what do they do to keep from getting in the family way?' He then explained that some men drew out their rod just before spending, others used a syringe, others a rubber bag over their long tom, etc. Julia asked if she wouldn't get in the family way. 'No, I guess not,' said he. 'If you do I'll take care of you.' Then he advised her not to let any man do it to her again till she got a husband. 'Then,' said he, 'you can let a dozen screw you if you are careful not to get caught. You are a woman now and will soon be getting a husband. You will give me some more, won't you, after you get married?' 'Yes,' said Julia, 'you may have all you want.' Then we arranged to meet again and he promised to tell us anything he might hear that was interesting. Julia enjoyed the delightful sensations his yard gave her while buried in her pussy so much that she could not keep still under him. He saw how fully she was enjoying it. After giving a few shoves which she promptly met he stopped and looked down in her face asked her if fucking was as good as she thought it would be. 'Oh yes,' said she, 'I wish I could stay this way forever.' They began to move again slowly at first but faster and faster after awhile, then this loud breathing and the die away. He wiped her again and after she got up and we fixed up the bed we went into the parlor again. I noticed that Julia walked a little awkwardly as if she was sore. Mr. Brown told us lots of stories of women who had been made happy by tasting stolen sweets and the time passed pleasantly till some time afternoon. Mr. Brown's charmer had long since regained its former magnificent state of erection but he didn't think it wise to put it into Julia again just then; it was some time after one o'clock when I saw Lizzie coming across the yard. I told Mr. Brown who she was and suggested that we should give her a surprise. So he let his pants down, pulled up his shirt and stood right in front of the door where she would come in, while Julia and I hid in the bed room. Pretty soon Lizzie came bounding in but she stopped suddenly as she saw the beautiful object before her and she looked at it in open wonder. Finally she stammered. 'Where – where are the girls?' We could hold in no longer. Lizzie at once regained her wits, but kept quiet for a few minutes. She could not keep her eyes off the beauty before her however and she soon began to handle it, then she commented on it. He was amused at her remarks and finally asked her if her pussy was big enough to take it in. 'No, it ain't,' said she, 'I wish it was.' 'Well, is Julia's?' he asked. 'No,' said she, 'it would take the biggest woman in town to take that' said she. 'Some small women have big mouths,' said he. 'I have had it in Julia twice to day.' 'I don't believe it' said Lizzie bluntly and she turned to Julia as if to get her to confirm her disbelief. 'Would you like to see me do it again?' he asked. Lizzie nodded assent.

Julia at once led the way to the bed and laying over across it pulled up her clothes and spread her legs. After getting between them he told Lizzie he wanted her to steer it, then she would know it was in sure. Without any hesitation she took hold of his beauty and placed its head at the right place and she kept hold of it till it was in so far she was forced to let go. 'Now do you believe it?' asked Mr. B. But Lizzie didn't reply, she was watching Julia, thinking it must hurt her to have such a big thing stuck into her, but when she saw no sign of pain, but evidences of pleasure she got down by Julia and in almost a whisper asked how it felt. 'It don't hurt a bit and it feels awfully good,' she replied. We watched them till it was all over. He didn't get off for some time but when he did his charmer seemed shorn of its glory, for it had shrunken in size and was soft and limp, hanging its head as if ashamed. We put the bed to rights again, then went back to the parlor, Lizzie got on his lap while he talked to us. He gave us some good advice about how to conduct ourselves so as to avoid being suspected. He cautioned us to tell no one of our meeting and managed for future meetings. He had told us too, to be careful when with young fellows for, said he, they will screw you if they can and some of them will boast of it. After he left us Lizzie and I asked Julia innumerable questions. She had at once acquired an enviable position in our estimation and she, herself, was disposed to put on airs. I met the girls quite often after that. They were as anxious as I to meet Mr. Brown again. We were out by the barn one day when we saw the boys, Abner and Van, coming. They urged us to go in the barn with them but we refused, though we stood and talked with them some time. Van put his arm around me and felt of my bosom while Abner felt of Julia's. They pleaded with us to go in the barn with them but Julia and I objected though Lizzie was willing. The boys went away evidently disappointed. Mr. Brown called one day, as usual Mr. H. – was away. I met him out by the gate. He enquired after Julia and said he wanted to see her again. 'Oh,' said I 'you want to screw her again. Well, she ain't here so you will have to screw the old woman.' 'Would you like to screw the old woman?' he asked. 'Oh, yes, do it,' said I. 'If I do' said he, 'you must not tell the girls.' I said I would not and he went on into the house; I followed soon after and was at once sent out as I expected. Before going out I pointed to the old lady and made some very suggestive motions which of course I didn't let her see, but Mr. Brown did and he laughed as I closed the door behind me. I lost no time in getting to my place of observation. The house was originally but a two roomed board house, to which a kitchen had been added at one time, a bed-room at another, then another bed-room, but it was an 'old ram shack-led' concern at the best. My hiding place was a narrow space between the bed-room and kitchen. From there I could hear what was said in any room in the house and could see into the old lady's bed-room. About the first question she asked was: 'Well, what is the latest scandal? Who's wife has been playing with her tail? He told her of some women that stories had been told about, then she told some thing she had heard about some girls that some fellow was suspected of having raised her petticoats. After some desultory talk I heard her say, 'What is the matter with you to-day? One would think you hadn't seen a woman for a month.' 'I haven't touched a woman's foot a long while' said he. 'You known when the last time was.' 'I'll bet,' said she, 'you have screwed half a dozen women since then.' He protested he hadn't even seen a woman's ankles. 'Why,' said he, 'I am getting so? I hardly dare turn over in bed at night for fear of breaking it off.' 'If your case is so bad as that,' said the old lady, 'you ought to get some relief.' 'Well, let's go in the bed-room and see if we can't do something for it,' said he. 'Wait till I see where Laura is,' said the old woman, as she started for the door. 'Never mind,' said Mr. Brown, 'I saw her down in the field just now, there is no danger from her.' I heard Mrs. H. – lock the door, then she and Mr. Brown entered the bed-room. They proceeded to business at once. Mrs. H. – pulled up her skirts, unbuttoned her drawers and took them off. Mr. Brown took off his coat, vest and pants, then pulling up his shirt he showed her what a terrible swelling he had. 'What a terrible state the darling is in to be sure,' said she taking it in her hand. 'I think it needs a hair poultice. That will soon take the swelling down and draw the matter out of it.' Retaining her hold of it she backed up to the bed and threw herself over on her back. She was evidently experienced in such matters for she took pains to get in a comfortable position before letting him get between her legs. I could not help admiring her beautiful legs, indeed I would not have thought her past forty from what I could see of her form. But Mr. Brown soon got into place and buried his charmer in her body. She hugged him closely as if she would have been glad to take him all in. Evidently the presence of his champion in her pussy gave her great pleasure for after the hug she gave him she drew a long breath and said, 'After all there is nothing in the world that gives such exquisite pleasure as fucking.' Knowing that I could hear every word and wishing to please me Mr. Brown kept her talking. In answer to his question if she enjoyed it as much now as she did when a girl she said she could hardly see any difference, and in the conversation she told that she first tasted stolen sweets when a girl of 16. Then he asked her to tell him about it. She said there was but little to tell. She went to a dance with her beau one night and got pretty well warmed up. When she went home, about 2 in the morning she asked him in hardly expecting him to do so. They took a seat on the sofa together and he put his arm about her waist. She had on a low necked dress and almost before she knew what he was about he had his hand in her bosom. Her amorous passions had been excited by the dancing, then his hand in her bosom so excited her that she could refuse him nothing.

He soon had his hand under her skirts where his fingers quickly excited her almost to frenzy.

She took off her clothes while he disrobed and then she said, 'we took a bout on the carpet.' I enjoyed listening to their conversation and watched their actions. After they went back to the parlor I quietly left my hiding place and managed to meet Mr. Brown out by the road where Mrs. H. could not see me, after leaving the house. After talking a moment about the old woman he enquired particularly about Julia. I saw he was afraid she might be knocked up as he expressed it, but I could give him no information about it. He wanted to meet her again soon and try to ascertain. As we were standing where no one could see us he put his hand under my skirts and felt of my pussy, but he didn't stay long. A few days after that, I met the boys over by the yard where the cows were. They were in the yard, I outside. They scolded because we would not go in the barn with them when they wanted us to and asked why we wouldn't. I said we knew what they wanted to do to us was the reason. Van asked what I thought they wanted to do to us. I said 'you want to fuck us' Van laughed, 'Right you are, that is just what we want to do.' Then he got down on the ground and put his arm through the fence and his hand up between my legs. I stood still only spreading my legs and let him feel. Pretty soon he asked me to go with him around back of the stable where no one could see us. 'I won't,' said I, 'you want to fuck me and I ain't big enough.' He said I was and urged strongly but when the boys saw I would not they urged me to bring Julia over. I promised to tell her that they wanted to see her but would promise nothing more. It was some time after that, two or three months at least, when Julia told me the folks she and Lizzie were living with were going away and would leave them there alone. I at once got permission to stay with them and I managed to let Mr. Brown know the circumstances. He and I got there soon after the folks left. Mr. Brown at once took Julia on his lap and while having his hand under her skirts he questioned her about her condition and was greatly pleased to ascertain that she had escaped getting in the family way. We locked the doors and then went to the girls bedroom where we all stripped. Lizzie and I didn't expect much attention from Mr. Brown for we knew Julia would receive most of it. He laid across the bed on his back, his charmer hard and stiff like a column of ivory with a red cap on it, attracting all our attention and admiration. We all tried to handle it at once. Finding we could not well do that Lizzie took hold of one of his hands and placed it on her nest. He got her in position so that he could better feel of her. After he had felt a minute she asked, 'Is my cunt big enough yet?' 'Hardly big enough yet,' said he, 'but I'll try it if you wish.' She didn't reply in words but quickly got on her back and spread her legs. He got on top of her then placed the head of his champion between the lips of her monkey. Before shoving any he rubbed its head about between the lips, evidently giving her much pleasure. Then he said: 'Now I am going to push, if it hurts you too much I'll stop.' Pretty soon she said: 'Oh stop, it hurts.' He at once stopped and got off. Lizzie wanted me to try it so I got in position. While he was rubbing the head of his staff in my slit I told him it felt good but when he began to push I too said it hurt. After he got off he asked Julia if she would try. She needed no urging. Instead however, of getting between her legs when she rolled over on her back, he got beside her and put his hand on her nest. Inserting a finger between its lips he began gently to rub and press her clitoris, often kissing her while doing so. I readily understood what his object was. He wished to get all her amorous passions aroused, so that the gratification of her desires would give her greater pleasure. When her actions showed that he had accomplished his purpose he got her in a position to suit him and got between her thighs. Placing the head of his instrument in the proper place he let it remain there a moment while he tightened his clasp about her. She had expected it to enter without difficulty, but her monkey had recovered from the stretching it had received so that his first shove failed to give him a complete entrance, but a second shove, which hurt her so that I thought she was going to scream. He overcame her resistance and that hard and shining shaft was again buried completely in her body. After gently kissing her he asked if it hurt her much when it went in. She said it did some. You need not fear that it will ever hurt again said he. After this time you can take in the biggest man in the state without its hurting any.

He moved gently within her, stopping occasionally to kiss her, or to toy with her breast which was getting hard, round and full. Soon her face began to flush, her eyes to sparkle and her actions more animated.

She was recovering from the unexpected hurt she felt when his charmer entered her, and was beginning to taste again the sweet pleasure only to be experienced by a woman while in the arms of a man as she was.

Still he did not hurry in his movements. He had fought too many such engagements not to know how best to cause his partner to enjoy the most of the sweetest pleasures. Mr. Brown retained control of himself but Julia's body soon became so thrilled with delight that she threw her head back, closed her eyes and moved her bottom so fast that he slid his hand down under her bottom to hold her up lest in her delirium of pleasure she might dislodge the stranger she was entertaining. After placing his hand under her bottom, he began to thrust more rapidly and only stopped to ask her if it was good. She languidly opened her eyes and helped up her lips to be kissed as she threw her arms about his neck. Then began the heaves and shoving again, soon increasing in rapidity and vehemence. After a few minutes the end came preceded by his loud breathing and her exclamations. After one tremendous shove as if to send his charge of life giving sperm as far into her body as possible he let his pleasure giving rod remain buried within her as his head slowly dropped and his muscles relaxed. Soon both were still. Lizzie and I had looked on, watching every motion, both enjoying the pleasure Julia was experiencing. We both became so excited that I squeezed my thighs together while Lizzie began to try to get relief by using her finger. After awhile Mr. Brown raised his head and Julia opened her eyes. Before withdrawing he gave her a few kisses, then got from between her thighs. Neither of them seemed inclined to say or do much for awhile. But Lizzie could not restrain herself, she began to ask them both many queer but puzzling questions, which they found it difficult to answer. At length Julia said to her. 'When you have been screwed you will know all about it.' Mr. Brown entertained us for an hour or two with very interesting stories all relating to that delightfully entertaining subject sexual intercourse.

His champion had long regained its former size and stiffness but he seemed in no hurry to give Julia another taste of its quality. We were all of us stark naked as I before intimated. Neither of us girls could resist the attractions his beautiful charmer possessed. Laying on his back with his arm stiffly standing he seemed pleased to have us examine and handle it. After we had been handling it for some time Julia got down on his belly and resting sometimes on her elbow and sometimes with her head on his belly, she took possession of it. She felt of the skin that would move on the shaft though so tightly stretched, then the glowing head attracted her attention and she even opened the orifice in the end as if to ascertain where all the pleasure giving sperm came from. She felt of the bag too, and the two balls it contained. But the shaft seemed to please her most, moving her head up to it she laid it against her cheek where she let it remain a little while. Then she kissed its rubby head again and again. At last her desires became so great that she moved her face up to his and whispered: 'Don't you want to fuck me again?' 'I will if you want me to,' he replied, but he didn't make any move. Presently she said 'I wish you would.' 'How would you like to fuck me?' he asked, drawing her on top of him, he told her to get astraddle, she needed no further suggestions. Getting a leg on either side of him, she took hold of his majesty and getting his head at the entrance to her grotto she let herself down and soon had him securely imprisoned. Mr. Brown kept still and let her do just as she pleased. She kept her bottom moving quite regularly at first but her pleasure soon became so great that she was in danger of losing her prisoner by her irregular motions. Clasping his arms about her he rolled her over on her back without letting the prisoner out. He then began to move the prisoner about in his close quarters. She again gave herself up to the delights she felt. She heaved, she squirmed, she threw her arms about his neck, every act telling of the exquisite pleasure she was enjoying. He too was experiencing thrilling pleasure in every nerve. Again he spent and again they lay in each others arms in that delicious die away languor that follows such amorous delights as they had been enjoying. Finally when they recovered their senses and he had got off, we all dressed ourselves for Mr. Brown said he dared not stay any longer. After he left I remained with the girls. I had never yet told Julia about the boys wanting her to come over to the stable but I then told her all about it. Lizzie said, 'Lets go to day,' but Julia had got about all she wanted for some days so she refused. I did not see the girls for a week or ten days after that, but I met them one day out by the barn, they having come from the direction of the dairy man's. Lizzie eagerly began to tell me that they had just come from over there, that they went with the boys out back of the stable, that Abner fucked Julia and that Van fucked her. Said she, 'He didn't hurt much for his prick ain't far so big as Mr. Brown's.' After that, the girls used to meet the boys two or three times a week, usually in the evening and often in the barn, and every time they indulged in amorous delights without restraint. I was with them many times and was often urged by the boys to let them have just one screw, but remembering Mr. Brown's advice, I refused. I noticed after awhile a change in Julia. She was in the family way. About three months after, Mr. Brown had been with her last she without any notice to any one was married to Abner. They went to house keeping near by for Abner still continued at the dairy. Lizzie went to another place to live where she was taken sick with inflamation of the bowels and died. Julia was delivered of a six months (?) baby just the picture of its father, Mr. Brown. I visited Julia very often, sometimes staying days with her. When the baby was about three months old Mr. Brown called to see him. I was there with Julia that day. After the baby had been duly admired Julia told him he was his. He was greatly pleased I could see, for as I said it was a handsome baby. He admired it and had it in his lap playing with its chubby hands finally he laid it down and drawing Julia in his lap said, 'Shan't we make another baby?' She made but little effort to get away, and he was soon handling her parts, then he got his hand under her skirts and unbuttoning her drawers felt of her pussy. As the drawers dropped to the floor and she stepped out of them he put his arm about her and led her to the bed. He laid her over on the bed and felt of her a few minutes, then getting between her legs he had no difficulty in inserting his instrument and quickly shoving its whole length in her. A lively engagement followed, both of them sharing in its pleasures. Of course I was allowed to look on as of old, but I realized a greater interest in what I saw and a greater desire than I had ever felt. After, he got off the bed and shook down her skirts, but didn't put on her drawers, expecting, no doubt, another bout after awhile. We went back to the parlor when he told us the latest scandal, etc. We seated ourselves on the lounge, one each side of him. He had not buttoned his pants, so when I saw his staff getting hard and stiff again, I took it in my hand. It somehow possessed a greater attraction than ever. He let me feel a few minutes, then drew me over across his lap and pulled my skirts off. My drawers being in the way, I jumped up and took them off, and resumed my place again. What sensations I felt as his hand rested a moment on my thighs. Spreading my legs his hand was at once placed on my pussy which was then surmounted by a lot of curly

brown hair. His burning fingers quickly excited in me sensations I
had never felt before. I can hardly tell how he did it but he very
soon set my blood to a fever heat and my senses in a whirl. Presently
he said, 'Let's go into the bed.' I led the way. He then nearly
undressed me and removed his own garments except his shirt. I
knew what he was going to do. It was what I had long wished for.
I too was going to experience the supremest pleasure of existence,
feel the pleasures of having that red-headed champion of him in
my body, feel it pulsating and throbbing as it filled and stretched
the delicate folds of my hungry receptacle. I pulled up my chemise
and got on the bed. Placing myself on my back I spread my legs
and awaited the attack. He didn't let me wait long. Getting
between my legs he first placed the head of his champion between
the lips of my nest. What pleasure just the contact of the parts gave
me. Yet I knew it was but a prelude of what was to come. He seem-
ingly was afraid of hurting me for he did not at once begin to shove.
I began to be eager to feel it entering me, to feel it buried completely within me. Ah, now he shoves, gently, easily, I feel it is
entering, but it meets some obstruction, still it has not hurt me.
Suddenly he gives a violent shove, then another – Something gives
away – I feel a sharp pain – he has overcome the obstacle and I
realize that now it is where I have so long desired to have it. The
pain had not been so great as I had anticipated and it was soon forgotten in the exquisite sensation that ensued. I can give no account
of what followed, for my senses were so drowned in bliss that I only
knew I was tasting more than heavenly pleasures. When I regained
my senses he was still within me. I knew he had spent for I could
feel it running down on my bottom. I expected he would get off
but he didn't. He remained between my legs with his shaft still in
my nest. 'Well, Laura,' said he, 'was it as good as you expected?'
'Yes, better,' said I. 'I didn't know any thing could make me feel so
good.' Still he kept his position. We had not talked long before I
felt his majesty swell and in a short time it was again throbbing and
moving in its prison. This time Mr. Brown did not hurry any, but

prolonged the pleasure a long while, just before he spent I felt his majesty swell and then I felt the sperm coming in warm jets. When he got off we dressed ourselves and returned to the parlor, Julia was not jealous a bit at my robbing her of anticipated pleasure. She insisted on Mr. Brown remaining to dinner with us which he did leaving only when prudence said it was not wise to stay any longer. Before he left Julia asked him to come again, as often as he pleased. Soon after that, I met a nice fellow who fell in love with me at once. After a short courtship, we were married. We had but few guests at the wedding but Mr. Brown was one of them. Shall I tell you the secrets of that first night? No, I don't need to. It was all your imagination can picture.

My husband was a man, every inch of him and he has a 'long Tom' as he calls it, big enough, long enough and stiff enough to fill any women's desires. I'll only say that I got no sleep till near day light, and my chemise was starched stiff in the morning.

John had a nice home ready on our return from our wedding trip, where I was installed as its mistress. One of the first to call after I got into my home was Mr. Brown.

I at once seated myself in his lap. He kissed me and inquired how I liked married life. I said 'It's bully,' but while we were talking he was taking liberties with me that no man ought to with another man's wife. I didn't object however, so he didn't stop till he had me nearly undressed, on my back on the bed with his staff into me as far as it could go, so as he could go no further of course he had to stop. He staid where he was, however, till he gave me another glimpse of paradise. After he had flooded my womb with great spouting jets of sperm, he got from between my legs, saying he had made twins for me. If I have any babies I wonder if I will be able to tell who their father is. You may wonder why I let Mr. Brown into my grotto and effections after my marriage, but the truth is one man is not enough for me, I can give John all he wants and then have enough left for two or three more men.

I have been admiring a good looking bachelor neighbour who lives over the way. I think with his brawn and muscle he could equal John or Mr. Brown, and every time I see him I can't help thinking of the good times we might have together if he would only try. But, dear reader, good bye.

EMMANUELLE ARSAN

from

Emmanuelle

Emmanuelle *was first published in French in 1975 and quickly became a byword for eroticism and spawned several imitations.*

EMMANUELLE boarded the plane in London that was to take her to Bangkok. At first the rich smell of leather, like that preserved in British cars after years of use, the other worldly lighting, and the thickness and silence of the carpets were all she could grasp of the environment she was entering for the first time.

She did not understand what was being said to her by the smiling man who was guiding her, but she was not upset. Although her heart may have been beating faster, it was only from a sensation of strangeness, not from apprehension. The blue uniforms, the thoughtfulness and authority of the personnel assigned to welcome and initiate her – everything combined to create a feeling of security and euphoria. A new universe was going to be hers for the next twelve hours of her life, a universe with different laws, more constraining, but perhaps more delectable for that very reason. The vigilance of freedom was replaced by the leisure and placidity of subjection.

The steward led her to her seat. It was what would normally have been a window seat, but there was no window. She could see nothing beyond the draped walls. It made no difference to her. She did not care about anything but abandoning herself to the powers of that deep seat, drifting into drowsiness between its woolly arms, against its foam shoulder, on its long, mermaid lap.

An English stewardess stopped in the aisle. Her hands flew up to the rack above Emmanuelle's head to put away her light, leather traveling case. She spoke French and the impression of semi-torpor that Emmanuelle had been feeling for the past two days (she had arrived in London only the day before) was dispelled.

As the stewardess leaned over her, her blondeness made Emmanuelle's long hair seem still more nocturnal. They were both dressed nearly alike, but a brassiere showed through the English girl's blouse, while the slightest movement revealed that Emmanuelle's breasts were free under hers. She was glad that the stewardess was young and that her eyes were like her own – flecked with gold.

Emmanuelle tried to think of something to ask that would please her. Maybe she should show an interest in the plane. But before she could speak, two children – a boy and a girl – pushed aside the velvet curtain that separated Emmanuelle's row of seats from the row in front. They looked so much alike that one had to assume they were twins. Emmanuelle noted at a glance the graceless, conventional clothes that stamped them as English schoolchildren, their reddish blond hair, their expression of affected coldness, and the haughtiness with which they spat out brief words to the stewardess. Although they were apparently only twelve or thirteen, their confident manner created a distance between them and her that she had no thought of reducing. They sedately planted themselves in the two seats across the aisle from Emmanuelle. At the same time the last of the four passengers for whom the compartment was reserved came in and she turned her attention to him.

He was at least a head taller than she was. His hair and mustache were black. She liked his amber-colored suit. She judged him to be elegant and well-bred, two qualities that, after all, covered most of what one hoped to find in a fellow passenger. She tried to guess his age from the wrinkles at the corners of his eyes – forty, perhaps fifty? He would be more agreeable, she thought, than the two pretentious children.

The stewardess had left the compartment and, through the gap in the curtains, Emmanuelle could now see her blue hip pressed against an invisible passenger. She tried to turn her eyes away. Her black hair whipped her cheeks and flowed over her face. Then the English girl straightened up, turned towards the rear of the plane, appeared between the curtains, pushing their long legs apart with her hands, and stepped toward Emmanuelle. 'Would you like me to introduce your traveling companions to you?' she asked; and, without waiting for an answer, she told her the man's name. Emmanuelle thought she heard 'Eisenhower,' which amused her and made her miss the names of the twins.

The man began talking to her in English. She had no idea what he was saying. Seeing her perplexity, the stewardess questioned the three others, then laughed, showing the tip of her tongue. 'What a pity!' she said lightheartedly. 'None of them knows a single word of French. This will be a good chance for you to brush up on your English!'

Before Emmanuelle could protest, the stewardess moved her fingers in a graceful, cryptic gesture to her passengers, turned on her heel and walked away. Emmanuelle was again alone. She felt like sulking, holding herself aloof from everything.

A loudspeaker hidden behind the draperies came to life. After a male voice had spoken in English, Emmanuelle recognized the stewardess speaking in French ('For me,' the thought), welcoming the passengers aboard the Flying Unicorn and giving flight instructions.

The awakening of the jet engines was indicated by a murmur and a slight quivering of the soundproof walls. Emmanuelle was not even aware that the plane was moving along the runway. And it was a long time before she realized that she was flying.

She did not realize it, in fact, until the red light went off and the man beside her stood up and offered, by gestures, to put away her packet, which she had kept on her knees without knowing why. She let him take it. He smiled, opened a book, and stopped looking at her. A waiter appeared, carrying a tray of glasses. She chose a cocktail by its color, but it was not the one she expected; it was stronger.

What must have been an afternoon on the other side of the silk wall went by without Emmanuelle's having time to do anything but eat pastry, drink tea, and leaf through a magazine that the stewardess had given her (she refused to accept a second one because she did not want to be distracted from the novelty of flying).

Then a waiter placed a little table in front of her and served various foods that were hard to identify, in unusually shaped containers. Her dinner seemed to last for hours but the discovery of the culinary game pleased her so much that she was in no hurry for it to end.

She felt light and carefree. She noticed that she had even lost her dislike of the twins. The stewardess came and went, never failing to say something cheerful to her as she passed. When she was absent, Emmanuelle was no longer impatient.

She wondered if it was time to go to sleep. But actually she was free to sleep whenever she chose in that winged cradle so far from the surface of the earth, in a region of space where there were neither winds nor clouds, and where she was not sure there was even night and day.

Emmanuelle's knees were bare in the golden light shining down from overhead, and the man was staring at them. Under the invisible nylon, the movement of their dimples made agile shadows in the toasted-bread color of their skin. She knew the excitement they caused. They seemed more naked than ever under the spotlight which had been turned on them. She felt as if she were coming out of the water after a moonlight swim. Her temples throbbed faster and her lips filled with blood. She closed her eyes and saw herself not partially but totally naked, and she knew that once again she would be helpless against the temptation of that narcissistic contemplation.

She resisted, but only to increase the joy of gradually slipping into surrender. Its nearness was announced by a diffuse languor, a kind of warm consciousness of her whole body, a desire for abandon, for opening, for fullness; nothing very different from the physical satisfaction she would have felt from stretching out on the warm sand of a sun-drenched beach. Then, little by little, the surface of her lips became more lustrous, her breasts swelled, and her legs tensed, attentive to the slightest control. Her brain began experimenting with images. They were disconnected and formless at first, but were enough to moisten her mucous membranes and arch her back.

The steady, subdued, almost imperceptible vibrations of the metal fuselage attuned her body to the frequency. Starting from her knees, a wave rose along her thighs, resonating on the surface, moving higher and higher, making her quiver.

Phantasms assailed her – lips pressed against her skin, genitals of men and women (whose faces remained ambiguous), penises eagerly rubbing against her, pushing their way between her knees, forcing her legs apart, opening her sex, penetrating it with laborious efforts that enraptured her. One after another, they plunged into the unknown of her body, thrusting into her unendingly, sating her flesh, and endlessly emptying their semen into her.

Thinking Emmanuelle was asleep, the stewardess cautiously tilted back her seat, transforming it into a bed, and spread a cashmere blanket over her long, languid legs. The man stood up and pushed his seat back to the same level as hers. The children had already dozed off. The stewardess wished everyone a good night and turned off the ceiling lights. Only two purple night lights prevented objects and people from losing all shape.

Emmanuelle had abandoned herself to the stewardess's care without opening her eyes. Her reverie, however, had lost none of its intensity or urgency. Her right hand now began to move over her belly, very slowly, restraining itself, descending toward her pubis. The thin blanket undulated above it. Her finger tips, pushing down on the soft silk of her skirt, whose narrowness made it difficult for her to spread her legs, found the bud of flesh in erection that they sought and pressed it tenderly. Her middle finger began the gentle, careful motion that would bring on orgasm. Almost immediately, the man's hand came down on hers.

She stopped breathing and felt her muscles and nerves tighten, as though her belly had been struck by a jet of ice water. Her sensations and thoughts were suspended, like a film when the projector has stopped, leaving a single image on the screen. She was neither afraid nor offended. She waited for what was going to follow her collapsed dreams.

The man's hand did not move. Merely by its weight, it applied pressure to her clitoris, on which her own hand was resting.

Nothing else happened for some time. She then became aware that his other hand was lifting the blanket and drawing it aside. It took hold of her knee and felt its curves and hollows. It rose slowly along her thigh and soon passed over the top of her stocking.

When it touched her bare skin, she started for the first time and tried to break the spell. She sat up awkwardly and turned halfway on her side. As though they wanted to punish her for her futile revolt, the man's hands abandoned her abruptly. But before she had time to react, they were on her again, this time at her waist. They deftly unfastened and unzipped her skirt, pulled it down to her knees, then moved up again. One of them slipped under her panties and caressed her flat, muscular belly, just above the high mound of her pubis, stroking it as though it were the neck of a thoroughbred. Its fingers ran along the folds of her groin and across the top of her public hair, tracing a triangle whose area they seemed to be estimating. The lower angle was very wide, a rather rare feature that had been appreciated by Greek sculptors.

Then the hand forced her thighs to spread further apart. It closed over her warm, swollen sex, caressing it as if to soothe it, without haste, following the furrow of its lips, dipping in lightly between them, passing over her erect clitoris and coming to rest on the thick curls of her pubis. As they moved to and fro between her legs, the fingers sank deeper between her moist membranes, slowing their advance, and seeming to hesitate as her tension increased. Biting her lips to stifle the sob that was rising from her throat, she panted with desire as the man brought her closer and closer to orgasm without letting her reach it.

Then his hand stopped moving and cupped the whole part of her body that it had inflamed. He leaned toward her, extending his other hand, took one of hers, and drew it inside his trousers. He helped her to grasp his rigid penis and guided her movements, regulating their length and cadence to suit his taste, slowing or accelerating them according to his degree of excitement, until he was convinced that he could rely on her intuition and good will and let her continue the manipulation in her own way.

She sat up to let her arm do its work properly, and he moved closer to her so that she could be sprayed by the sperm he felt welling up from the depths of his glands. He succeeded in restraining himself for a long time, while her bent fingers rose and fell, becoming less timid as they prolonged their caresses, no longer limiting themselves to elementary back-and-forth motions, but opening slightly, skillfully, to slide along the big, swollen vein of his arched penis (lightly scratching it with her filed nails), as far down as possible, as close to his testicles as the tightness of his trousers would permit, then rising again with lascivious twists. His member had grown so much that it seemed endless, but she finally reached its tip and covered it with the folds of loose skin in the hollow of her damp palm before beginning another downward journey, squeezing him tightly again, stretching his foreskin, alternately strangling his tumescent flesh and relaxing her grip on it, barely grazing it or tormenting it, massaging it in broad strokes or irritating it with quick, merciless little movements . . .

When his satisfied penis finally disgorged its semen in long, white, odorous spurts, she received it with strange exaltation along her arms, on her bare belly, on her throat, face, and mouth, and in her hair. It seemed that it would never stop. She felt as if it were flowing down her throat, as if she were drinking it . . . She was seized with an unknown intoxication, a shameless delight. When she let her arm fall, he took hold of her clitoris with his finger tips and brought her to orgasm.

A buzzing sound indicated that the loudspeaker was about to be used. The stewardess's voice, deliberately softened so the passengers would not be awakened too abruptly, announced that the plane would land at Bahrein in about twenty minutes. It would leave at midnight, local time. A light meal would be served at the airport.

The light in the compartment gradually came on again, imitating the slowness of a sunrise. Emmanuelle used the blanket, which had slipped down to her feet, to wipe away the sperm that had spattered her. She pulled her skirt up over her hips. When the stewardess came in, Emmanuelle was sitting up on her seat, without having raised its back, still trying to make herself presentable.

'Did you sleep well?' the stewardess asked.

Emmanuelle fastened the waist of her skirt. 'My blouse is all wrinkled,' she said.

She looked at the damp spots that spread out in both directions from below her collar. She rolled back the lapels of her blouse and the pink tip of a breast appeared. Her neckline remained open and four pairs of English eyes were glued to the profile of her bare breast.

'Don't you have anything to change into?' asked the stewardess.

'No,' said Emmanuelle.

The two women looked each other in the eye and recognized their complicity; they were both equally excited. The man observed them. There was not a single wrinkle in his suit, his shirt was as neat as when he had boarded the plane, his tie was perfectly straight.

'Come with me,' said the stewardess.

Emmanuelle stood up, stepped past the man, and followed the young English stewardess into the ladies' lounge. It was filled with mirrors, cushioned footstools, white leather upholstery, and shelves laden with lotions in crystal bottles.

'Wait.'

The stewardess slipped away and returned moments later, carrying a little suitcase. She lifted its calfskin lid and removed a russet sweater of orlon, wool, and silk, so light that it was crumpled into a ball that fit into her closed fist. When she shook it out it seemed to swell suddenly like a balloon. Emmanuelle clapped her hands with admiration. 'You're lending it to me?' she asked.

'No. I'm giving it to you. I'm sure it will look good on you.'

'But . . .'

The stewardess put her finger over Emmanuelle's lips as they rounded to protest her embarrassment. Her tender eyes sparkled. Emmanuelle could not look away from them. She moved her face close to them. But the stewardess spun around and handed her a bottle of toilet water. 'Rub yourself with this, it's delightful!'

Emmanuelle refreshed her face, arms, and neck, started to wipe between her breasts with the pad she had saturated with the perfumed liquid, then changed her mind and quickly unbuttoned the rest of her blouse.

She made it fall to the white carpet by throwing back her arms. Suddenly dizzied by her half-nakedness, she took a deep breath. She turned to the stewardess and looked at her with candid jubilation. The stewardess bent down, picked up the rumpled blouse and pressed it against her face. 'Oh, it smells so good!' she said, laughing mischievously.

Emmanuelle was disconcerted. The reminder of the incredible scene in her compartment seemed out of place to her now. Her only thought, which was turning in her mind as though in a cage, was to get rid of her skirt and stockings, to be completely naked for that beautiful girl. Her fingers were already toying with the buckle of her belt.

'How thick and black your hair is!' the stewardess exclaimed, playfully running a brush over the waves that hung down Emmanuelle's naked back to below her waist. 'It's so shiny, so silky! I wish my hair were as beautiful as yours.'

'But I like yours!' protested Emmanuelle.

Oh, if only the stewardess would undress, too! Emmanuelle desired her so much that her voice was husky when she implored: 'Isn't it possible to take a bath on this plane?'

'Of course. But you'd better wait – the bathrooms at the airport are more comfortable. Anyway, you wouldn't have time, we're going to land in five minutes.'

Emmanuelle was unable to resign herself. She pulled on the zipper of her skirt.

'Hurry and put on my sweet little sweater,' the English girl said reproachfully, handing it to her.

She helped her put her head through the narrow opening. The elastic sweater was clinging and thin, the lips of her breasts stood out as visibly as if they had been painted reddish brown. The stewardess seemed to notice them for the first time. 'What a seductive sight!' She pressed on one of the sharp nipples with her forefinger, as though she were ringing a doorbell. Emmanuelle's eyes twinkled.

'Is it true,' Emmanuelle asked, 'that all airline stewardesses are virgins?'

The English girl burst out laughing, then, before Emmanuelle had time to react, she opened the door and pulled her outside. 'Go back to your seat, quickly! The red light is on, we're about to land.'

Emmanuelle scowled. Aside from everything else, she had no desire to sit with the man in her compartment again.

The stopover was boring. What good did it do to know she was in the Arabian desert if she could see nothing of it? The airport building, aseptic and chromed, too glaringly lighted, refrigerated, airtight, and soundproof, bore a singular resemblance to the interior of the artificial satellite in the televised newscast that was being shown in the waiting room. She glumly took a bath, then drank tea and ate pastry with four or five other passengers, one of whom was 'her' man.

She looked at him with astonishment, trying to understand what had taken place between them an hour earlier. That episode did not fit in with the rest of her life. But thinking about it was too complicated, too risky. She began making diligent efforts to empty the part of her brain that persisted in asking questions.

By the time the movement of the others, rather than the incomprehensible voice of the loudspeaker, told her she had to return to the plane, she was no longer quite sure of what it was that she was trying so hard to forget.

When the passengers were back aboard the plane, they saw that it had been cleaned, tidied up, and aired. Fresh perfume had been sprayed in the compartments. The reclining seats were covered with new blankets. Big, luminously white pillows, swollen with down, made the midnight-blue velvet on which they rested still more tempting. The steward came to ask if anyone would like a drink. No? Well, then, sleep well. The stewardess also came in to wish everyone a good night. That ceremony delighted Emmanuelle. She felt herself becoming happy again – in a positive way, whole-heartedly, with certainty. She wanted the world to be exactly as it was. Everything on earth was absolutely right.

She lay back in her seat. She lifted her legs one after the other, bending and unbending her knees, working the muscles of her thighs, rubbing her ankles together with a soft rustling of nylon.

'After all,' she mused, 'it's not just my knees that are worth looking at, but all of my legs. No one can deny that they're really pretty; they're like two little brooks covered with dry leaves and swollen with perversity, amusing themselves by passing over each other. And they're not the only good things about me. I also like my skin, and the way it turns golden in the sun, like a grain of corn, without ever reddening. I like my behind, too. And the tiny little raspberries at the tips of my breasts, with their collars of red sugar. I wish I could lick them . . .'

The ceiling lights dimmed. With a sigh of well-being, she pulled up the blanket, scented with a fragrance of pine needles.

When only the night lights were on, she turned over on her side and tried to see the man. Till now, when she had stretched out beside him, she had not dared to look at him directly. Her gaze met his. They looked into each other's eyes for a moment, with no expression other than one of perfect tranquillity. She recognized the spark of slightly amused and protective interest that she had noticed when they first met. (When had that been, exactly? Was it only seven hours ago?) The expression on his face was what she liked most about him.

His presence suddenly became agreeable to her again. She smiled and closed her eyes. She had a vague yearning for something, but did not know what. She found no other diversion than to resume rejoicing at being beautiful; her own image lingered in her head like a favorite refrain. Her heart beat faster as she sought in her mind the invisible cove that she knew to be buried under its promontory of black grass, where the two brooks came together, and she felt their current licking at its edges. When the man raised himself on one elbow and leaned toward her, she opened her eyes and let him kiss her. The taste of his lips on hers had the freshness of sea salt.

When he began pulling off her sweater she sat up and lifted her arms to make it easier for him. She relished the excitement of seeing her breasts emerge from under the russet garment, looking even rounder and larger in the near-darkness than in daylight. To leave him the whole pleasure of undressing her, she did not help him when he groped for the zipper of her skirt, although she did raise her hips so that he could slide it down without difficulty. This time her narrow skirt did not remain twisted around her knees – she was completely free of it.

His active hands rid her of her thin panties. When he had unhooked her garter belt, she rolled down her stockings herself and dropped them to the floor in front of her seat, where they joined her skirt and sweater.

Only when she was entirely undressed did he take her in his arms and begin caressing her from her hair to her ankles, forgetting nothing. She now had so powerful a desire to make love that her heart hurt and her throat was constricted. She thought she would never be able to breathe again, to return to daylight. She was afraid, she felt like calling out, but the man was holding her too tightly, putting one hand between her buttocks, widening the quivering little crevice, with one whole finger buried in it. At the same time he kissed her avidly, licking her tongue, and drinking her saliva.

She whimpered softly without knowing the exact cause of her distress. Was it the finger that was probing so deeply inside her, or the mouth that was feeding on her, swallowing each breath, each gasp? Was she tormented by desire or ashamed of her lasciviousness? She was haunted by the memory of the long, arched form that she had held in her hand, magnificent and erect, arrogant, hard, unbearably hot. She moaned so loudly that the man took pity on her. She at last felt his bare penis, as big as she had expected, touch her belly, and she pressed against it with all the softness of her body.

They remained like that for a long time, without moving; then, seeming to make up his mind abruptly, he lifted her in his arms, drew her over him, and put her down beside him in his seat, on the aisle.

She was less than three feet away from the English children. She had forgotten they even existed; she now realized that they were not asleep and that they were looking at her. The boy was nearer to her, but the girl had huddled against him to see better. Motionless and breathless, they were staring at her with widened eyes in which she could see nothing but fascinated curiosity. At the thought of being possessed in front of them, of abandoning herself to that excess of debauchery, she felt a kind of dizziness. But at the same time she was eager to begin and let them see everything.

She was lying on her right side with her legs bent forward while the man held her by the hips from behind. He slipped one leg between hers and entered her with a straight, irresistible thrust that was made easy by the absolute rigidity of his penis and the moistness of her flesh. It was not until he had reached the deepest point of her vagina and stopped there long enough to sigh with pleasure that he began moving his member back and forth with long, regular strokes.

Delivered of her anxiety, she panted, became warmer and more liquid with each onslaught of his phallus. Through the mist of her ecstasy, she marveled at the thought that her organs had not atrophied during all the months when they had not been stimulated by a male goad. Now that she was rediscovering that pleasure, she wanted to enjoy it as long and completely as possible.

The man showed no sign of being about to tire. For a moment she wondered how long he had been in her, but there was no way for her to guess the time that had gone by.

She held back her orgasm, effortlessly and without frustration, because she had trained herself since childhood to prolong the pleasure of waiting. Even more than the final spasm itself, she loved that growing sensitivity, that extreme tension of her being, which she knew so well how to give herself when she was alone, and her fingers stroked the trembling stem of her clitoris for hours, with the lightness of a violin bow, refusing to yield to the supplication of her own flesh, until at last the pressure of her sensuality broke through. The explosion was as terrifying as the convulsions of death, but she was always reborn from it immediately, fresher, and more alert than ever.

She looked at the children. Their faces had lost their haughtiness; they had become more human. They were neither excited nor snickering, but attentive and almost respectful. She tried to imagine what was going on in their heads, the bewilderment they must be feeling at the event they were witnessing, but her thoughts unraveled, her brain was seized with spells of faintness, and she was much too happy to care about anyone else.

When the acceleration of her partner's movements, a certain stiffness of his hands as they gripped her buttocks, and the sudden expansion and pulsation of the organ that was piercing her made her realize that he was about to ejaculate, she let herself go. The spurting sperm whipped her pleasure to a frenzied pitch. During the whole time he was emptying himself in her he stayed deep in her vagina, pressed against her cervix, and even in the midst of her spasm she still had imagination enough to enjoy the mental image of his penis disgorging creamy torrents that were lapped up by the oval opening of her uterus, as greedy and active as a mouth.

He finished his orgasm and she too became calm, filled with a sense of well-being without remorse, increased by his sliding motion as he withdrew, the contact of the blanket that she felt him spreading over her, the comfort of the reclining seat, and the warm, increasing opacity of the sleep that was covering her.

The plane had passed through the night as though crossing a bridge, blind to the deserts of India, to the bays, estuaries, and rice paddies below. When Emmanuelle opened her eyes, the mountains of Burma were iridescent in the light of a sunrise that she could not see, while inside the compartment the purple glow of the night lights left her unaware of the exotic landscape and the time of day.

The white blanket had slid off her lap and she was lying naked, curled up like a cold child. Her conqueror was asleep.

Awakening by degrees, she lay still. Nothing of what she might have been thinking could be seen on her face. She slowly stretched her legs, drew back her shoulders, and rolled over on her back, groping for the blanket. But her hand stopped in midair – a man was standing in the aisle, looking at her.

From his position above her, he seemed gigantic and she told herself that he was also incredibly handsome. That was no doubt why she forgot her nakedness, or at least was not embarrassed by it. 'He's a Greek statue,' she thought. A fragment of a poem, which was not Greek, flashed into her mind: 'Deity of the ruined temple . . .' She wished there were primroses and yellowed herbs strewn at the feet of the god, and foliage twined around his pedestal. Her gaze moved from the short, soft hair that curled above his ears and forehead down the straight bridge of his nose, to his delicately curved lips, and his marble chin. Two firm tendons sculpted the lines of his neck down to where they met his shirt, half-open over a hairless chest. Her eyes continued to study him. There was an enormous bulge beneath his white flannel trousers, near her face.

The apparition bent down, picked up her clothes scattered over the floor – skirt, sweater, panties, garter belt, stockings, and shoes – then straightened up and said, 'Come.'

She put her feet down on the carpet and took the hand he was holding out to her. Then, having stood up with a lithe effort, she walked forward, naked, as though altitude and the night had brought her into a different world.

The stranger led her into the lounge where she had already gone with the stewardess. He leaned his back against the silk-padded wall and placed her so that she was facing him. She nearly cried out when she saw the reptile that had risen before her from its patch of golden underbrush. Because she was much shorter than he was, the blunted triangle of his glans touched her between her breasts.

He took her by the waist and lifted her effortlessly. She clasped her fingers over the back of his neck and felt his muscles harden beneath her palms, then, when he lowered her onto his penis, she spread her legs so that it could penetrate her. Tears flowed down her cheeks while he entered her cautiously, tearing her. Pressing her knees against his hips and the wall, she did her best to help the herculean serpent crawl into the depths of her body. She writhed, clawed his neck as she clung to it, sobbed, moaned, and cried out unintelligible words. In her frenzy she was not even aware that he was ejaculating, quickly, with such a savage thrust of his pelvis that he seemed determined to force his way through her till he reached her heart. When he withdrew, with his face radiant, he kept her standing against him. His wet phallus cooled her smarting skin. 'Did you like it?' he asked.

Emmanuelle put her cheek on the Greek god's chest. She felt his semen moving in her. 'I love you,' she murmured. 'Do you want to take me again?'

He smiled. 'I'll come back,' he said, 'Get dressed now.' He bent down and kissed her on the hair so chastely that she did not dare to say anything more. Before she had realized that he was leaving her, she found herself alone.

With slow gestures, as though she were performing a rite (or because she had not yet entirely recovered the rhythm of reality), she turned on the shower and let the water flow over her, covered her body with lather, carefully rinsed herself, rubbed her skin with warm, fragrant towels, sprayed her neck, armpits, and pubic hair with a perfume that evoked the greenery of a forest, and brushed her hair. Her image was reflected on three sides by long mirrors. It seemed to her that she had never been so fresh or aglow with more beauty. Would the stranger return as he had promised?

She waited till the loudspeaker announced that the plane was approaching Bangkok. Then, resentfully, with her heart in turmoil, she dressed and returned to her compartment. She took her bag and her jacket from the baggage rack and put them on her lap when she sat down. An obliging hand had raised the back of her seat and placed a cup of tea and a tray of rolls beside it. The man in the next seat, whom she glanced at absent-mindedly, was visibly surprised. 'But . . . aren't you going on to Tokyo?' he asked in English, with a note of dismay in his voice.

Emmanuelle guessed rather easily what he had said and shook her head. His face darkened. He asked another question, which she did not understand and, anyway, was in no mood to answer. She looked straight ahead with a chagrined expression.

He took out a notebook and held it in front of her, motioning her to write in it. He probably wanted her to leave him her name, or an address where he could reach her. But she shook her head again, stubbornly. She wondered if the stranger with the smell of warm stone, the fantastic genie of the ruined temple, would get off at Bangkok with her or fly on to Japan.

She looked for him among the passengers when they had gotten off the plane and were waiting, clustered under its wings in the morning of the tropical airport, for someone to lead them to the cement and glass buildings whose futuristic silhouettes stood out against a sky that was already white with heat. But she saw no one as tall as he or who had his autumnal hair. The stewardess smiled at her; Emmanuelle scarcely noticed her. She was already being pushed toward the iron customs gates. Someone crossed a barrier, flashed a pass, and called her. She ran forward with a cry of joy and threw herself into the outstretched arms of her husband.

JOHN UPDIKE

from

Rabbit is Rich

Rabbit is Rich, set in 1978, was first published in 1981 and is one of a sequence of novels featuring Harry Angstrom, the Rabbit in the title. Rabbit unexpectedly finds himself prosperous as Chief Sales Representative of a Toyota agency in Brewer, Pennsylvania. For Rabbit, sex is life, and he is always ready to enjoy any woman who comes his way.

LUNCH at the resort is served by the pool or brought by tray to the beach, but dinner is a formal affair within a vast pavilion whose rafters drip feathery fronds yards long and at whose rear, beside the doors leading into the kitchen, a great open barbecue pit sends flames roaring high, so that shadows twitch against the background design of thatch and carved masks, and highlights spark in the sweating black faces of the assistant chefs. The head chef is a scrawny Belgian always seen sitting at the bar between meals, looking sick, or else conferring in accents of grievance with one of the missionary-prim native women who run the front desk. Monday night is the barbecue buffet, with a calypso singer during the meal and dancing to electrified marimbas afterward; but all six of the holidayers from Diamond County agree they are exhausted from the night at the casino and will go to bed early. Harry after nearly drowning in Cindy's arms fell asleep on the beach and then went inside for a nap. While he was sleeping, a sudden sharp

tropical rainstorm drummed for ten minutes on his tin roof; when
he awoke, the rain had passed, and the sun was setting in a band of
orange at the mouth of the bay, and his pals had been yukking it
up in the bar ever since the shower an hour ago. Something is
cooking. They seem, the three women, very soft-faced by the light
of the candle set on the table in a little red netted hurricane lamp,
amid papery flowers that will be wilted before the meal is over.
They keep touching one another, their sisterhood strengthened
and excited down here. Cindy is wearing a yellow hibiscus in her
hair tonight, and that Arab thing, unbuttoned halfway down. She
more than once reaches past Webb's drink and stringy brown hands
as they pose on the tablecloth to touch Janice on a wrist, remembering 'that fresh colored boy behind the bar today, I told him I
was down here with my husband and he shrugged like it made no
difference whatsoever!' Webb looks sage, letting the currents pass
around him, and Ronnie sleepy and puffy but still full of beans, in
that grim playmaker way of his. Harry and Ronnie were for three
years on the Mt. Judge basketball varsity together and more than
once Rabbit had to suppress a sensation that though he was the star
Coach Tothero liked Ronnie better, because he never quit trying
and was more 'physical' around the backboards. The world runs on
push. Rabbit's feeling has been that if it doesn't happen by itself it's
not worth making happen. Still, that Cindy. A man could kill for
a piece of that. Pump it in, and die like a male spider. The calypso
singer comes to their table and sings a long dirty song about the
Big Bamboo. Harry doesn't understand all the allusions but the
ladies titter after every verse. The singer smiles and the song smiles
but his bloody eyes glitter like those of a lizard frozen on the wall
and his skull when bent over the guitar shows circlets of gray. A
dying art. Harry doesn't know if they are supposed to tip him or
just applaud. They applaud and quick as a lizard's tongue his hand
flickers out to take the bill Webb, leaning back, has offered. The
old singer moves on to the next table and begins that one about
Back to back, and Belly to belly. Cindy giggles, touches Janice on

the forearm, and says, 'I bet all the people back in Brewer will think we've swapped down here.'

'Maybe we should then,' Ronnie says, unable to suppress a belch of fatigue.

Janice, in that throaty mature woman's voice cigarettes and age have given her but that Harry is always surprised to hear she has, asks Webb, who sits beside her, gently, 'How do you feel about that sort of thing, Webb?'

The old fox knows he has the treasure to barter and takes his time, pulling himself up in his chair to release an edge of coat he's sitting on, a kind of dark blue captain's jacket with spoked brass buttons, and takes his pack of Marlboro Lights from his side pocket. Rabbit's heart races so hard he stares down at the table, where the bloody bones, ribs and vertebrae, of their barbecue wait to be cleared away. Webb drawls, 'Well, after two marriages that I'd guess you'd have to say were not fully successful, and some of the things I've seen and done before, after, and between, I must admit a little sharing among friends doesn't seem to me so bad, if it's done with affection and respect. Respect is the key term here. Every party involved, and I mean every party, has to be willing, and it should be clearly understood that whatever happens will go no further than that particular occasion. Secret affairs, that's what does a marriage in. When people get romantic.'

Nothing romantic about him, the king of the Polaroid pricks. Harry's face feels hot. Maybe it's the spices in the barbecue settling, or the length of Webb's sermon, or a blush of gratitude to the Murketts, for arranging all this. He imagines his face between Cindy's thighs, tries to picture that black pussy like a curved snug mass of eyebrow hairs, flattened and warmed to fragrance from being in underpants and framed by the white margins the bikini bottom had to cover to be decent. He will follow her slit down with his tongue, her legs parting with that same weightless slither he felt under water today, down and in, and around the corner next to his nose will be that whole great sweet ass he has a thousand times watched jiggle as she dried herself from swimming in the pool at the Flying Eagle, under the nappy green shadow of Mt. Pemaquid. And her tits, the fall of them forward when she obediently bends over. Something is happening in his pants, like the stamen of one of these floppy flowers on the tablecloth jerking with shadow as the candleflame flickers.

'Down the way,' the singer sings at yet another table, 'where the nights are gay, and the sun shines daily on the moun-tain-top.' Black hands come and smoothly clear away the dark bones and distribute dessert menus. There is a walnut cake they offer here that Harry especially likes, though there's nothing especially Caribbean about it, it's probably flown in from Fort Lauderdale.

Thelma, who is wearing a sort of filmy top you can see her cocoa-colored bra through, is gazing into middle distance like a schoolteacher talking above the heads of her class and saying, '. . . simple female curiosity. It's something you hardly ever see discussed in all these articles on female sexuality, but I think it's what's behind these male strippers rather than any real desire on the part of the women to go to bed with the boys. They're just curious about the penises, what they look like. They *do* look a lot different from each other, I guess.'

'That how you feel?' Harry asks Janice. 'Curious?'

She lowers her eyes to the guttering hurricane lamp. 'Of course.'

'Oh I'm not,' Cindy says, 'not the shape. I don't think I am. I really am not.'

'You're very young,' Thelma says.

'I'm thirty,' she protests. 'Isn't that supposed to be my sexual prime?'

As if rejoining her in the water, Harry tries to take her side. 'They're ugly as hell. Most of the pricks I've seen are.'

'You don't see them erect,' Thelma lightly points out.

'Thank God for that,' he says, appalled, as he sometimes is, by this coarse crowd he's in.

'And yet he loves his own,' Janice says, keeping that light and cool and as it were scientific tone that has descended upon them, in the hushed dining pavilion. The singer has ceased. People at other tables are leaving, moving to the smaller tables at the edge of the dance floor by the pool.

'I don't love it,' he protests in a whisper. 'I'm stuck with it.'

'It's you,' Cindy quietly tells him.

'Not just the pricks,' Thelma clarifies, 'it has to be the whole man who turns you on. The way he carries himself. His voice, the way he laughs. But it all refers to that.'

Pricks. Can it be? They let the delicate subject rest, as dessert and coffee come. Revitalized by food and the night, they decide after all to sit with Stingers and watch the dancing a while, under the stars that on this night seem to Harry jewels of a clock that moves with maddening slowness, measuring out the minutes until he sinks himself in Cindy as if a star were to fall and sizzle into this Olympic-sized pool. Once, on some far lost summer field of childhood, someone, his mother it must have been though he cannot hear her voice, told him that if you stare up at the night sky while you count to one hundred you are bound to see a shooting star, they are in fact so common. But though he now leans back from the Stinger and the glass table and the consolatory, conspiratory murmur of his friends until his neck begins to ache, all the stars above him hang unbudging in their sockets. Webb Murkett's gravelly voice growls, 'Well, kiddies. As the oldest person here, I claim the privilege of announcing that I'm tired and want to go to bed.' And as Harry turns his face from the heavens there it is, in a corner of his vision, vivid and brief as a scratched match, a falling star, doused in the ocean of ink. The women rise and gather their skirts about them; the marimbas, after a consultation of fluttering, fading notes, break into 'Where Are the Clowns?' This plaintive pealing is lost behind them as they move along the pool, and past the front desk where the haggard, alcoholic resort manager is trying to get through long-distance to New York, and across the hotel's traffic circle with its curbs of white-washed coral, down into the shadowy realm of concrete paths between bushes of sleeping flowers. The palms above them grow noisy as the music faces. The *shoosh* of surf draws nearer. At the moonlit point where the paths diverge into three, goodnights are nervously exchanged but no one moves; then a woman's hand reaches out softly and takes the wrist of a man not her husband. The others follow suit, with no person looking at another, a downcast and wordless tugging serving to separate the partners out and to draw them down the respective paths to each woman's bungalow. Harry hears Cindy giggle at a distance, for it is not her hand with such gentle determination pulling him along, but Thelma's.

She has felt him pull back, and tightens her grip, silently. On the beach, he sees, a group has brought down a hurricane lamp, with their drinks; the lamp and their cigarettes glow red in the shadows, while the sea beyond stretches pale as milk beyond the black silhouette of a big sailboat anchored in the bay, under the half-moon tilted onto its back. Thelma lets go of his arm to fish in her sequinned purse for the bungalow key. 'You can have Cindy tomorrow night,' she whispers. 'We discussed it.'

'O.K., great,' he says lamely, he hopes not insultingly. He is figuring, this means that Cindy wanted that pig Harrison, and Janice got Webb. He had been figuring Janice would have to take Ronnie, and felt sorry for her, except from the look of him he'd fall asleep soon, and Webb and Thelma would go together, both of them yellowy stringy types. Thelma closes the bungalow door behind them and switches on a straw globe light above the bed. He asks her, 'Well, are tonight's men the first choice for you ladies or're you just getting the second choice out of the way?'

'Don't be so competitive, Harry. This is meant to be a loving sharing sort of thing, you heard Webb. One thing we absolutely agreed on, we're not going to carry any of it back to Brewer. This is all the monkey business there's going to be, even if it kills us.' She stands there in the center of her straw rug rather defiantly, a thin-faced sallow woman he scarcely knows. Not only her nose is pink in the wake of her sunburn but patches below her eyes as well, a kind of butterfly is on her face. Harry supposes he should kiss her, but his forward step is balked by her continuing firmly, 'I'll tell you one thing though, Harry Angstrom. You're *my* first choice.'

'I am?'

'Of course. I adore you. *Adore* you.'

'Me?'

'Haven't you ever sensed it?'

Rather than admit he hasn't, he hangs there foolishly.

'Shit,' Thelma says. 'Janice did. Why else do you think we weren't invited to Nelson's wedding?' She turns her back, and starts undoing her earring before the mirror, that just like the one in his and Janice's bungalow is framed in woven strips of bamboo. The batik hanging in here is of a tropical sunset with a palm in the foreground instead of the black-mammy fruit-seller he and Janice have, but the batik manufacturer is the same. The suitcases are the Harrisons', and the clothes hanging on the painted pipe that does for a closet. Thelma asks, 'You mind using Ronnie's toothbrush? I'll be a while in there, you better take the bathroom first.'

In the bathroom Harry sees that Ronnie uses shaving cream, Gillette Foamy, out of a pressure can, the kind that's eating up the ozone so our children will fry. And that new kind of razor with the narrow single-edge blade that snaps in and out with a click on the television commercials. Harry can't see the point, it's just more waste, he still uses a rusty old two-edge safety razor he bought for $1.99 about seven years ago, and lathers himself with an old imitation badger-bristle on whatever bar of soap is handy. He shaved before dinner after his nap so no need now. Also the Harrisons use chlorophyll Crest in one of those giant tubes that always buckles and springs a leak when he and Janice try to save a couple of pennies and buy one. He wonders whatever happened to Ipana and what was it *Consumer Reports* had to say about toothpastes a few issues back, probably came out in favor of baking soda, that's what he and Mim used to have to use, some theory Mom had about the artificial flavoring in toothpaste contributing to tartar. The trouble with consumerism is, the guy next door always seems to be doing better at it than you are. Just the Harrisons' bathroom supplies make him envious. Plain as she is, Thelma carries a hefty medicine kit, and beauty aids, plus a sun block called Eclipse, and Solarcaine. Vaseline, too, for some reason. Tampax, in a bigger box than Janice ever buys. And a lot of painkiller, aspirin in several shapes and Darvon and more pills in little prescription bottles than he would have expected. People are always a little sicker than you know. Harry debates whether he should take his leak sitting down to spare Thelma the sound of its gross splashing and rejects the idea, since she's the one wants to fuck him. It streams noisily into the bowl it seems forever, embarrassingly, all those drinks at dinner. Then he sits down on the seat anyway, to let out a little air. Too much shell-fish. He imagines he can smell yesterday's crabmeat and when he stands tests with a finger down there to see if he stinks. He decides he does. Better use a washcloth. He debates which washcloth is Ronnie's, the blue or the brown. He settles on the brown and scrubs what counts. Getting ready for the ball. He erases his scent by giving the cloth a good rinsing no matter whose it is.

When he steps back into the room Thelma is down to her underwear, cocoa bra and black panties. He didn't expect this, nor to be so stirred by it. Breasts are strange: some look bigger in clothes than they are and some look smaller. Thelma's are the second kind; her bra is smartly filled. Her whole body, into her forties, has kept that trim neutral serviceability nurses and grade-school teachers surprise you with, beneath their straight faces. She laughs, and holds out her arms like a fan dancer. 'Here I am. You look shocked. You're such a sweet prude, Harry – that's one of the things I adore. I'll be out in five minutes. Try not to fall asleep.'

Clever of her. What with the sleep debt they're all running down here and the constant booze and the trauma in the water today –

his head went under and a bottomless bile-green volume sucked at his legs – he was weary. He begins to undress and doesn't know where to stop. There are a lot of details a husband and wife work out over the years that with a strange woman pop up all over again. Would Thelma like to find him naked in the bed? Or on it? For him to be less naked than she when she comes out of the bathroom would be rude. At the same time, with this straw-shaded light swaying above the bed on so bright, he doesn't want her to think seeing him lying there on display that he thinks he's a *Playgirl* centerfold. He knows he could lose thirty pounds and still have a gut. In his underpants he crosses to the bamboo-trimmed bureau in the room and switches on the lamp there whose cheap wooden base is encrusted with baby seashells glued on. He takes off his underpants. The elastic waistband has lost its snap, the only brand of this type to buy is Jockey, but those cut-rate stores in Brewer don't like to carry it, quality is being driven out everywhere. He switches off the light over the bed and in shadow stretches himself out, all of him, on top of the bedspread, as he is, as he was, as he will be before the undertakers dress him for the last time, not even a wedding ring to relieve his nakedness, when he and Janice got married men weren't expected to wear wedding rings. He closes his eyes to rest them for a second in the red blankness there, beneath his lids. He has to get through this, maybe all she wants to do is talk, and then somehow be really rested for tomorrow night. Getting there. . . . That slither underwater. . . .

Thelma with it seems the clatter of an earthquake has come out of the bathroom. She is holding her underclothes in front of her, and with her back to him she sorts the underpants into the dirty pile the Harrisons keep beside the bureau, behind the straw wastebasket, and the bra, clean enough, back into the drawer, folded. This is the second time in this trip, he thinks drowsily, that he has seen her ass. Her body as she turns eclipses the bureau lamp and the front of her gathers shadow to itself; she advances timidly, as if wading into water. Her breasts sway forward as she bends to turn the light he switched off back on. She sits down on the edge of the bed.

His prick is still sleepy. She takes it into her hand. 'You're not circumcised.'

'No, they somehow weren't doing it at the hospital that day. Or maybe my mother had a theory, I don't know. I never asked. Sorry.'

'It's lovely. Like a little bonnet.' Sitting on the edge of the bed, more supple naked than he remembers her seeming with clothes on, Thelma bends and takes his prick in her mouth. Her body in the lamplight is a pale patchwork of faint tan and peeling pink and the natural yellowy tint of her skin. Her belly puckers into flat folds like stacked newspapers and the back of her hand as it holds the base of his prick with two fingers shows a dim lightning of blue veins. But her breath is warm and wet and the way that in lamplight individual white hairs snake as if singed through the mass of dull brown makes him want to reach out and stroke her head, or touch the rhythmic hollow in her jaw. He fears, though, interrupting the sensations she is giving him. She lifts a hand quickly to tuck back a piece of her hair, as if to let him better see.

He murmurs, 'Beautiful.' He is growing thick and long but still she forces her lips each time down to her fingers as they encircle him at his base. To give herself ease she spreads her legs; between her legs with one aslant across the bed edge he sees emerging from a pubic bush more delicate and reddish than he would have dreamed a short white string. Unlike Janice's or Cindy's as he imagined it, Thelma's pussy is not opaque; it is a fuzz transparent upon the bruise-colored labia that with their tongue of white string look so lacking and defenseless Harry could cry. She too is near tears, perhaps from the effort of not gagging. She backs off and stares at the staring eye of his glans, swollen free of his foreskin. She pulls up the bonnet again and says crooningly, teasingly, 'Such a serious little face.' She kisses it lightly, once, twice, flicking her tongue, then bobs again, until it seems she must come up for air. 'God,' she sighs. 'I've wanted to do that for so long. Suck you. Come. Come,

Harry. Come in my mouth. Come in my mouth and all over my face.' Her voice sounds husky and mad saying this and all through her words Thelma does not stop gazing at the little slit of his where a single cloudy tear has now appeared. She licks it off.

'Have you really,' he asks timidly, 'liked me for a while?'

'Years,' she says. 'Years. And you never noticed. You shit. Always under Janice's thumb and mooning after silly Cindy. Well you know where Cindy is now. She's being screwed by my husband. He didn't want to, he said he'd rather go to bed with me.' She snorts, in some grief of self-disgust, and plunges her mouth down again, and in the pinchy rush of sensation as he feels forced against the opening of her throat he wonders if he should accept her invitation.

'Wait,' Harry says. 'Shouldn't I do something for you first? If I come, it's all over.'

'If you come, then you come again.'

'Not at my age. I don't think.'

'Your age. Always talking about your age.' Thelma rests her face on his belly and gazes up at him, for the first time playful, her eyes at right angles to his disconcertingly. He has never noticed their color before: that indeterminate color called hazel but in the strong light overhead, and brightened by all her deep-throating, given a tawny pallor, an unthinking animal translucence. 'I'm too excited to come,' she tells him. 'Anyway, Harry, I'm having my period and they're really bloody, every other month. I'm scared to find out why. In the months in between, these terrible cramps and hardly any show.'

'See a doctor,' he suggests.

'I see doctors all the time, they're useless. I'm dying, you know that, don't you?'

'Dying?'

'Well, maybe that's too dramatic a way of putting it. Nobody knows how long it'll take, and a lot of it depends upon me. The one thing I'm absolutely supposed not to do is go out in the sun. I was crazy to come down here, Ronnie tried to talk me out of it.'

'Why did you?'

'Guess. I tell you, I'm crazy, Harry. I got to get you out of my system.' And it seems she might make that sob of disgusted grief again, but she has reared up her head to look at his prick. All this talk of death has put it half to sleep again.

'This is this lupus?' he asks.

'Mmm,' Thelma says. 'Look. See the rash?' She pulls back her hair on both sides. 'Isn't it pretty? That's from being so stupid in the sun Friday. I just wanted so badly to be like the rest of you, not to be an invalid. It was terrible Saturday. Your joints ache, your insides don't work. Ronnie offered to take me home for a shot of cortisone.'

'He's very nice to you.'

'He loves me.'

His prick has stiffened again and she bends to it. 'Thelma.' He has not used her name before, this night. 'Let me do something to you. I mean, equal rights and all that.'

'You're not going down into all that blood.'

'Let me suck these sweet things then.' Her nipples are not bumply like Janice's but perfect as a baby's thumb-tips. Since it is his treat now he feels free to reach up and switch off the light over the bed. In the dark her rashes disappear and he can see her smile as she arranges herself to be served. She sits crosslegged, like Cindy did on the boat, women the flexible sex, and puts a pillow in her lap for his head. She puts a finger in his mouth and plays with her nipple and his tongue together. There is a tremble running through her like a radio not quite turned off. His hand finds her ass, its warm dents; there is a kind of glassy texture to Thelma's skin where Janice's has a touch of fine, fine sandpaper. His prick, lightly teased by her fingernails, has come back nicely. 'Harry.' Her voice presses into his ear. 'I want to do something for you so you won't forget me, something you've never had with anybody else. I suppose other women have sucked you off?'

He shakes his head yes, which tugs the flesh of her breast.

'How many have you fucked up the ass?'

He lets her nipple slip from his mouth. 'None. Never.'

'You and Janice?'

'Oh no. It never occurred to us.'

'Harry. You're not fooling me?'

How dear that was, her old-fashioned 'fooling.' From talking to all those third-graders. 'No, honestly. I thought only queers . . . Do you and Ronnie?'

'All the time. Well, a lot of the time. He loves it.'

'And you?'

'It has its charms.'

'Doesn't it hurt? I mean, he's big.'

'At first. You use Vaseline. I'll get ours.'

'Thelma, wait. Am I up to this?'

She laughs a syllable. 'You're up.' She slides away into the bathroom and while she is gone he stays enormous. She returns and anoints him thoroughly, with an icy expert touch. Harry shudders. Thelma lies down beside him with her back turned, curls forward as if to be shot from a cannon, and reaches behind to guide him. 'Gently.'

It seems it won't go, but suddenly it does. The medicinal odor of displaced Vaseline reaches his nostrils. The grip is tight at the base but beyond, where a cunt is all velvety suction and caress, there is no sensation: a void, a pure black box, a casket of perfect nothingness. He is in that void, past her tight ring of muscle. He asks, 'May I come?'

'Please do.' Her voice sounds faint and broken. Her spine and shoulder blades are taut.

It takes only a few thrusts, while he rubs her scalp with one hand and clamps her hip steady with the other. Where will his come go? Nowhere but mix with her shit. With sweet Thelma's sweet shit. They lie wordless and still together until his prick's slow shrivelling withdraws it. 'O.K.,' he says. 'Thank you. That I won't forget.'

'Promise?'

'I feel embarrassed. What does it do for you?'

'Makes me feel full of you. Makes me feel fucked up the ass. By lovely Harry Angstrom.'

'Thelma,' he admits, 'I can't believe you're so fond of me. What have I done to deserve it?'

'Just existed. Just shed your light. Haven't you ever noticed, at parties or at the club, how I'm always at your side?'

'Well, not really. There aren't that many sides. I mean, we see you and Ronnie –'

'Janice and Cindy noticed. They knew you were who I'd want.'

'Uh – not to, you know, milk this, but what is it about me that turns you on?'

'Oh darling. Everything. Your height and the way you move, as if you're still a skinny twenty-five. The way you never sit down anywhere without making sure there's a way out. Your little provisional smile, like a little boy at some party where the bullies might get him the next minutes. Your good humor. You *believe* in people so – Webb, you hang on his words where nobody else pays any attention, and Janice, you're so proud of her it's pathetic. It's not as if she can *do* anything. Even her tennis, Doris Kaufmann was telling us, really –'

'Well it's nice to see her have fun at something, she's had a kind of dreary life.'

'See? You're just terribly generous. You're so grateful to be anywhere, you think that tacky club and that hideous house of Cindy's are heaven. It's wonderful. You're glad to be alive.'

'Well, I mean, considering the alternative –'

'It kills me. I love you *so much* for it. And your hands. I've always loved your hands.' Having sat up on the edge of the bed, she takes his left hand, lying idle, and kisses the big white moons of each fingernail. 'And now your prick, with its little bonnet. Oh Harry I don't care if this kills me, coming down here, tonight is worth it.'

That void, inside her. He can't take his mind from what he's discovered, that nothingness seen by his single eye. In the shadows, while humid blue moonlight and the rustle of palms seep through the louvers by the bed, he trusts himself to her as if speaking in prayer, talks to her about himself as he has talked to none other: about Nelson and the grudge he bears the kid and the grudge the boy bears him, and about his daughter, the daughter he thinks he has, grown and ignorant of him. He dares confide to Thelma, because she has let him fuck her up the ass in proof of love, his sense of miracle at being himself, himself instead of somebody else, and his old inkling, now fading in the energy crunch, that there was something that wanted him to find it, that he was here on earth on a kind of assignment.

'How lovely to think that,' Thelma says. 'It makes you' – the word is hard for her to find – 'radiant. And sad.' She gives him advice on some points. She thinks he should seek out Ruth and ask her point-blank if that is his daughter, and if so is there anything he can do to help? On the subject of Nelson, she thinks the child's problem may be an extension of Harry's; if he himself did not feel guilty about Jill's death and before that Rebecca's, he would feel less threatened by Nelson and more comfortable and kindly with him. 'Remember,' she says, 'he's just a young man like you once were, looking for his path.'

'But he's not like me!' Harry protests, having come at last into a presence where the full horror of this truth, the great falling-off, will be understood. 'He's a goddam little Springer, through and through.'

Thelma thinks he's more like Harry than he knows. Wanting to learn to hang glide – didn't he recognize himself in that? And the thing with two girls at once. Wasn't he, possibly, a bit jealous of Nelson?

'But I never had the impulse to screw Melanie,' he confesses. 'Or Pru either, much. They're both out of this world, somehow.'

Of course, Thelma says. 'You shouldn't want to fuck them. They're your daughters. Or Cindy either. You should want to fuck *me*. I'm your generation, Harry. I can *see* you. To those girls you're just an empty heap of years and money.'

And, as they drift in talk away from the constellations of his life, she describes her marriage with Ronnie, his insecurities and worries beneath that braggart manner that she knows annoys Harry. 'He was never a star like you, he never had that for a moment.' She met him fairly well along in her twenties, when she was wondering if she'd die a spinster schoolteacher. Being old as she was, with some experience of men, and with a certain gift for letting go, she was amused by the things he thought of. For their honeymoon breakfast he jerked off into the scrambled eggs and they ate his fried jism with the rest. If you go along with everything on that side of Ronnie, he's wonderfully loyal, and docile, you could say. He has no interest in other women, she knows this for a fact, a curious fact even, given the nature of men. He's been a perfect father. When he was lower down on the totem pole at Schuylkill Mutual, he lost twenty pounds, staying awake nights worrying. Only in these last few years has the weight come back. When the first diagnosis of her lupus came through, he took it worse than she did, in a way. 'For a woman past forty, Harry, when you've had children. . . . If some Nazi or somebody came to me and they'd take either me or little Georgie, say – he's the one that's needed most help, so he comes to mind – it wouldn't be a hard choice. For Ronnie I think it might be. To lose me. He thinks what I do for him not every woman would. I suspect he's wrong but there it is.' And she admits she likes his cock. But what Harry might not appreciate, being a man, is that a big one like Ronnie's doesn't change size that much when it's hard, just the angle changes. It doesn't go from being a little bonneted sleeping baby to a tall fierce soldier like this. She has worked him up again, idly toying as she talks, while the night outside their louvered window has grown utterly still, the last drunken shout and snatch of music long died,

nothing astir but the incessant sighing of the sea and the piping of
some high-pitched cricket they have down here. Courteously he
offers to fuck her through her blood, and she refuses with an almost
virginal fright, so that he wonders if on the excuse of her flow she
is not holding this part of herself back from him, aloof from her
love and shamelessness, pure for her marriage. She has explained,
'When I realized I was falling in love with you, I was so *mad* at
myself, I mean it couldn't contribute to *any*thing. But then I came
to see that something must be missing between me and Ronnie, or
maybe in any life, so I tried to accept it, and even quietly enjoy it,
just watching you. My little hairshirt.' He has not kissed her yet on
the mouth, but now guessing at her guilty withholding of herself
from being fucked he does. Her lips feel cool and dry, considering.
Since she will not admit him to her cunt, as compromise he mas-
turbates her while sitting on her face, glad he thought of washing
where he did. Her tongue probes there and her fingers, as cool on
top of his as if still filmed with Vaseline, guide his own as they find
and then lose and find again the hooded little center that is *her*. She
comes with a smothered cry and arches her back so this darkness at
the center of her pale and smooth and unfamiliar form rises hun-
grily under his eyes, a cloud with a mouth, a fish lunging upwards
out of water. Getting her breath, she returns the kindness and with
him watches the white liquid lift and collapse in glutinous strings
across her hand. She rubs his jism on her face, where it shines. The
stillness outside is beginning to brighten, each leaf sharp in the soft
air. Drunk of fatigue and self-exposure he begs her to tell him
something that he can do to her that Ronnie has never done. She
gets into the bathtub and has him urinate on her. 'It's hot!' she
exclaims, her sallow skin drummed upon in designs such as men
and boys drill in the snow. They reverse the experience, Thelma
awkwardly straddling, and having to laugh at her own impotence,
looking for the right release in the maze of her womanly insides.
Above him as he waits her bush has a masculine jut, but when her
stream comes, it dribbles sideways; women cannot *aim*, he sees.

And her claim of heat seems to him exaggerated; it is more like coffee or tea one lets cool too long at the edge of the desk and then must drink in a few gulps, this side of tepid. Having tried together to shower the ammoniac scent of urine off their skins, Thelma and Harry fall asleep among the stripes of dawn now welling through the louvers as if not a few stolen hours but an entire married life of sanctioned intimacy stretches unto death before them.

MARILYN FRENCH

from
The Women's Room

The Women's Room (1978) *was an international bestseller and has established itself as a landmark in feminist writing. It traces, with sometimes shocking frankness, a girl's journey from the shallow excitements of casual affairs through to the dawning awareness of the exhilaration of liberation.*

MIRA got a little high that night, and so did Ben, and somehow – later she could not remember whose suggestion it was, or if there had been no suggestion at all, but simple single purpose – he ended up in her car, driving her to her apartment and when they arrived, he got out and saw her to the door and of course she asked him in for a nightcap and of course he came.

They were laughing as they climbed the steps, and they had their arms around each other. They were designing the perfect world, trying to outdo each other in silliness, and giggling to the point of tears at their own jokes. Mira fumbled with her key, Ben took it from her, dropped it, both of them giggling, picked it up and opened the door.

She poured them brandies. Ben following her to the kitchen, leaning over the counter and gazing at her as she prepared the drinks, talking, talking. He followed her out of the kitchen and right into the bathroom, until she turned with a little surprise and he caught himself, cried '*Oh!*' and laughed, and stepped out, but stood right beside the closed door talking to her through it while she peed. Then sat close beside her on the couch, talking, talking, laughing, smiling at her with shining eyes. And when he got up to get refills, she followed him into the kitchen and leaned across the counter gazing at him as he prepared the drinks, and he kept looking at her as he did it, and poured too much water in her glass. And they sat even closer this time, and there needed no forethought or calculation for the moment when they reached across and took each other's hands and it was only a few moments later that Ben was on her, leaning against her, his face searching in her face for something madly wanted that did not reside in faces, but searched, kept searching, and she too, in his. His body was lying on her now, his chest against her breasts, and the closeness of their bodies felt like completion. Her breasts were pressed flat under him: they felt soft and hard at once. Their faces stayed together, mouths searching, probing, opening as if to devour, or rubbing softly together. Their cheeks too rubbed softly like the cheeks of tiny children just trying to feel another flesh, and hard, his beard, shaved though he was, harsh and hurtful on her cheek. He had her head in his hands, and he held it firmly, possessively, and gently, all at once, and he dipped his face into hers, searching for nourishment, hungry, hungry. They rose together, like one body, and like one body walked into the bedroom, not separating even in the narrow hallway, just squeezing through together.

For Mira, Ben's lovemaking was the discovery of a new dimension. He loved her body. Her pleasure in this alone was so extreme that it felt like the discovery of a new ocean, mountain, continent. He loved it. He crowed over it as he helped her to undress, he kissed it and caressed it and exclaimed, and she was quieter, but adored his with her eyes as she helped him to undress, ran her hands over the smooth skin of his back, grabbed him from behind around the waist and kissed his back, the back of his neck, his shoulders. She was shy of his penis at first, but when he held her close and nestled against her, he pressed his penis against her body, and her hand went out to it, held it, caressed it. Then he wrapped his legs around her, covered her, holding on to her tightly, and kissed her eyes, her cheeks, her hair. She pulled away from him gently and took his hands and kissed them, and he took hers and kissed the tips of her fingers.

She lay back again as he pressed against her, and he caressed her breasts. She felt that her body was floating out to sea on a warm gentle wave that had orders not to drown her, but she didn't even care if she drowned. Then, rather suddenly, he put his mouth to her breasts and nursed at them, and quickly entered her and quickly came, silently, with only an expelled breath, and a pang of self-pity hit her, her eyes filled with tears. No, no, not again, it couldn't be the same, it wasn't fair, was there really something wrong with her? He lay on top of her, holding her closely for a long time afterward, and she had time to swallow the tears and paste a smile back on her face. She patted his back gently and reminded herself that she had at least had pleasure from it this time, and maybe that was a good sign. He had given her, if nothing else, more pleasure than she had ever had from her body before.

After a time, he leaned back and lay on his side close to her. They lighted cigarettes and sipped their drinks. He asked her about her girlhood: what kind of child had she been? She was surprised. Women ask such things, sometimes, but not men. She was delighted. She lay back and threw herself into it, talking as if it were happening there and then. Her voice changed and curled around its subject: she was five, she was twelve, she was fourteen. She hardly noticed at first that he had begun to caress her body again. It seemed simply natural that they would touch each other. He was gently rubbing her belly and sides, her shoulders. She put her cigarette out and caressed his shoulders. Then he was leaning over her, kissing her belly, rubbing his hands on her thighs, on the insides of her thighs. Desire rose up in her more fiercely than before. She caressed his hair, then his head moved down, and she tightened up, her eyes widened, he was kissing her genitals, licking them, she was horrified, but he kept stroking her belly, her leg, he kept doing it and when she tried to tighten her legs, he held them gently apart, and she lay back again and felt the warm wet pressure and her innards felt fluid and giving, all the way to her stomach. She tried to pull him up, but he would not permit it, he turned over, he kissed her back, her buttocks, he put his finger on her anus and rubbed it gently, and she was moaning and trying to turn over, and finally, she succeeded, and then he had her breast in his mouth and the hot shoots were climbing all the way to her throat. She wrapped her body around him, clutching him, no longer kissing or caressing, but only clinging now, trying to get him to come inside her, but he wouldn't. She surrendered her body to him, let him take control of it, and in an ecstasy of passivity let her body float out to the deepest part of the ocean. There was only body, only sensation: even the room had ceased to exist. He was rubbing her clitoris, gently, slowly, ritually, and she was making little gasps that she could hear from a distance. Then he took her breast in his mouth again and wrapped his body around her and entered her. She came almost immediately and gave a sharp cry, but he kept going, and she came over and over again in a series of sharp pleasures that were the same as pain. Her face and body were wet, so were his, she felt, and still the pangs came, less now, and she clutched him to her, holding him as if she really might drown. The orgasms subsided, but still he thrust himself into her. Her legs were aching, and the thrust no longer felt like pleasure. Her muscles were weary, and she was unable to keep the motion going. He pulled out and turned her over and propped her on a pillow so that her ass was propped up, and entered her vagina from behind. His hand stroked her breast gently, he was humped over her like a dog. It was a totally different feeling, and as he thrust more and more sharply, she gave out little cries. Her clitoris was being triggered again, and it felt sharp and fierce and hot and as full of pain as pleasure and suddenly he came and thrust fiercely and gave off a series of loud cries that were nearly sobs, and stayed drooped over her like a flower, heaving, his wet face against her back.

When he pulled out, she turned over and reached up to him and pulled him down and held him. He put his arms around her and they lay together for a long time. His wet penis was against her leg, and she could feel semen trickling out of her onto the sheets. It began to feel cold, but neither of them moved. Then they moved a few inches and looked into each other's faces. They stroked each other's faces, then began to laugh. They hugged each other hard, like friends rather than lovers, and sat up. Ben went into the bathroom and got some tissues and they dried themselves and the sheets. He went back and started water running in the tub. Mira was lying back against the pillow, smoking.

'Come on, woman, get up!' he ordered, and she looked at him startled, and he reached across and put his arms around her and lifted her from the bed, kissing her at the same time, and helped her to her feet, and they went together to the bathroom and both peed. The water was at bath level by then. Ben had put Myra's bath lotion in the water, and it was bubbly and smelled fresh, and they got in together and sat with bent knees intertwined, and gently threw water at each other and lay back enjoying the warmth and caressed each other beneath and above the water.

'I'm hungry,' she said.

'I'm famished,' he said.

Together, they pulled everything out of the refrigerator, and produced a feast of Jewish salami and feta cheese and hard-boiled eggs and tomatoes and black bread and sweet butter and half-sour pickles and big black Greek olives and raw Spanish onions and beer, and trotted all of it back to bed with them and sat there gorging themselves and talking and drinking and laughing and touching each other with tender fingertips. And finally they set the platters and plates and beer cans on the floor and Ben nuzzled his face in her breast, but this time she pushed him down and got on top of him and, refusing to let him move, she kissed and caressed his body and slid her hands down his sides and along the insides of his thighs, held his balls gently, then slid down and took his penis in her mouth and he gasped with pleasure and she moved her hands and head slowly up and down with it, feeling the vein throb, feeling it harden and melt little drops of semen, and wouldn't let him move until suddenly she raised her head and he looked startled and she got on top of him and set her own rhythms, rubbing her clitoris against him as she moved and she came, she felt like a goddess, triumphant, riding the winds, and she kept coming and he came too then, and she bent down her chest and clutched him, both of them moaning together, and ended, finally, exhausted.

They fell back on the rumpled sheets for a while, then Mira lighted a cigarette. Ben got up and smoothed the bedclothes out, and fluffed up the pillows, and got in beside her and pulled up the sheets and blankets and took a drag of her cigarette and put his arms behind his head and just lay there smiling.

It was five o'clock, and the sky above the houses was light, lightening, a pale streak of light blue. They were not tired, they said. They turned their heads toward each other, and just smiled, kept smiling. Ben took another drag of her cigarette, then she put it out. She reached out and switched off the lamp, and together they snuggled down in the sheets. They were still turned to each other, and they twisted their bodies together. They fell immediately asleep. When they awakened in the morning, they were still intertwined.

ALMUDENA GRANDES

from

The Ages of Lulu

Almudena Grandes was born in Madrid in 1960. The Ages of Lulu (Las Edades de Lulu), *her first novel, was published in Spain in 1989 and in Britain, translated by Sonia Soto, in 1993. Lulu's need to experience the sexual exploits of her fantasies is conceived on the night she loses her virginity at fifteen.*

IT was five years, two months and eleven days since I'd last seen him. His face, with its large nose and square jaw, had hardly changed. The grey hadn't gained much ground either, his hair was still mostly black. He was quite a bit thinner, though. This surprised me – Marcelo always said the food was quite good in Philadelphia – but he'd got thinner, and it made him look even taller and more gangling. That was one of the things I'd always liked most about him – he'd always looked as if he was about to come apart, not enough flesh for all those bones.

His age suited him.

While the guy with the sideburns introduced the speakers in an exasperatingly ponderous manner, he lit a cigarette and glanced round the hall. He was looking in every direction except mine.

The hollow inside was devouring me.

I felt very hot. And very scared.

I didn't look at him straight on but I noticed that he'd gone very still.

He was staring at me intently, his eyes half closed, a strange look on his face. Then he smiled, and only then did he move his lips, silently, two syllables, as if pronouncing my name.

He recognized me.

I acted according to my plan. I slowly unbuttoned my coat, uncovering my horrendous, brown school uniform. I tried to look sure of myself, but inside I felt like a bad old magician, only just keeping up appearances but expecting the eight wooden skittles he's juggling to come crashing down on top of him. Pablo put his hand over his face, and stayed like that for a few seconds, before looking at me again. He was still smiling.

He spoke very little that afternoon, and very badly. He went blank a couple of times and stammered; he seemed to be unable to construct a sentence of more than three words. He didn't take his eyes off me, and my neighbours were looking at me curiously.

When the old guy with the sideburns kicked off the question-and-answer session, I got up from my seat.

To my surprise, my legs still held me up.

I walked the length of the row, very slowly, without tripping, and left the lecture theatre. I crossed the hall without looking back, went through the glass doors at the entrance and only had time to take about eight or nine steps before he stopped me. He put his arm on mine, took me by the elbow, made me turn round and, after looking at me closely for a few seconds, he touched me with his magic wand.

'I'm so pleased, Lulu, you haven't grown up at all.'

He accepted all I offered him with exquisite elegance. He read all the signs without making any comment. He spoke little, just enough. He willingly fell into my traps. He let me find out all I wanted to know.

He took me to his place, a very large but furniture-packed loft in the centre of town.

'What's happened to the workshop in Moreto?'

'My mother sold it a couple of years ago.' He seemed sorry. 'She's bought herself a truly ghastly little house in Majadahonda.'

Then, in silence, he ran his eyes over me, slowly, from my head to my toes. He held my arms above my head and I kept them there while he pulled my jumper off. He undid my blouse, removed it and looked into my face, smiling. I wasn't wearing a bra and he still remembered everything. He leaned forward, seized me by the ankles and pulled them suddenly upwards, making me fall on the sofa. He drew my legs towards him until they were on top of his. I was now lying down. He undid the clasps on my skirt. Before removing it, he took one of my hands, held it up to his face and looked at it closely, lingering over the round, blunt fingertips. That was one detail I'd overlooked. Even though I knew I shouldn't, I broke the silence.

'Do you like long nails, painted red?'

My hand still in his, he gave me an ironic smile.

'Does it matter?'

I couldn't answer that it did, it mattered a lot, so I gave a vague shrug.

'No, I don't like them,' he admitted at last. That's lucky, I thought.

He finished undressing me, slowly. He took off my shoes, my stockings and then put my shoes back on. He looked at me a moment, without moving. Then he stretched out his open hand and slid it softly over me, from the instep of my foot to my neck, several times. He seemed so calm, his gestures so steady and light that for a moment I thought he didn't really desire me, that this was only an echo of his former desire, now long gone. Maybe I'd grown too much, after all.

He slipped his arm under me and sat me up. I was now sitting on his knees. He put his arms around me and kissed me. The mere contact with his tongue reverberated throughout my body, sending shivers down my spine. He is the meaning of my life, I thought. It was an old thought, that I'd endlessly repeated to myself during his absence, and violently pushed aside in recent months, for being mean and pathetic, and useless. There were still so many great causes to fight for in the world, but at that moment, as he kissed me and rocked me in his arms, it was the only truth, the plain and simple truth: he was the only thing that gave meaning to my life.

I caught his hand and covered my face with it. I held it still a moment, feeling the pressure of his fingertips, and gave his palm a long, moist kiss, then I bent his fingers, one by one, hiding the thumb under the other four, put my hand round his fist and pressed my cheeks and lips against his knuckles.

I was trying to make him see that I loved him.

'I've got something for you . . .'

He put me aside very gently, stood up and crossed the room. He took out a long narrow box from one of the desk drawers.

'I bought it for you about three years ago, in a moment of weakness . . .' He smiled at me. 'Don't tell anyone about it. I think I find it embarrassing now, but at the time I'd get these crazy urges every so often, especially when I was on my own. I'd get in the car and head off to New York, to Fourteenth Street and Eighth Avenue. It's a really lively place – how can I explain what it's like . . .' He was silent for a moment, thinking it over. Then his face lit up. 'Yeah, that's it, Fourteenth Street is like a kind of Bravo Murillo but wilder; it's full of people, and bars and shops. It would take me over four hours there and back, just to go and eat tuna *empanadas* and sing 'Asturias, Beloved Homeland' in a bar owned by a guy from Langreo. I'd get blind drunk, and then I'd feel better. In one of those stupid fits of nostalgia, I bought you this.' He sat down next to me and handed me the box. 'At the risk of sounding vulgar, I'll tell you, it was very expensive, and I was broke at the time, but I bought it for you anyway, because I owed it to you. I've felt strangely responsible for you all these years. I never dared send it to you, though. The truth is, I expected to find you all grown up, and grown women don't always appreciate toys . . .'

The box, carefully wrapped in cellophane, contained a dozen plastic objects in white, beige and red – an electric vibrator with a grooved surface, surrounded by a set of detachable covers and accessories. There were also two small batteries, in a bag.

I had no problem showing I was satisfied. I was very pleased, and not just because he'd remembered me.

'Thanks a lot, I love it.' I gave him a big smile. 'You should have sent it to me, I could have really done with it. I suppose it's my size . . .' He was watching me and laughing. 'If you like, I could try it out . . .. now.'

I tore off the cellophane and carefully examined the contents. I found the slot for the batteries without too much trouble and loaded the vibrator. I turned the little switch at its base and it started to tremble. I increased the power until it was dancing in the palm of my hand. It was funny, just like on Christmas morning as a child, when after fitting two batteries into its back, an ordinary, inert doll, would start to talk or move its head. I realized that I was smiling.

I looked at Pablo, he was smiling too.

'Which do you think is the best?'

He didn't answer, he just stood up and went to sit in an armchair leaning against the wall opposite, about seven feet away, exactly facing me.

Now I'll show you, I thought, I'll show you if I've grown up or not. I felt good, very sure of myself. I had a feeling that this was my only winning card. I'd thought about it often in the last few days and I hadn't been able to come up with a concrete plan, or any definite tactics, but he'd made it all very easy for me. He was attracted to me, and I remembered that he liked dirty little girls – all right then, I'd show him just how dirty I could be, really dirty. I remembered the headmistress's words and I urged myself on. The only thing I was worried about was that my performance might be a little too theatrical, even slightly hysterical, and not convincing enough. I didn't care about anything else. I have a strange sense of propriety. A lady exclaiming 'Isn't he sweet!' at a handicapped child in a wheelchair; a parvenu kicking up a fuss when the fifteen-year-old waiter at a little bar on the beach says they don't have whole-meal bread; or a pair of rich, fat cats in swanky clothes who won't give beggars more than five pesetas – that's the sort of thing that makes me feel ashamed. The other kind of propriety, the conventional kind, is something I've never had.

I slowly opened my legs and slid my finger along my pussy, just once, before starting to chatter.

'I think I'll begin with this one.' I extracted from the box a flesh-coloured plastic cover, which was a pretty faithful reproduction of the real thing, veins and all. 'Do you know something? I don't like being so tall any more. I used to be really proud of it but now I'd like to be about ten inches shorter, like Susana – do you remember Susana?'

'The one with the recorder?' His expression, both thoughtful and amused, was the one I had made an effort to retain in my mind's eye all these years.

'That's right, the one with the recorder. You've got a good memory . . .' I was looking straight into his eyes the whole time, trying to affect the cold, calculating expression which characterizes expertly lascivious women, but my sex, as yet empty, was throbbing and swelling all the time, and I've never been able to stay calm when I felt like that. 'There we are, but it's huge! I suppose you won't be embarrassed if I put it in right now, will you?' He shook his head. I rubbed myself a couple of times with the new toy before unhurriedly sinking it inside me. I became distracted and wasn't able to observe his reaction, although this had been my main purpose. It was the first time I'd used one of these things and my own reactions absorbed me entirely.

'Do you like it?' His question upset my concentration.

'Yes, I do . . .' I was silent a moment and looked at him, before going on. 'But it's not really like a man's cock, like I'd imagined, first because it's not hot, and then, I've got to move it myself, so there's not that element of surprise – do you know what I mean?

There's no change of rhythm, like when it stops, and then suddenly speeds up, that's what I like best, when it speeds up . . .'

'You've fucked a lot all these years, haven't you?'

'I haven't done too badly . . .' Now I was moving my hand more quickly. I was vigorously pumping the fake penis against the walls of my vagina, and it felt good. It was starting to feel a bit too good, so I stopped suddenly and decided to change the cover; I didn't want to precipitate things. 'Is this one with the spikes meant to hurt?'

'I don't know, I don't think so.'

'Well, we'll see . . . I was telling you something, ah yes, the thing about Susana. Because she's five feet tall, all blokes seem huge to her – it's brilliant. Every time I ask her she always says the same: "it was this big,"' I spread my hands wide apart, '"enormous", but like, complaining. I can't understand her, she's always complaining. I'd love it, but because I'm so big, well, they never quite fill me up, so it's a disadvantage really, being so tall, you're too long all over . . .'

'Yeah . . .' He was laughing loudly and watching me. I knew he was enjoying it all so I decided to link this story with another one from a completely different source. I'd never have believed I could tell him about it, but at that moment it didn't seem important.

'Hey, you know what? The spikes don't hurt. Now I'm going to put this on, let's see what happens.' I took out a kind of red cap, covered in little bumps, and fitted it onto the tip. 'Yeah, and a funny thing, talking of Susana, a couple of months ago I dreamt about you one night, and dildoes played a big part in the dream.' I stopped for a moment. I wanted to examine his face, but I couldn't detect anything special. 'Well, it turns out, Susana's become a little goody-goody recently. She used to be the sluttiest in the class, at school, but a couple of years ago she got a fiancé, terribly serious, a real old square, he's about twenty-nine . . .'

'I'm thirty-two . . .' At first he looked at me with the same expression as my mother when she caught me poking around in the larder, then he burst out laughing.

'Yeah, but you're not a square.'

'Why not?'

'Because you're not, like Marcelo – he isn't square either, even though he's got a kid and everything. Well, anyway, the thing is Susana's fiancé is really loaded. He's got an ad agency but not an ounce of humour. The other night we went out for dinner – the two of them, Chelo, who brought quite an amusing guy, and me. I didn't have anybody to take, seriously, look, if I'd had this then, maybe I could have worn it.' I took the vibrator out from inside me and started to remove the accessories. I wanted to try it with nothing on – it would probably be less effective like that. The spikes were starting to excite me too much. 'The fact is we got drunk, including Susana, and we told him the story about the recorder. Chelo's bloke laughed a lot, he thought it was really funny, but Susana's got furious. He said it wasn't funny at all, he definitely didn't find that kind of stupidity funny. I told them I thought that was a bit odd and that when you'd found out, it really turned you on. Didn't it?' He nodded. 'Did you bring me a recorder back from New York too?'

'No.'

'What a pity!' At that I couldn't help laughing, but I managed to get a grip on myself after a few seconds, and went on. 'Well, the fact is, that night I dreamt we were both driving along in a really big, flash car, with a really handsome black chauffeur, who called you Sir and had a really big cock. I don't know how, but I knew he had a really big one.' His smile, different now, made me worry that he suspected what kind of dream this really was, so I started to improvise, to try and make the whole thing seem more likely. 'I was wearing a long, sixteenth-century style, dove-grey dress with a huge décolleté, a white ruff and hoop skirt with a tulle bustle over my bottom and loads of jewellery all over the place, but you were just dressed in ordinary trousers and a thick red jumper, and we stopped in Fuencarral Street, which was really Berlin, even though all the street signs were in Spanish. Everything was the same as it is in real life, and we went into a shoe shop, with loads of shoes in the windows, of course . . . Hey, you don't mind if I carry on with my finger, do you, just for a little bit? I need a rest.'

'Please, feel free.'

'Thank you, so kind, right, where was I, ah yes. In the shoe shop there was an assistant dressed up as an old-fashioned page, but his clothes weren't really like mine. His costume looked French, like Louis XIV, lots of lace and a powdered wig, you know the kind of thing, and then I sat down very nicely on a seat. You remained standing by my side and the assistant came up to you and said, "What can I do for you, Sir?" because the funniest thing is, you can't imagine what the relationship was between you and me, you'll never guess . . .'

'Father and daughter?'

'Yes . . .' I stammered. 'How did you guess?'

'Pah, I said the first thing that came into my head.'

'Don't you find it incredible?' My amazement, tinged with embarrassment, genuine embarrassment, despite my proverbial lack of shame, threatened to paralyze me at any moment.

'No. It's charming.' His words dispelled my doubts. 'Then what happened? I wasn't getting you kitted out for school, was I?'

'No way.' I laughed. The unpleasant feeling had completely disappeared, and I was feeling better and better, and more convincing. I went back to stroking myself so he could see me, moving slowly on the carpet, arousing him from a distance. That really excited me, but I also felt a terrible urge to go over and touch him. 'You told the shop assistant that you were going off to Philadelphia for a couple of weeks, to give a course on Saint John of the Cross to those poor savages – the Indians, I mean – and that you were worried about leaving me all alone like that, because I was a shameless little hussy and there was no knowing what I might do, so you'd thought of inserting a dildo inside me to comfort me and keep me company while you were away. The assistant agreed it was a good idea. "These young girls nowadays," he said, "you can never be too careful." Then the man went into the back room and came back with these two stands. I don't know what to call them – a pair of metal poles with rings at the top – and he put them in front of me, one on either side. I knew what I had to do. I lifted up my skirts, spread my legs and put a heel in the ring at the top of each stand, like when you go to the gynaecologist. I was wearing long white bloomers down to my knees, but all open underneath, with a buttonhole embroidered with little flowers, and the shop assistant put his finger inside me. He looked at you and said, "I can't try any of them out, she's completely dry. If you like, I can try to do something about it," and you agreed, so then he kneeled in front of me and started to lick my cunt. He did it really well and it felt good, but when I was about to come you said, "That's enough," and he stopped . . .'

'That was rather disagreeable of me, wasn't it?' He was smiling, drumming his fingers on his flies.

'Yes,' I answered, 'you were definitely very rude. Well, then the man started to fit me with big golden dildoes, longer and bigger ones, and as I was already quite aroused, well, I came right in the middle of the fitting. You liked that. The shop assistant wasn't very pleased, but he didn't say anything. In the end he put a horrible one inside me, it really hurt, but you loved it and you said, "Yes, that one, that one," so he pushed a little bit more and it went right inside me, the whole thing, and I couldn't get it out. I cried and complained, "I don't want this one," I told you, but you went to the till and paid. You helped me up and led me out, saying you'd miss the plane, because you were going to Philadelphia by plane, from Paris, oh, I mean Berlin, but I couldn't walk, I just couldn't. I had to keep my legs wide apart and I could feel it inside, that great big rod. When we got in the car, the chauffeur asked what was the matter, and you lifted my skirt for him to see. He put the tip of his finger inside me and exclaimed, "Size 56, wonderful, that's the best one," and I said to you, whimpering, "How are we going to be able to say goodbye if I've got this inside?" and you said, "Don't worry, there are other ways," and you forced me to kneel on top of the back seat. You lifted up my skirt, and put a finger in my bottom . . . and then I woke up. I was soaking, and I thought about you.' I looked at him, for a long time. He didn't say anything but just smiled, then I spoke again. 'Did you like my dream?'

ALINA REYES

from

The Butcher

Alina Reyes' first novel, The Butcher, *was published to great acclaim in France in 1988, and in Britain, translated by David Watson, in 1991.*

NEITHER of us said a word. I watched the movement of the wind-screen wipers. I grew sluggish with the smell of my wet hair next to my cheeks.

He opened the door, took me by the hand. My sandals were full of water, my feet squelched against the plastic soles. He led me to the lounge, sat me down, brought me a coffee. Then he turned on the radio and asked me to excuse him for five minutes. He had to take a shower.

I went over to the window, pulled the curtain open a little and watched the rain falling.

The rain made me want to piss. When I came out of the toilet I pushed open the bathroom door. The room was warm and all steamed up. I saw the broad silhouette through the shower curtain. I pulled it open a little and looked at him. He reached out a hand but I pulled away. I offered to scrub his back. I stepped onto the rim, put my hands under the warm water and picked up the soap, turning it over between my palms until I worked up a thick lather.

I began to rub his back, starting at the neck and shoulders, in circular movements. He was big and pale, firm and muscular. I worked my way down his spine, a hand on each side. I rubbed his sides, moving round a little onto his stomach. The soap made a fine scented froth, a cobweb of small white bubbles flowing over the wet skin, a slippery soft carpet between my palm and his back.

I went up and down the spine several times, from the small of the back to the base of the neck up to the first little hairs, the ones the barber shaves off for short haircuts with his deliciously vibrating razor.

I set off again from the shoulders and soaped each arm in turn. Although the limbs were relaxed, I felt bulging knots of muscle. His forearms were covered with dark hairs; I had to really wet the soap to make the lather stick. I worked back towards the deep hairy armpits.

I lathered up my hands again and massaged his buttocks in a revolving motion. Though on the big side, his buttocks had a harmonious shape, curving gracefully from the small of the back and joining the lower limbs without flab. I went over and over their roundness to know their form with my palms as well as with my eyes. Then I moved down the hard solid legs. The hairy skin covered barriers of muscle. I felt I was penetrating a new, wilder region of the body down to the strange treasure of the ankles.

Then he turned towards me. I raised my head and saw his swelling balls, his taut cock, straight above my eyes.

I got up. He didn't move. I took the soap between my hands again and began to clean his broad, solid, moderately hairy chest.

I began to move slowly down over his distended stomach, surrounded by powerful abdominal muscles. It took some time to cover the whole surface. His navel stood out, a small white ball outlined by the rounded mass, a star around which my fingers gravitated, straining to delay the moment when they would succumb to the downward pull towards the comet erected against the harmonious round form of the stomach.

I knelt down to massage his abdomen. I skirted round the genital area slowly, quite gently, towards the inside of the thighs.

His penis was incredibly large and erect.

I resisted the temptation to touch it, continuing to stroke over the pubis and between the legs. He was now lying back against the wall, his arms spread, with both hands pressed against the tiles, his stomach jutting forward. He was groaning.

I felt he was going to come before I even touched him.

I moved away, sat down fully under the shower spray, and with my eyes still fixed on his over-extended penis, I waited until he calmed down a little.

The warm water ran over my hair, inside my dress. Filled with steam, the air frothed around us, effacing all shapes and sounds.

He had been at the peak of excitement, and yet had made no move to hasten the denouement. He was waiting for me. He would wait as long as I wanted to make the pleasure last, and the pain.

I knelt down in front of him again. His cock, already thickly inflated, sprang up.

I moved my hands over his balls, back up to their base near the anus. His cock stood up again, more violently. I held it in my other hand, squeezed it, began slowly pulling it up and down. The soapy water I was lathered with provided perfect lubrication. My hands were filled with a warm, living, magical substance. I felt it beating like the heart of a bird, I helped it ride to its deliverance. Up, down, always the same movement, always the same rhythm, and the moans above my head. And I was moaning too, with the water from the shower sticking my dress to me like a tight silken glove, with the world stopped at the level of my eyes, of his belly, at the sound of the water trickling over us and of his cock sliding under my fingers, at the warm and tender and hard things between my hands, at the smell of the soap, of the soaking flesh and of the sperm mounting under my palm.

The liquid spurted out in bursts, splashing my face and my dress.

He knelt down as well, and licked the tears of sperm from my face. He washed me the way a cat grooms itself, with diligence and tenderness.

His plump white hand, his pink tongue on my cheek, his washed-out blue eyes, the eyelids still heavy as if under the effect of a drug. And his languid heavy body, his body of plenitude . . .

A green tender field of showers in the soft breeze of the branches . . . It is autumn, it is raining, I am a little girl, I am walking in the park and my head is swimming because of the smells, of the water on my skin and my clothes, I see a fat man over there on the bench looking at me so intently that I pee myself, standing up, I am walking and I am peeing myself, it is my warm rain on the park, on the ground, in my knickers, I rain, I give pleasure . . .

He took off my dress, slowly.

Then he stretched me out on the warm tiles and, with the shower still running, began planting kisses all over my body. His powerful hands lifted me up and turned me over with extreme delicacy. Neither the hardness of the floor nor the pleasure of his fingers could bruise me.

I relaxed completely. And he placed the pulp of his lips, the wetness of his tongue in the hollow of my arms, under my breasts, on my neck, behind my knees, between my buttocks, he put his mouth all over, the length of my back, the inside of my legs, right to the roots of my hair.

He lay me on my back on the ground, on the warm slippery tiles, lifted my hips with both hands, his fingers firmly thrust into the hollow as far as the spine, his thumbs on my stomach. He placed my legs over his shoulders and brought his tongue up to my vulva. I arched my back sharply. Thousands of drops of water from the shower hit me softly on my stomach and on my breasts. He licked me from my vagina to my clitoris, regularly, his mouth stuck to my

outer lips. My sex became a channelled surface from which pleasure streamed, the world disappeared, I was no more than this raw
flesh where soon gigantic cascades splashed, in sequence, continually, one after the other, forever.

Finally the tension slackened, my buttocks fell back onto his
arms, I recovered gradually, felt the water on my stomach, saw the
shower once more, and him, and me.

He had dried me off, put me in the warm bed, and I had fallen
asleep.

I woke up slowly to the sound of the rain against the tiles. The
sheets and pillow were warm and soft. I opened my eyes. He was
lying next to me, looking at me. I placed my hand on his sex. He
wanted me again.

I wanted nothing else but that. To make love, all the time,
without rage, with patience, persistence, methodically. Go on to
the end. He was like a mountain I must climb to the summit, like
in my dreams, my nightmares. It would have been best to emascu-
late him straight away, to eat this still hard still erect still demanding piece of flesh, to swallow it and keep it in my belly, for ever
more.

I drew close, raised myself a little, put my arms around him.
He took my head between his hands, led my mouth to his,
thrust his tongue in all at once, wiggled it at the back of my
throat, wrapped it and rolled it over mine. I began biting his lips
till I tasted blood.

Then I mounted on top of him, pressed my vulva against his sex,
rubbed it against his balls and his cock. I guided it by hand and
pushed it into me and it was like a giant flash, the dazzling entry of
the saviour, the instantaneous return of grace.

I raised my knees, bent my legs around him and rode him vigorously. Each time when at the crest of the wave I saw his cock
emerge glistening and red I held it again and tried to push it even
further in.

I was going too fast. He calmed me down gently. I unfolded my legs and lay on top of him. I lay motionless for a moment, contracting the muscles of my vagina around his member.

I chewed him over the expanse of his chest; an electric charge flowed through my tongue, my gums. I rubbed my nose against the fat of his white meat, inhaled its smell, trembling. I was squinting with pleasure. The world was no more than a vibrant abstract painting, a clash of marks the colour of flesh, a well of soft matter I was sinking into with the joyous impulse of perdition. A vibration coming from my eardrums took over my head, my eyes closed. An extraordinarily sharp awareness spread with the waves surging through my skull, it was like a flame, and my brain climaxed, alone and silent, magnificently alone.

He rolled over onto me, and rode me in turn, leaning on his hands so as not to crush me. His balls rubbed against my buttocks, at the entry to my vagina, his hard cock filled me, slid and slid along my deep walls, I dug my nails into his buttocks, he breathed more heavily . . . We came together, on and on, our fluids mingled, our groans mingled, coming from further than the throat, the depths of our chests, sounds alien to the human voice.

It was raining. Enveloped in a large T-shirt which he had lent me I was leaning on the window-sill, kneeling on the chair placed against the wall.

If I knew the language of the rain, of course, I would write it down, but everyone recognises it, and is able to recall it to their memory. Being in a closed space while outside all is water, trickling, drowning . . . Making love in the cramped backseat of a car, while the windows and roof resonate with the monotonous raindrops . . . The rain undoes bodies, makes them full of softness and damp patches . . . slimy and slobbering like snails . . .

He was also wearing a T-shirt, lying on the couch, his big buttocks, his big genitals, and his big legs bare.

He came over to me and pressed his hard cock against my buttocks. I wanted to turn round but he grabbed me by the hair, pulled my head back and began to push himself into my anus. It hurt, and I was trapped on the chair, condemned to keep my head pointing skywards.

Finally he entered fully, and the pain subsided. He began to move up and down, I was full of him, I could feel nothing except his huge monster cock right inside, whilst outside the bucketing rain poured down pure liquid light.

Continuing to jerk himself in me, to dig at me like a navvy while keeping my head held back, he slid two fingers into my vagina, then pulled them out. So I put in my own and felt the hard cock pounding behind the lining, and I began to fondle myself to the same rhythm. He speeded up his thrusts, my excitement grew, a mixture of pain and pleasure. His stomach bumped against my back with each thrust of his hips, and he penetrated me a bit further, invaded me a bit further. I wanted to free my head but he pulled my hair even harder, my throat was horribly stretched, my eyes were turned stubbornly towards the emptying sky, and he struck me and hammered me to the depths of myself, he shook up my body and then filled me with his hot liquid which came out in spurts, striking me softly, pleasurably.

A large drop would regularly drip somewhere with the sound of hollow metal. He let go of my hair, I let my head sink against the casement and began to sway imperceptibly.

I had him undress and stretch out on his back on the ground. With the expanders on his exercise machine I tied his arms to the foot of the bed, his legs to those of the table.

We were both tired. I sat down in the armchair and looked at him for a moment, spread-eagled and motionless.

His body pleased me like that, full of exposed imprisoned flesh, burst open in its splendid imperfection. Uprooted man, once more pinned to the ground, his sex like a fragile pivot exiled from the shadows and exposed to the light of my eyes.

Everything would have to be a sex; the curtains the moquette, the expanders and the furniture, I would need a sex instead of my head, another instead of his.

We would both need to be hanging from an iron hook face to face in a red fridge, hooked by the top of the skull or the ankles, head down, legs spread, our flesh face to face, rendered powerless to the knife of our sexes burning like red-hot irons, brandished, open. We would need to scream ourselves to death under the tyranny of our sexes, what are our sexes?

Last summer, first acid, I lost my hands first of all, and then my name, the name of my race, lost humanity from my memory, from the knowledge of my head and of my body, lost the idea of man, of woman, or even of creature; I sought for a while, who am I? My sex. My sex remained to the world, with its desire to piss. The only place where my soul had found refuge, had become concentrated, the only place where I existed, like an atom, wandering between sky and grass, between green and blue, with no other feeling than that of a pure atom-sex, just, barely, driven by the desire to piss, gone astray, blissful, in the light, Saint-Laurent peninsula, it was one summer's day, no it was autumn, it took me all night and the next morning to come down, but for months afterwards when I pissed I lost myself, the moment of dizziness that's it, I draw myself back entirely into my sex as if into a navel, my being is there in that sensation in the centre of the body, the rest of the body annihilated, I no longer know myself, have no form nor title, the ultimate trip each time and sometimes still, just an instant, like being hung head down in the great spiral of the universe, but only you know what those moments mean, afterwards I say to myself 'is that really who I am?' and 'how beautiful the world is, with all those bunches of black grapes, how good it is to go grape-picking at the height of summer, with the sun catching the grapes and the eyes of the pickers, the vines are twisted, how I'd love to piss at the end of the row!', and there are all sorts of stupid things like that in our bodies, so good do we feel after that weird dizziness which we miss a little, nevertheless, already.

I got up, knelt with my legs apart above his head. Still out of range of his face, I pulled open my outer lips with my fingers and gave him a long look at my vulva.

Then I stroked it slowly, with a rotating movement, from my anus to my clitoris.

I would have wanted grey skies where hope is focused, where quivering trees spread their fairy arms, capricious, hot-headed dreams in the grass kissed by the wind, I would have wanted to feel between my legs the huge breath of the millions of men on earth. I would have wanted, look, look at what I want . . .

I pushed the fingers of my left hand into my vagina, continued to rub myself. My fingers are not my fingers, but a heavy ingot, a thick square ingot stuck inside me, dazzling with gold to the dark depths of my dream. My hands went faster and faster. I rode the air in spasms, threw my head back, weeping onto his eyes as I came.

I regained the armchair. His face had turned red, he grew erect again, fairly softly. He was defenceless.

When I was small, I knew nothing about love. Making love, that magic word, the promise of that unbelievably wonderful thing which would happen all the time as soon as we were big. I had no idea about penetration, not even about what men have between their legs, in spite of all those showers with my brothers. You can look and look in vain, what do you know, when you have the taste for mystery? ·

When I was even smaller, no more than four, they talked in front of me thinking that I wasn't listening; Daddy told about a madman who ran screaming through the woods at night. I open the gate of my grandmother's garden, and all alone with my alsatian bitch I enter the woods. At the first gap in the trees, on a mound of sand, I lie down with the bitch, up against her warm flank, an arm round her neck. She puts out her tongue and she waits, like me. No one. The pines draw together and bend over us, in a tender, scary gesture. In the middle of the woods there is a long concrete drain, bordered with brambles where blackberries grow, and where one day a kart driver, hurtled violently off the track in front of me and put his eyes out. There is a blockhouse with a black mouth disguised as a door, and right at the end a washing plant devoured by moss and grass. Preserved in the watercourse is the hardened print of an enormous foot.

I went and lay on the ground next to him, laid my head on his stomach, my mouth against his cock, one hand on his balls, and I went to sleep. Certainly the footprint in the wet cement was of a big, strong, blond and probably handsome soldier.

When I woke up next to his penis I took it in my mouth, sucked it in several times with my tongue, felt it swell and touch the back of my throat. I massaged his balls, licked them, then returned to his cock. I placed it in the hollow of both my eyes, on my forehead, on my cheeks, against my nose, on my mouth, my chin, my throat, put my neck on it, squeezed it between my shoulder blades and my bent head, in my armpit, then the other, brushed against it with my breasts till I almost reached a climax, rubbed it with my stomach, my back, my buttocks, my thighs, squeezed it between my arms and my folded legs, pressed the sole of my foot against it, until I had left a trace of it over the whole of my body.

Then I put it back in my mouth and gave it a long suck, like you suck your thumb, your mother's breast, life, while he moaned and panted, always, until he ejaculates, in a sharp lamentation, and I drink his sperm, his sap, his gift.

NICHOLSON BAKER

from

Vox

*Vox was published in 1992 and was an immediate success. Fay Weldon wrote:
'. . . let the prudish grit their teeth and let us all read his (Nicholson Baker's)
book, this paean in praise of mutual masturbation.' Vox takes the form of a tele-
phone conversation in which the unnamed man and woman take it in turns to
arouse each other.*

'LAWRENCE had come up with the idea of going to the circus – this
was our very first time out, by the way, though I'd known him for
a while – so he was careful not to be too impressed. While we were
walking out to the car he said, "I guess those elephants really
respond to training." He thought the elephant wasn't biting the
woman's leg, but rather that its tongue was actually hooked under
her knee. I was dubious, but it was an interesting idea. It was touching to see how pleased Lawrence was that I'd liked the circus. We
were standing out by my car in the parking lot, just drenched with
sweat, he was plucking at his shirt and squinting at me, and we were
supposed to go to this clam-shack place and have an early dinner
on a picnic table outside, and I just didn't want to do that. So I
thought what the hell, and I said, "You look hot. Why don't you
come back to my apartment and you'll have a shower, and I'll have
a shower and then I'll make some dinner and we'll do the clam
shack another time, okay?" He agreed instantly – he was delighted

to have the responsibility for the success of this date taken out of his hands. So he had a shower, and I happened to have a pair of very baggy shorts with an elastic waistband that fit him fine, and a big T-shirt, and then I had a shower, and I put on a pair of shorts and a dark red T-shirt, and everything was fine.'

'But separate showers, no nudity.'

'No, very chaste,' she said.

'What was he doing when you got out of the shower?'

'He was peering inside a Venetian paperweight.'

'Classic. He'd obviously heard your shower turn off, and then he'd stood there, holding the paperweight to his face for ten minutes, so that you would be sure to discover him in that casual pose, appreciating your trinket.'

'Quite possible. Anyhow, he sat in the kitchen and we talked rather formally while I made a spiral kind of pasta and microwaved a packet of creamed chipped beef – this is a great dish, incidentally, Stouffer's creamed chipped beef over any kind of pasta noodles – I have it about once a week. Lawrence made an elaborate pretense of being impressed by this super easy recipe, and when I poured the spirals from the drainer into a bowl he came over to where I was standing and he said, "I have to see this." I was going to simply slice the packet of creamed chipped open and dump it over the spirals, which is what I normally do, but I was feeling sneaky, I'd just had a shower, and you know about me and showers, but I hadn't dithered, despite the *major* striptease fantasy I'd had at the circus, because obviously I couldn't, since a man was in my apartment, so I was feeling devious, and so I got out some olive oil and poured a little of it on the spirals, and he – he was definitely not in the know about cooking, and I'm certainly not much of a cook myself – but he said, "So *that's* how you keep them from sticking and clumping." I stirred them up, and they made an embarrassingly luscious sexy sound, and I just decided, fuck it, I've dressed this person, I'm feeding this person, I'm going to seduce this person, right now, today, so I said, I said, "How very strange," I said, "I just remembered something I haven't thought of in years. I just remembered this kid in my junior high – you remind me of him in some ways – I just remembered his commenting that a certain girl must have used olive oil to put on her jeans." Well, I saw Lawrence's little eyeballs roll at this. He said something obvious about extra virgin cold pressed and he snuffled out a nervous laugh and I thought, yes, I am in charge here, I am going to see this person's penis get hard, and even though I have a smoldering yeast problem and so can't really have full-fledged sex I am going to have my way with this person somehow. It was probably that Venezuelan ball-twirling screamer that put me in that mood, now that I think back. I mean, I felt powerful and shrewd and effortlessly in control and everything else I usually don't feel. I cut open the packet of creamed chipped and I said, musingly, "My grandmother was very careful about money – she always used to say that she was as tight as the bark on a tree. And I used to think about what that really would feel like, whether bark does feel tight to the inner wood of the tree. I used to put on my jeans and take them off, thinking about that." Lawrence said, "Really!" I said, "Yeah, although actually I didn't like my jeans to be at all tight, even then. I liked them loose. The appeal was the rough fabric, and the rough stitching, very barklike, the appeal was of being in this sort of complete male embrace, but then when you took them off, being all smooth and curved." Lawrence nodded seriously. So I said, making the leap, I said, "And when I started getting my legs waxed, which is quite an expensive little procedure, I also thought of that phrase, *as tight as the bark on a tree*, when Leona, my waxer, began putting the little warm wax strips on my legs and letting them solidify for an instant and ripping them off." I said, "In fact, I just had my legs waxed yesterday." Lawrence said, "Is that right?" and I said, "Yes, it's amazing how much freer you feel after your legs are waxed – it's almost as if you've become physically more limber – you want to leap around, and make high kicks, cavort." I waited for that to sink in and then I said, "Leona's a tiny Ukrainian woman, and she makes this growly sound as she rips the strips of muslin and wax off, *rrr*, and when she's done both my legs and there's no more hurting, she rubs lotion into them, and it's a surprisingly sensual experience." Lawrence was silent for a second and then he said, "I'm inexperienced with depilatory techniques. I've never known anyone who had her legs waxed." I said, "Let's have dinner." '

'What a tactician!'

'Not really. Anyhow, we had dinner, which was pretty tame. Lawrence had many virtues, he had a kind of bony broad-shoulderedness, and a deliberate way of blinking and looking at you when you spoke, and he was quite smart – he was a patent lawyer.'

'Ah. Patent in*fringe*ment?'

'Yes indeed. But he had no conversational skills at all. He was putty in my hands. No, I'm actually making myself seem more completely sure of my powers than I felt – but still, I was pretty much in control. I started asking him how electrical things worked – you know, like what shortwave radio was, and how cordless telephones worked, and why it is that at drive-ins now you can hear the movie on the FM radio in your car. And he was full of interesting information, once you jump-started him that way. But the thing was, I kept a faint racy undertone going in the conversation. For instance, I'd say, "What do you think those ham-radio buffs really talked about? Do you think some of them were secretly gay, and they left their wives asleep and crept down to their finished basements in the middle of the night to have long conversations with *friends* in New Zealand or wherever?" He said, "I suppose it's a possibility." And about the drive-ins I said things like, "It must be much more comfortable and *private* in drive-ins now, because you can close the window completely, you don't have that metal thing hanging there with the tinny sound, covered with yellow chipped paint, like a chaperone, you're not attached to anything around you, it's much more like being in a car on the expressway." He said he didn't know exactly how drive-ins supplied the FM sound, because he hadn't been to a drive-in since he was eight years old, but he said that technically speaking it was an easy problem to solve, for instance there was a thing advertised in the back of *Popular Science* that picks up any sound in the room and broadcasts it to FM radios within several hundred yards, it's called a Bionic Mike Transmitter. I said, "Ooo, a Bionic Mike Transmitter!" He said, "Oh sure, it's this device that you can leave in this room, for instance, and it will broadcast any sound in the room to any nearby FM radio, if it's correctly tuned." He said, "Of course it's advertised with a big warning about how it's not meant for illegal surveillance. But probably that's what it's used for." I said, "You mean that whatever I did, whatever intimate private activity I engaged in, would be heard by the people swooshing by in the cars on the expressway?" He said, "If they were tuned correctly, yes." I said, "Hmmm." You see, my living room is on the second floor, about three hundred feet from a raised part of the expressway.'

'In some eastern city,' he said.

'That's right,' she said.

'So what did Lawrence do when you expressed a keen interest in his description of the Bionic Mike Transducer?'

'Transmitter. He asked if he could have a fourth helping of creamed chipped beef. Then we were finished and I started to clear the table and he said, "I'll wash up." I said, "No, forget it, I'll do it later," but he said, "No no really, I like washing up." So I said fine, and he cleaned the kitchen, quite efficiently, while I told him the plot of *Dial M for Murder*, really lingering over the hot letter that's found on the body of the man with the pair of scissors in his back. You know? Lawrence listened carefully – he'd never seen the movie, if you can believe it. He said he didn't like black-and-white movies. I said. "Fine, don't like them, *Dial M for Murder* is in color." He said, "Oh." And then he said, "Well, I think Hitchcock was a fairly sick individual anyway." I said, "You're probably right." Then he dried his hands with a paper towel and turned toward me holding the glass bottle of olive oil and he said, "Now, where does this go?" I said, "Well, where would you like it to go?" And he said, "I don't know." So I said, "Well sometimes, after I get my legs waxed, the day after, they're still a little tender, and I've found that olive oil really helps them feel better." Which wasn't true, they feel fine the day after, but anyway"

'Erotic license.'

'Exactly. He said, "But that would be terribly messy!" I said, "So I'll stand in the bathtub." And he said, "But won't it be cold and clammy?" So I turned the bottle of oil on its side and put it in the microwave for twenty seconds. He felt it and he shook his head and said, "I think it needs a full minute." So we leaned on the counter, looking at the microwave, while it heated the oil. When the five beeps beeped, Lawrence took it out, and we went to the bathroom together. I stood in the bathtub and pulled my shorts up high on my legs, and very solemnly he poured a little pool of olive oil on his fingers and rubbed it just above my knee.'

'He was kneeling himself?'

'Yes. The bathtub wasn't really wet anymore – I mean it was still humid from both the showers, but we didn't have the water running or anything. He said, "You're very smooth." I said, "Thank you." A rather powerful smell of olive oil surrounded us, and I began to feel quite Mediterranean and Bacchic, and honestly somewhat like a mushroom being lightly sautéed. He stared at his hand going over my skin, blinking at it. I pulled the sides of my shorts up higher so he could do more of my thighs, and I said, "Leona is very thorough. No follicle is left unmolested." Then, whoops, I wondered whether that was maybe too kinky for him and whether he might think that I was trying to give him the idea that Leona had gone over the edge and waxed off all my pubic hair, horrifying thought, so I said, "I mean, within limits." He just kept on dolloping oil on his fingers and rubbing it in. After a while I turned around and held on to the showerhead and he did the backs of my legs. He wasn't artful at all, he didn't know how to knead the deep muscles, but I could feel the intelligence and interest in his fingers when they came to each new dry curve. His hands went right up underneath the bagginess of my shorts. I liked that. He didn't say anything. Once I think he cleared his throat. Finally he said, "Okay, I think that's everything." I turned around and looked down at him: he was sitting with his legs crossed, looking at my legs, very closely, really letting his eyes travel over them. He had curly hair – he needed a haircut, in fact. He had the top of the olive oil in one hand and the bottle in the other, and before he stood up he pressed the circle of the plastic top back and forth up the inside of both my legs, in a zigzag. Then he stood up and handed me the bottle. He was blushing. I smiled at him and I said, "Are you suffering from any sticking or clumping?" And he said, "Yeah, some." So I pulled on the waistband of his shorts and poured about a tablespoonful of oil in there.'

'No kidding!'

'Yes, well, he looked at me with shock. And I know I wouldn't have been able to do it if they hadn't really been my *own* shorts that I'd lent him. I said, "I'm awfully sorry, I don't know what I was thinking. Take those off and I'll see if I have another pair." So he marched that peculiar march that men do as they are taking off their pants. He was not erect by any means, but he wasn't dormant either. I said, "Did the olive oil feel warm?" And he said, "Yes." So I said, "Would you like some more?" and he said, "Maybe." So I held the mouth of the bottle right where his public hair bushed out, high on his cock, I mean near the base, not near the tip, because he was still drooping down, and I tipped it as if to pour it over him, but I didn't actually let any come out. I just held it there. And the expectation of the warmth of the oil made his cock rise a little. I tipped the bottle even more, so that the olive oil was right in the neck, ready to pour out, but still I didn't actually pour it. And his erection rose a little more, wanting the oil. It was like some kind of stage levitation. His hands were in little boyish fists at his sides. When he was almost horizontal, but still angling slightly downward, suddenly I poured the entire rest of the bottle over him, just *glug glug glug glug glug*, so that it flowed down its full cock length and fell with a buzzing sound onto the bathtub. And this was not a trivial amount of oil, this was about maybe a third of the bottle. The waste was itself exciting. It was like covering him in some amber glaze. He hurriedly moved his legs farther apart so he wouldn't get oil spatter on his feet. By the time there were only a few last drips falling from the bottle, he was totally, I mean totally, hard. And of course with this success I had second thoughts. I almost wanted him to leave right then so that I could come in the shower by myself. I stepped out of the tub and I said, "Sorry, I got carried away. And the problem is, I have this darn yeast situation, so I can't really do anything with that magnificent thing, much as I'd like to." He said, "Ah, that's all right, I'll just go home and take care of myself, that's no problem," he said, "but your *tub*, on the other hand, is a mess. Ask me to clean it and I will." I said, "Oh don't worry about that, it's just oil, it's nothing." But he was on his own private trajectory, and he said, "That's right, it's oil, plus I have to say the tub is not terribly clean to begin with." I said, "No no no, don't even think of it, really." He picked up an old dry Rescue pad that was in a corner and he held it up and he said, "Look, tell me to clean your tub." He's standing there, a pantless patent lawyer, semi-erect, wearing my Danger Mouse T-shirt, holding the tiny curled-up green Rescue pad with a fierce expression. *He wanted to clean my tub.* I said, "Well, great. Please do. Sure." He asked for some Ajax, so I brought some from the kitchen, along with a folding chair so I could sit and watch. Well, this Lawrence turned out to be some kind of demon scrub-wizard. He hands me my bottles of shampoo, one by one. My tub is now naked! He squats in it, so that his testicles are practically gamboling in the giant teardrop of oil that's on the bottom, and he takes the Ajax and he taps its rim against the edge of the tub, all the way around, so that these *curtains* of pale blue powder fall down the sides, kind of an aurora borealis effect, and then he moistens his Rescue pad and he starts scrubbing and scrubbing, every curve, every seam, talk about circling motions, my lord! He did the place where the shampoo bottles had been, that I'd simply defined as a safe haven for mildew, he was in there, *grrr, grrr*, twisting and jamming that little sponge. Not that my tub is filthy, it isn't, it's just not sparkling, and there *is* a faint rich smell of mildew or something vaguely biological, which I kind of like, because it's so closely associated by now with my private shower activity. But here I was watching this guy *in* my shower! He took down the Water Pik massage head and he rinsed off the parts he'd done, and he began to herd all the oil down the drain with hot water, and the oil and the Ajax had mixed and formed this awful stuff, like a *roux* first, and then when the water mixed in it became this yellow sort of foam, which didn't daunt him, he took care of it. And then he started scrubbing his way toward the fittings, using liberal amounts of Ajax alternating with hot water. He said, "You don't worry about scratching, do you?" I said I didn't. So he gnarled around the cold-water tap and he gnarled around the hot-water tap and he circled fiercely around the clitty thing that controls the drain, and then when the whole rest of the tub was absolutely *gleaming*, he went to the drain itself – he set aside the filter thing, and he reached two fingers way in, and he pulled out this revolting slime locket and splapped it against the side of the tub, and then he really went to work on that drain, around and around the rim of chrome, and deeper, right down to those dark crossbars, that I'd never gotten to, he worked the scrubber sponge in there, *grrr*, more Ajax, more circling, more hot water. I mean I was in a transport!'

'I bet.'

'Then I held out the trash can, and he threw out the drain slime and the Rescue pad, and he rinsed his hands, and he stood, and in the midst of this newly cleaned tub he started to rinse off his cock and his legs, where a little oil had fallen, and I watched the water go over him, I watched the way the even spray of the showerhead in his hand made all the hairs on his legs into these perfect perfect rows, like some ideal crop, and he was quite hairy, and so I slipped off my shorts and unders and sat on the far end of the bathtub and propped my left foot against a washcloth handle and I hung my

right leg out over the edge of the bathtub, so I was wide open, and
I said, "I'm a bit rank, too, do me," so he started playing the water
over my legs and then directly on my . . . femalia, and I held my
lips open so that he could see my inner wishbone, and the drops of
water exploding on it, and as he sprayed me, he began to get hard
again. But I can't come with just water, so I started strumming
myself, while he sprayed my hand, which was a lovely feeling, and
I held out my left hand and he maneuvered closer to me and I took
hold of his cock and tried to begin to jerk it off, but I didn't do
very well, because my own finger on my clit felt so good, and I
couldn't seem to keep the two kinds of masturbating motion going
with my left and right hand independently, I was making big odd
circles with his cock, so instead I took the showerhead from him
and I said, "You're on your own," and I sprayed his cock and some
of his Danger Mouse T-shirt, that is, *my* Danger Mouse T-shirt,
while he began stroking away, staring at my legs and my pussy, and
I liked spraying him quite a lot, I liked aiming the water at his fist,
I liked the sight of his wet T-shirt, and he had, this is rather bad of
me to say, but he had a kind of gruesome-looking cock, a real
monster, and the relief of not having that girth in me was itself
almost enough to put me over the top, and it looked quite a bit
more distinguished through the glint of the spray. But I also wanted
the water on me − I wanted to spray him, but I wanted the water
flowing on me as well − and suddenly it seemed like the most
natural thing in the world, I remembered the elephant woman
lifting her knee, and so I reached forward and pulled his hips toward
me so that his legs straddled my left leg, and I lifted my knee, and
he clamped his thighs around it, and I let my other leg sprawl so
that I was absolutely wide open, and now, when I sprayed his cock
and his hand the water streamed down his thighs and then down
my thigh and on to me. And it was exactly what I wanted, and it
started to feel so good, and I said so, and suddenly he started
stroking himself incredibly fast, it was this blur, like a *sewing*
machine, and he produced this major jet of sperm at a diagonal

right into the circular spray of the water, so that it fought against all the drops and was sort of torn apart by them, and he was clamping my leg, my smooth leg, extremely tight with those perfectly water-groomed thighs, and I shifted adroitly so that the poached sperm and hot-water runoff wouldn't pour directly into me and possibly cause trouble, but so that it still poured over me. And then he took the showerhead again, and still holding his cock and still clamping my knee very tight, he sprayed slowly across my hand and my thighs very close with the water until I closed my eyes and came, imagining I was in front of a circus audience. So that was nice.'

ACKNOWLEDGMENTS

The publisher is grateful to the following for permission to reproduce copyright material from:

History of My Life by Giacomo Casanova, Translated by Willard R. Trask, copyright © 1960 by F. A. Brockhaus, English translation copyright © 1966 by Harcourt Brace & Company, reprinted by permission of Harcourt Brace & Company.

The Journals of James Boswell by James Boswell. Copyright © Yale University 1991. Reproduced by permission of Yale University Press and Reed International. Published originally by McGraw Hill and Heinemann.

Emmanuelle by Emmanuelle Arsan. Reproduced by permission of Harper Collins Publishers Limited and Editions du Chêne.

Rabbit is Rich by John Updike. Copyright © 1981 by John Updike. Reprinted by permission of Alfred A. Knopf, Inc and Hamish Hamilton Ltd.

The Women's Room by Marilyn French. Copyright © 1977 by Marilyn French. Reproduced by permission of Simon & Schuster, Inc and André Deutsch Ltd.

The Ages of Lulu by Almudena Grandes. Reproduced by permission of Abacus.

The Butcher by Alina Reyes. Translated by David Watson. Reproduced by permission of Reed International.

Vox by Nicholson Baker published by Chatto & Windus. Copyright © 1992 by Nicholson Baker. Reprinted by permission of Random House, Inc and the Melanie Jackson Agency.